THE ALASKAN

It was as if the man was deliberately insulting her.

James Oliver Curwood

THE ALASKAN

A Novel of the North

With Illustrations by
WALT LOUDERBACK

BIBLIOBAZAAR

THE ALASKAN

To the strong-hearted men and women of Alaska, the new empire rising in the North, it is for me an honor and a privilege to dedicate this work.

JAMES OLIVER CURWOOD

Owosso, Michigan

August 1, 1923

LIST OF ILLUSTRATIONS

CHAPTER I

Captain Rifle, gray and old in the Alaskan Steamship service, had not lost the spirit of his youth along with his years. Romance was not dead in him, and the fire which is built up of clean adventure and the association of strong men and a mighty country had not died out of his veins. He could still see the picturesque, feel the thrill of the unusual, and—at times—warm memories crowded upon him so closely that yesterday seemed today, and Alaska was young again, thrilling the world with her wild call to those who had courage to come and fight for her treasures, and live—or die.

Tonight, with the softly musical throb of his ship under his feet, and the yellow moon climbing up from behind the ramparts of the Alaskan mountains, something of loneliness seized upon him, and he said simply:

"That is Alaska."

The girl standing beside him at the rail did not turn, nor for a moment did she answer. He could see her profile clear-cut as a cameo in the almost vivid light, and in that light her eyes were wide and filled with a dusky fire, and her lips were parted a little, and her slim body was tense as she looked at the wonder of the moon silhouetting the cragged castles of the peaks, up where the soft, gray clouds lay like shimmering draperies.

Then she turned her face a little and nodded. "Yes, Alaska," she said, and the old captain fancied there was the slightest ripple of a tremor in her voice. "Your Alaska, Captain Rifle."

Out of the clearness of the night came to them a distant sound like the low moan of thunder. Twice before, Mary Standish had heard it, and now she asked: "What was that? Surely it can not be a storm, with the moon like that, and the stars so clear above!"

"It is ice breaking from the glaciers and falling into the sea. We are in the Wrangel Narrows, and very near the shore, Miss Standish. If it were day you could hear the birds singing. This is what we call the Inside Passage. I have always called it the water-wonderland of the world, and yet, if you will observe, I must be mistaken—for we are almost alone on this side of the ship. Is it not proof? If I were right, the men and women in there—dancing, playing cards, chattering—would be crowding this rail. Can you imagine humans like that? But they can't see what I see, for I am a ridiculous old fool who remembers things. Ah, do you catch that in the air, Miss Standish—the perfume of flowers, of forests, of green things ashore? It is faint, but I catch it."

"And so do I."

She breathed in deeply of the sweet air, and turned then, so that she stood with her back to the rail, facing the flaming lights of the ship.

The mellow cadence of the music came to her, soft-stringed and sleepy; she could hear the shuffle of dancing feet. Laughter rippled with the rhythmic thrum of the ship, voices rose and fell beyond the lighted windows, and as the old captain looked at her, there was something in her face which he could not understand.

She had come aboard strangely at Seattle, alone and almost at the last minute—defying the necessity of making reservation where half a thousand others had been turned away—and chance had brought her under his eyes. In desperation she had appealed to him, and he had discovered a strange terror under the forced calm of her appearance. Since then he had fathered her with his attentions, watching closely with the wisdom of years. And more than once he had observed that questing, defiant poise of her head with which she was regarding the cabin windows now.

She had told him she was twenty-three and on her way to meet relatives in Nome. She had named certain people. And he had believed her. It was impossible not to believe her, and he admired her pluck in breaking all official regulations in coming aboard.

In many ways she was companionable and sweet. Yet out of his experience, he gathered the fact that she was under a tension. He knew that in some way she was making a fight, but, influenced by the wisdom of three and sixty years, he did not let her know he had guessed the truth.

He watched her closely now, without seeming to do so. She was very pretty in a quiet and unusual way. There was something irresistibly attractive about her, appealing to old memories which were painted clearly in his heart. She was girlishly slim. He had observed that her eyes were beautifully clear and gray in the sunlight, and her exquisitely smooth dark hair, neatly coiled and luxuriant crown of beauty, reminded him of puritanism in its simplicity. At times he doubted that she was twenty-three. If she had said nineteen or twenty he would have been better satisfied. She puzzled him and roused speculation in him. But it was a part of his business to see many things which others might not see—and hold his tongue.

"We are not quite alone," she was saying. "There are others," and she made a little gesture toward two figures farther up the rail.

"Old Donald Hardwick, of Skagway," he said. "And the other is Alan Holt."

"Oh, yes."

She was facing the mountains again, her eyes shining in the light of the moon. Gently her hand touched the old captain's arm. "Listen," she whispered.

"Another berg breaking away from Old Thunder. We are very near the shore, and there are glaciers all the way up."

"And that other sound, like low wind—on a night so still and calm! What is it?"

"You always hear that when very close to the big mountains, Miss Standish. It is made by the water of a thousand streams and rivulets rushing down to the sea. Wherever there is melting snow in the mountains, you hear that song."

"And this man, Alan Holt," she reminded him. "He is a part of these things?"

"Possibly more than any other man, Miss Standish. He was born in Alaska before Nome or Fairbanks or Dawson City were thought of. It was in Eighty-four, I think. Let me see, that would make him—"

"Thirty-eight," she said, so quickly that for a moment he was astonished.

Then he chuckled. "You are very good at figures."

He felt an almost imperceptible tightening of her fingers on his arm.

"This evening, just after dinner, old Donald found me sitting alone. He said he was lonely and wanted to talk with someone—like me. He almost frightened me, with his great, gray beard and shaggy hair. I thought of ghosts as we talked there in the dusk."

"Old Donald belongs to the days when the Chilkoot and the White Horse ate up men's lives, and a trail of living dead led from the Summit to Klondike, Miss Standish," said Captain Rifle. "You will meet many like him in Alaska. And they remember. You can see it in their faces—always the memory of those days that are gone."

She bowed her head a little, looking to the sea. "And Alan Holt? You know him well?"

"Few men know him well. He is a part of Alaska itself, and I have sometimes thought him more aloof than the mountains. But I know him. All northern Alaska knows Alan Holt. He has a reindeer range up beyond the Endicott Mountains and is always seeking the last frontier."

"He must be very brave."

"Alaska breeds heroic men, Miss Standish."

"And honorable men—men you can trust and believe in?"

"Yes."

"It is odd," she said, with a trembling little laugh that was like a bird-note in her throat. "I have never seen Alaska before, and yet something about these mountains makes me feel that I have known them a long time ago. I seem to feel they are welcoming me and that I am going home. Alan Holt is a fortunate man. I should like to be an Alaskan."

"And you are—"

"An American," she finished for him, a sudden, swift irony in her voice. "A poor product out of the melting-pot, Captain Rifle. I am going north—to learn."

"Only that, Miss Standish?"

His question, quietly spoken and without emphasis, demanded an answer. His kindly face, seamed by the suns and winds of many years at sea, was filled with honest anxiety as she turned to look straight into his eyes.

"I must press the question," he said. "As the captain of this ship, and as a father, it is my duty. Is there not something you would like to tell me—in confidence, if you will have it so?"

For an instant she hesitated, then slowly she shook her head. "There is nothing, Captain Rifle."

"And yet—you came aboard very strangely," he urged. "You will recall that it was most unusual—without reservation, without baggage—"

"You forget the hand-bag," she reminded him.

"Yes, but one does not start for northern Alaska with only a hand-bag scarcely large enough to contain a change of linen, Miss Standish."

"But I did, Captain Rifle."

"True. And I saw you fighting past the guards like a little wildcat. It was without precedent."

"I am sorry. But they were stupid and difficult to pass."

"Only by chance did I happen to see it all, my child. Otherwise the ship's regulations would have compelled me to send you ashore. You were frightened. You can not deny that. You were running away from something!"

He was amazed at the childish simplicity with which she answered him.

"Yes, I was running away—from something."

Her eyes were beautifully clear and unafraid, and yet again he sensed the thrill of the fight she was making.

"And you will not tell me why—or from what you were escaping?"

"I can not—tonight. I may do so before we reach Nome. But—it is possible—"

"What?"

"That I shall never reach Nome."

Suddenly she caught one of his hands in both her own. Her fingers clung to him, and with a little note of fierceness in her voice she hugged the hand to her breast. "I know just how good you have been to me," she cried. "I should like to tell you why I came aboard—like that. But I can not. Look! Look at those wonderful mountains!" With one free hand she pointed.

"Behind them and beyond them lie the romance and adventure and mystery of centuries, and for nearly thirty years you have been very near those things, Captain Rifle. No man will ever see again what you have seen or feel what you have felt, or forget what you have had to forget. I know it. And after all that, can't you—won't you—forget the strange manner in which I came aboard this ship? It is such a simple, little thing to put out of your mind, so trivial, so unimportant when you look back—and think. Please Captain Rifle—please!"

So quickly that he scarcely sensed the happening of it she pressed his hand to her lips. Their warm thrill came and went in an instant, leaving him speechless, his resolution gone.

"I love you because you have been so good to me," she whispered, and as suddenly as she had kissed his hand, she was gone, leaving him alone at the rail.

* * * *

CHAPTER II

Alan Holt saw the slim figure of the girl silhouetted against the vivid light of the open doorway of the upper-deck salon. He was not watching her, nor did he look closely at the exceedingly attractive picture which she made as she paused there for an instant after leaving Captain Rifle. To him she was only one of the five hundred human atoms that went to make up the tremendously interesting life of one of the first ships of the season going north. Fate, through the suave agency of the purser, had brought him into a bit closer proximity to her than the others; that was all. For two days her seat in the dining-salon had been at the same table, not quite opposite him. As she had missed both breakfast hours, and he had skipped two luncheons, the requirements of neighborliness and of courtesy had not imposed more than a dozen words of speech upon them. This was very satisfactory to Alan. He was not talkative or communicative of his own free will. There was a certain cynicism back of his love of silence. He was a good listener and a first-rate analyst. Some people, he knew, were born to talk; and others, to trim the balance, were burdened with the necessity of holding their tongues. For him silence was not a burden.

In his cool and causal way he admired Mary Standish. She was very quiet, and he liked her because of that. He could not, of course, escape the beauty of her eyes or the shimmering luster of the long lashes that darkened them. But these were details which did not thrill him, but merely pleased him. And her hair pleased him possibly even more than her gray eyes, though he was not sufficiently concerned to discuss the matter with himself. But if he had pointed out any one thing, it would have been her hair—not so much the color of it as the care she evidently gave it, and the manner in which she dressed it. He noted that it was dark, with varying flashes of luster in it under the dinner lights. But what he approved of most of all were the smooth, silky coils in which she fastened it to her pretty head. It was an intense relief after looking on so many frowsy heads, bobbed and marcelled, during his six months' visit in the States. So he liked her, generally speaking, because there was not a thing about her that he might dislike.

He did not, of course, wonder what the girl might be thinking of him—with his quiet, stern face, his cold indifference, his rather Indian-like litheness, and the single patch of gray that streaked his thick, blond hair. His interest had not reached anywhere near that point.

Tonight it was probable that no woman in the world could have interested him, except as the always casual observer of humanity. Another and greater thing gripped him and had thrilled him since he first felt the throbbing pulse of the engines of the new steamship *Nome* under his feet at Seattle. He was going *home*. And home meant Alaska. It meant the mountains, the vast tundras, the immeasurable spaces into which civilization had not yet come with its clang and clamor. It meant friends, the stars he knew, his herds, everything he loved. Such was his reaction after six months of exile, six months of loneliness and desolation in cities which he had learned to hate.

"I'll not make the trip again—not for a whole winter—unless I'm sent at the point of a gun," he said to Captain Rifle, a few moments after Mary Standish had left the deck. "An Eskimo winter is long enough, but one in Seattle, Minneapolis, Chicago, and New York is longer—for me."

"I understand they had you up before the Committee on Ways and Means at Washington."

"Yes, along with Carl Lomen, of Nome. But Lomen was the real man. He has forty thousand head of reindeer in the Seward Peninsula, and they had to listen to him. We may get action."

"May!" Captain Rifle grunted his doubt. "Alaska has been waiting ten years for a new deck and a new deal. I doubt if you'll get anything. When politicians from Iowa and south Texas tell us what we can have and what we need north of Fifty-eight—why, what's the use? Alaska might as well shut up shop!"

"But she isn't going to do that," said Alan Holt, his face grimly set in the moonlight. "They've tried hard to get us, and they've made us shut up a lot of our doors. In 1910 we were thirty-six thousand whites in the Territory. Since then the politicians at Washington have driven out nine thousand, a quarter of the population. But those that are left are hard-boiled. We're not going to quit, Captain. A lot of us are Alaskans, and we are not afraid to fight."

"You mean—"

"That we'll have a square deal within another five years, or know the reason why. And another five years after that, we'll he shipping a million reindeer carcasses down into the States each year. Within twenty years we'll be shipping five million. Nice thought for the beef barons, eh? But rather fortunate, I think, for the hundred million Americans who are turning their grazing lands into farms and irrigation systems."

One of Alan Holt's hands was clenched at the rail. "Until I went down this winter, I didn't realize just how bad it was," he said, a note hard as iron in his voice. "Lomen is a diplomat, but I'm not. I want to fight when I see such things—fight with a gun. Because we happened to find gold up here, they think Alaska is an orange to be sucked as quickly as possible, and that when the sucking process is over, the skin will be worthless. That's modern, dollar-chasing Americanism for you!"

"And are you not an American, Mr. Holt?"

So soft and near was the voice that both men started. Then both turned and stared. Close behind them, her quiet, beautiful face flooded with the moon-glow, stood Mary Standish.

"You ask me a question, madam," said Alan Holt, bowing courteously. "No, I am not an American. I am an Alaskan."

The girl's lips were parted. Her eyes were very bright and clear. "Please pardon me for listening," she said. "I couldn't help it. I am an American. I love America. I think I love it more than anything else in the world—more than my religion, even. *America,* Mr. Holt. And America doesn't necessarily mean a great many of America's people. I love to think that I first came ashore in the *Mayflower.* That is why my name is Standish. And I just wanted to remind you that Alaska *is* America."

Alan Holt was a bit amazed. The girl's face was no longer placidly quiet. Her eyes were radiant. He sensed the repressed thrill in her voice, and he knew that in the light of day he would have seen fire in her cheeks. He smiled, and in that smile he could not quite keep back the cynicism of his thought.

"And what do you know about Alaska, Miss Standish?"

"Nothing," she said. "And yet I love it." She pointed to the mountains. "I wish I might have been born among them. You are fortunate. You should love America."

"Alaska, you mean!"

"No, America." There was a flashing challenge in her eyes. She was not speaking apologetically. Her meaning was direct.

The irony on Alan's lips died away. With a little laugh he bowed again. "If I am speaking to a daughter of Captain Miles Standish, who came over in the *Mayflower,* I stand reproved," he said. "You should be an authority on Americanism, if I am correct in surmising your relationship."

"You are correct," she replied with a proud, little tilt of her glossy head, "though I think that only lately have I come to an understanding of its significance—and its responsibility. I ask your pardon again for interrupting you. It was not premeditated. It just happened."

She did not wait for either of them to speak, but flashed the two a swift smile and passed down the promenade.

The music had ceased and the cabins at last were emptying themselves of life.

"A remarkable young woman," Alan remarked. "I imagine that the spirit of Captain Miles Standish may be a little proud of this particular olive-branch. A chip off the old block, you might say. One would almost suppose he had married Priscilla and this young lady was a definite though rather indirect result."

He had a curious way of laughing without any more visible manifestation of humor than spoken words. It was a quality in his voice which one could not miss, and at times, when ironically amused, it carried a sting which he did not altogether intend.

In another moment Mary Standish was forgotten, and he was asking the captain a question which was in his mind.

"The itinerary of this ship is rather confused, is it not?"

"Yes—rather," acknowledged Captain Rifle. "Hereafter she will ply directly between Seattle and Nome. But this time we're doing the Inside Passage to Juneau and Skagway and will make the Aleutian Passage via Cordova and Seward. A whim of the owners, which they haven't seen fit to explain to me. Possibly the Canadian junket aboard may have something to do with it. We're landing them at Skagway, where they make the Yukon by way of White Horse Pass. A pleasure trip for flabby people nowadays, Holt. I can remember—"

"So can I," nodded Alan Holt, looking at the mountains beyond which lay the dead-strewn trails of the gold stampede of a generation before. "I remember. And old Donald is dreaming of that hell of death back there. He was all choked up tonight. I wish he might forget."

"Men don't forget such women as Jane Hope," said the captain softly.

"You knew her?"

"Yes. She came up with her father on my ship. That was twenty-five years ago last autumn, Alan. A long time, isn't it? And when I look at Mary Standish and hear her voice—" He hesitated, as if betraying a secret, and then he added: "—I can't help thinking of the girl Donald

Hardwick fought for and won in that death-hole at White Horse. It's too bad she had to die."

"She isn't dead," said Alan. The hardness was gone from his voice. "She isn't dead," he repeated. "That's the pity of it. She is as much a living thing to him today as she was twenty years ago."

After a moment the captain said, "She was talking with him early this evening, Alan."

"Miss Captain Miles Standish, you mean?"

"Yes. There seems to be something about her that amuses you."

Alan shrugged his shoulders. "Not at all. I think she is a most admirable young person. Will you have a cigar, Captain? I'm going to promenade a bit. It does me good to mix in with the sour-doughs."

The two lighted their cigars from a single match, and Alan went his way, while the captain turned in the direction of his cabin.

To Alan, on this particular night, the steamship *Nome* was more than a thing of wood and steel. It was a living, pulsating being, throbbing with the very heart-beat of Alaska. The purr of the mighty engines was a human intelligence crooning a song of joy. For him the crowded passenger list held a significance that was almost epic, and its names represented more than mere men and women. They were the vital fiber of the land he loved, its heart's blood, its very element—"giving in." He knew that with the throb of those engines romance, adventure, tragedy, and hope were on their way north—and with these things also arrogance and greed. On board were a hundred conflicting elements—some that had fought for Alaska, others that would make her, and others that would destroy.

He puffed at his cigar and walked alone, brushing sleeves with men and women whom he scarcely seemed to notice. But he was observant. He knew the tourists almost without looking at them. The spirit of the north had not yet seized upon them. They were voluble and rather excitedly enthusiastic in the face of beauty and awesomeness. The sour-doughs were tucked away here and there in shadowy nooks, watching in silence, or they walked the deck slowly and quietly, smoking their cigars or pipes, and seeing things beyond the mountains. Between these two, the newcomers and the old-timers, ran the gamut of all human thrill for Alan, the flesh-and-blood fiber of everything that went to make up life north of Fifty-four. And he could have gone from man to man and picked out those who belonged north of Fifty-eight.

Aft of the smoking-room he paused, tipping the ash of his cigar over the edge of the rail. A little group of three stood near him, and he recognized them as the young engineers, fresh from college, going up to work on the government railroad running from Seward to Tanana. One of them was talking, filled with the enthusiasm of his first adventure.

"I tell you," he said, "people don't know what they ought to know about Alaska. In school they teach us that it's an eternal icebox full of gold, and is headquarters for Santa Claus, because that's where reindeer come from. And grown-ups think about the same thing. Why"—he drew in a deep breath—"it's nine times as large as the state of Washington, twelve times as big as the state of New York, and we bought it from Russia for less than two cents an acre. If you put it down on the face of the United States, the city of Juneau would be in St. Augustine, Florida, and Unalaska would be in Los Angeles. That's how big it is, and the geographical center of our country isn't Omaha or Sioux City, but exactly San Francisco, California."

"Good for you, sonny," came a quiet voice from beyond the group. "Your geography is correct. And you might add for the education of your people that Alaska is only thirty-seven miles from Bolshevik Siberia, and wireless messages are sent into Alaska by the Bolsheviks urging our people to rise against the Washington government. We've asked Washington for a few guns and a few men to guard Nome, but they laugh at us. Do you see a moral?"

From half-amused interest Alan jerked himself to alert tension. He caught a glimpse of the gaunt, old graybeard who had spoken, but did not know him. And as this man turned away, a shadowy hulk in the moonlight, the same deep, quiet voice came back very clearly:

"And if you ever care for Alaska, you might tell your government to hang a few such men as John Graham, sonny."

At the sound of that name Alan felt the blood in him run suddenly hot. Only one man on the face of the earth did he hate with undying hatred, and that man was John Graham. He would have followed, seeking the identity of the stranger whose words had temporarily stunned the young engineers, when he saw a slim figure standing between him and the light of the smoking-room windows. It was Mary Standish. He knew by her attitude that she had heard the words of the young engineer and the old graybeard, but she was looking at *him*. And he could not remember that he had ever seen quite that same look in a woman's face before. It was not fright. It was more an expression of horror which comes from thought and mental vision rather than physical things. Instantly it annoyed Alan Holt. This was the second time she had betrayed a too susceptible reaction in matters which did not concern her. So he said, speaking to the silent young men a few steps away:

"He was mistaken, gentlemen. John Graham should not be hung. That would be too merciful."

He resumed his way then, nodding at them as he passed. But he had scarcely gone out of their vision when quick footsteps pattered behind him, and the girl's hand touched his arm lightly.

"Mr. Holt, please—"

He stopped, sensing the fact that the soft pressure of her fingers was not altogether unpleasant. She hesitated, and when she spoke again, only her finger-tips touched his arm. She was looking shoreward, so that for a moment he could see only the lustrous richness of her smooth hair. Then she was meeting his eyes squarely, a flash of challenge in the gray depths of her own.

"I am alone on the ship," she said. "I have no friends here. I want to see things and ask questions. Will you . . . help me a little?"

"You mean . . . escort you?"

"Yes, if you will. I should feel more comfortable."

Nettled at first, the humor of the situation began to appeal to him, and he wondered at the intense seriousness of the girl. She did not smile. Her eyes were very steady and very businesslike, and at the same time very lovely.

"The way you put it, I don't see how I can refuse," he said. "As for the questions—probably Captain Rifle can answer them better than I."

"I don't like to trouble him," she replied. "He has much to think about. And you are alone."

"Yes, quite alone. And with very little to think about."

"You know what I mean, Mr. Holt. Possibly you can not understand me, or won't try. But I'm going into a new country, and I have a passionate desire to learn as much about that country as I can before I get there. I want to know about many things. For instance—"

"Yes."

"Why did you say what you did about John Graham? What did the other man mean when he said he should be hung?"

There was an intense directness in her question which for a moment astonished him. She had withdrawn her fingers from his arm, and her slim figure seemed possessed of a sudden throbbing suspense as she waited for an answer. They had turned a little, so that in the light of the moon the almost flowerlike whiteness of her face was clear to him. With her smooth, shining hair, the pallor of her face under its lustrous darkness, and the clearness of her eyes she held Alan speechless for a moment, while his brain struggled to seize upon and understand the something about her which made him interested in spite of himself. Then he smiled and there was a sudden glitter in his eyes.

"Did you ever see a dog fight?" he asked.

She hesitated, as if trying to remember, and shuddered slightly. "Once."

"What happened?"

"It was my dog—a little dog. His throat was torn—"

He nodded. "Exactly. And that is just what John Graham is doing to Alaska, Miss Standish. He's the dog—a monster. Imagine a man with a colossal financial power behind him, setting out to strip the wealth from a new land and enslave it to his own desires and political ambitions. That is what John Graham is doing from his money-throne down there in the States. It's the financial support he represents, curse him! Money—and a man without conscience. A man who would starve thousands or millions to achieve his ends. A man who, in every sense of the word, is a murderer—"

The sharpness of her cry stopped him. If possible, her face had gone whiter, and he saw her hands clutched suddenly at her breast. And the look in her eyes brought the old, cynical twist back to his lips.

"There, I've hurt your puritanism again, Miss Standish," he said, bowing a little. "In order to appeal to your finer sensibilities I suppose I must apologize for swearing and calling another man a murderer. Well, I do. And now—if you care to stroll about the ship—"

From a respectful distance the three young engineers watched Alan and Mary Standish as they walked forward.

"A corking pretty girl," said one of them, drawing a deep breath. "I never saw such hair and eyes—"

"I'm at the same table with them," interrupted another. "I'm second on her left, and she hasn't spoken three words to me. And that fellow she is with is like an icicle out of Labrador."

And Mary Standish was saying: "Do you know, Mr. Holt, I envy those young engineers. I wish I were a man."

"I wish you were," agreed Alan amiably.

Whereupon Mary Standish's pretty mouth lost its softness for an instant. But Alan did not observe this. He was enjoying his cigar and the sweet air.

* * * * *

26

CHAPTER III

Alan Holt was a man whom other men looked at twice. With women it was different. He was, in no solitary sense of the word, a woman's man. He admired them in an abstract way, and he was ready to fight for them, or die for them, at any time such a course became necessary. But his sentiment was entirely a matter of common sense. His chivalry was born and bred of the mountains and the open and had nothing in common with the insincere brand which develops in the softer and more luxurious laps of civilization. Years of aloneness had put their mark upon him. Men of the north, reading the lines, understood what they meant. But only now and then could a woman possibly understand. Yet if in any given moment a supreme physical crisis had come, women would have turned instinctively in their helplessness to such a man as Alan Holt.

He possessed a vein of humor which few had been privileged to discover. The mountains had taught him to laugh in silence. With him a chuckle meant as much as a riotous outburst of merriment from another, and he could enjoy greatly without any noticeable muscular disturbance of his face. And not always was his smile a reflection of humorous thought. There were times when it betrayed another kind of thought more forcefully than speech.

Because he understood fairly well and knew what he was, the present situation amused him. He could not but see what an error in judgment Miss Standish had made in selecting him, when compared with the intoxicating thrill she could easily have aroused by choosing one of the young engineers as a companion in her evening adventure. He chuckled. And Mary Standish, hearing the smothered note of amusement, gave to her head that swift little birdlike tilt which he had observed once before, in the presence of Captain Rifle. But she said nothing. As if challenged, she calmly took possession of his arm.

Halfway round the deck, Alan began to sense the fact that there was a decidedly pleasant flavor to the whole thing. The girl's hand did not merely touch his arm; it was snuggled there confidently, and she was necessarily so close to him that when he looked down, the glossy coils of her hair were within a few inches of his face. His nearness to her, together with the soft pressure of her hand on his arm, was a jolt to his stoicism.

"It's not half bad," he expressed himself frankly. "I really believe I am going to enjoy answering your questions, Miss Standish."

"Oh!" He felt the slim, little figure stiffen for an instant. "You thought—possibly—I might be dangerous?"

"A little. I don't understand women. Collectively I think they are God's most wonderful handiwork. Individually I don't care much about them. But you—"

She nodded approvingly. "That is very nice of you. But you needn't say I am different from the others. I am not. All women are alike."

"Possibly—except in the way they dress their hair."

"You like mine?"

"Very much."

He was amazed at the admission, so much so that he puffed out a huge cloud of smoke from his cigar in mental protest.

They had come to the smoking-room again. This was an innovation aboard the *Nome*. There was no other like it in the Alaskan service, with its luxurious space, its comfortable hospitality, and the observation parlor built at one end for those ladies who cared to sit with their husbands while they smoked their after-dinner cigars.

"If you want to hear about Alaska and see some of its human make-up, let's go in," he suggested. "I know; of no better place. Are you afraid of smoke?"

"No. If I were a man, I would smoke."

"Perhaps you do?"

"I do not. When I begin that, if you please, I shall bob my hair."

"Which would be a crime," he replied so earnestly that again he was surprised at himself.

Two or three ladies, with their escorts, were in the parlor when they entered. The huge main room, covering a third of the aft deck, was blue with smoke. A score of men were playing cards at round tables. Twice as many were gathered in groups, talking, while others walked aimlessly up and down the carpeted floor. Here and there were men who sat alone. A few were asleep, which made Alan look at his watch. Then he observed Mary Standish studying the innumerable bundles of neatly rolled blankets that lay about. One of them was at her feet. She touched it with her toe.

"What do they mean?" she asked.

"We are overloaded," he explained. "Alaskan steam-ships have no steerage passengers as we generally know them. It isn't poverty that rides steerage when you go north. You can always find a millionaire or two on the lower deck. When they get sleepy, most of the men you see in there will unroll blankets and sleep on the floor. Did you ever see an earl?"

He felt it his duty to make explanations now that he had brought her in, and directed her attention to the third table on their left. Three men were seated at this table.

"The man facing us, the one with a flabby face and pale mustache, is an earl—I forget his name," he said. "He doesn't look it, but he is a real sport. He is going up to shoot Kadiak bears, and sleeps on the floor. The group beyond them, at the fifth table, are Treadwell mining men, and that fellow you see slouched against the wall, half asleep, with whiskers nearly to his waist, is Stampede Smith, an old-time partner of George Carmack, who discovered gold on Bonanza Creek in Ninety-six. The thud of Carmack's spade, as it hit first pay, was the 'sound heard round the world,' Miss Standish. And the gentleman with crumpled whiskers was the second-best man at Bonanza, excepting Skookum Jim and Taglish Charlie, two Siwah Indians who were with Carmack when the strike was made. Also, if you care for the romantic, he was in love with Belinda Mulrooney, the most courageous woman who ever came into the north."

"Why was she courageous?"

"Because she came alone into a man's land, without a soul to fight for her, determined to make a fortune along with the others. And she did. As long as there is a Dawson sour-dough alive, he will remember Belinda Mulrooney."

"She proved what a woman could do, Mr. Holt."

"Yes, and a little later she proved how foolish a woman can be, Miss Standish. She became the richest woman in Dawson. Then came a man who posed as a count, Belinda married him, and they went to Paris. *Finis*, I think. Now, if she had married Stampede Smith over there, with his big whiskers—"

He did not finish. Half a dozen paces from them a man had risen from a table and was facing them. There was nothing unusual about him, except his boldness as he looked at Mary Standish. It was as if he knew her and was deliberately insulting her in a stare that was more than impudent in its directness. Then a sudden twist came to his lips; he shrugged his shoulders slightly and turned away.

Alan glanced swiftly at his companion. Her lips were compressed, and her cheeks were flaming hotly. Even then, as his own blood boiled, he could not but observe how beautiful anger made her.

"If you will pardon me a moment," he said quietly, "I shall demand an explanation."

Her hand linked itself quickly through his arm.

"Please don't," she entreated. "It is kind of you, and you are just the sort of man I should expect to resent a thing like that. But it would be absurd to notice it. Don't you think so?"

In spite of her effort to speak calmly, there was a tremble in her voice, and Alan was puzzled at the quickness with which the color went from her face, leaving it strangely white.

"I am at your service," he replied with a rather cold inclination of his head. "But if you were my sister, Miss Standish, I would not allow anything like that to go unchallenged."

He watched the stranger until he disappeared through a door out upon the deck.

"One of John Graham's men," he said. "A fellow named Rossland, going up to get a final grip on the salmon fishing, I understand. They'll choke the life out of it in another two years. Funny what this filthy stuff we call money can do, isn't it? Two winters ago I saw whole Indian villages starving, and women and little children dying by the score because of this John Graham's money. Over-fishing did it, you understand. If you could have seen some of those poor little devils, just skin and bones, crying for a rag to eat—"

Her hand clutched at his arm. "How could John Graham—do that?" she whispered.

He laughed unpleasantly. "When you have been a year in Alaska you won't ask that question, Miss Standish. *How*? Why, simply by glutting his canneries and taking from the streams the food supply which the natives have depended upon for generations. In other words, the money he handles represents the fish trust—and many other things. Please don't misunderstand me. Alaska needs capital for its development. Without it we will not only cease to progress; we will die. No territory on the face of the earth offers greater opportunities for capital than Alaska does today. Ten thousand fortunes are waiting to be made here by men who have money to invest.

"But John Graham does not represent the type we want. He is a despoiler, one of those whose only desire is to turn original resource into dollars as fast as he can, even though those operations make both land and water barren. You must remember until recently the government of

Alaska as manipulated by Washington politicians was little better than that against which the American colonies rebelled in 1776. A hard thing for one to say about the country he loves, isn't it? And John Graham stands for the worst—he and the money which guarantees his power.

"As a matter of fact, big and legitimate capital is fighting shy of Alaska. Conditions are such, thanks to red-tapeism and bad politics, that capital, big and little, looks askance at Alaska and cannot be interested. Think of it, Miss Standish! There are thirty-eight separate bureaus at Washington operating on Alaska, five thousand miles away. Is it a wonder the patient is sick? And is it a wonder that a man like John Graham, dishonest and corrupt to the soul, has a fertile field to work in?

"But we are progressing. We are slowly coming out from under the shadow which has so long clouded Alaska's interests. There is now a growing concentration of authority and responsibility. Both the Department of the Interior and the Department of Agriculture now realize that Alaska is a mighty empire in itself, and with their help we are bound to go ahead in spite of all our handicaps. It is men like John Graham I fear. Some day—"

Suddenly he caught himself. "There—I'm talking politics, and I should entertain you with pleasanter and more interesting things," he apologized. "Shall we go to the lower decks?"

"Or the open air," she suggested. "I am afraid this smoke is upsetting me."

He could feel the change in her and did not attribute it entirely to the thickness of the air. Rossland's inexplicable rudeness had disturbed her more deeply than she had admitted, he believed.

"There are a number of Thlinkit Indians and a tame bear down in what we should ordinarily call the steerage. Would you like to see them?" he asked, when they were outside. "The Thlinkit girls are the prettiest Indian women in the world, and there are two among those below who are—well—unusually good-looking, the Captain says."

"And he has already made me acquainted with them," she laughed softly. "Kolo and Haidah are the girls. They are sweet, and I love them. I had breakfast with them this morning long before you were awake."

"The deuce you say! And that is why you were not at table? And the morning before—"

"You noticed my absence?" she asked demurely.

"It was difficult for me not to see an empty chair. On second thought, I think the young engineer called my attention to it by wondering if you were ill."

"Oh!"

"He is very much interested in you, Miss Standish. It amuses me to see him torture the corners of his eyes to look at you. I have thought it would be only charity and good-will to change seats with him."

"In which event, of course, your eyes would not suffer."

"Probably not."

"Have they ever suffered?"

"I think not."

"When looking at the Thlinkit girls, for instance?"

"I haven't seen them."

She gave her shoulders a little shrug.

"Ordinarily I would think you most uninteresting, Mr. Holt. As it is I think you unusual. And I rather like you for it. Would you mind taking me to my cabin? It is number sixteen, on this deck."

She walked with her fingers touching his arm again. "What is your room?" she asked.

"Twenty-seven, Miss Standish."

"This deck?"

"Yes."

Not until she had said good night, quietly and without offering him her hand, did the intimacy of her last questions strike him. He grunted and lighted a fresh cigar. A number of things occurred to him all at once, as he slowly made a final round or two of the deck. Then he went to his cabin and looked over papers which were going ashore at Juneau. These were memoranda giving an account of his appearance with Carl Lomen before the Ways and Means Committee at Washington.

It was nearly midnight when he had finished. He wondered if Mary Standish was asleep. He was a little irritated, and slightly amused, by the recurring insistency with which his mind turned to her. She was a clever girl, he admitted. He had asked her nothing about herself, and she had told him nothing, while he had been quite garrulous. He was a little ashamed when he recalled how he had unburdened his mind to a girl who could not possibly be interested in the political affairs of John Graham and Alaska. Well, it was not entirely his fault. She had fairly catapulted herself upon him, and he had been decent under the circumstances, he thought.

He put out his light and stood with his face at the open port-hole. Only the soft throbbing of the vessel as she made her way slowly through the last of the Narrows into Frederick Sound came to his ears. The ship, at last, was asleep. The moon was straight overhead, no longer silhouetting the mountains, and beyond its misty rim of light the world was dark. Out of this darkness, rising like a deeper shadow, Alan could make out faintly the huge mass of Kupreanof Island. And he wondered, knowing the perils of the Narrows in places scarcely wider than the length of the ship, why Captain Rifle had chosen this course instead of going around by Cape Decision. He could feel that the land was more distant now, but the *Nome* was still pushing ahead under slow bell, and he could smell the fresh odor of kelp, and breathe deeply of the scent of forests that came from both east and west.

Suddenly his ears became attentive to slowly approaching footsteps. They seemed to hesitate and then advanced; he heard a subdued voice, a man's voice—and in answer to it a woman's. Instinctively he drew a step back and stood unseen in the gloom. There was no longer a sound of voices. In silence they walked past his window, clearly revealed to him in the moonlight. One of the two was Mary Standish. The man was Rossland, who had stared at her so boldly in the smoking-room.

Amazement gripped Alan. He switched on his light and made his final arrangements for bed. He had no inclination to spy upon either Mary Standish or Graham's agent, but he possessed an inborn hatred of fraud and humbug, and what he had seen convinced him that Mary Standish knew more about Rossland than she had allowed him to believe. She had not lied to him. She had said nothing at all—except to restrain him from demanding an apology. Evidently she had taken advantage of him, but beyond that fact her affairs had nothing to do with his own business in life. Possibly she and Rossland had quarreled, and now they were making up. Quite probable, he thought. Silly of him to think over the matter at all.

So he put out his light again and went to bed. But he had no great desire to sleep. It was pleasant to lie there, flat on his back, with the soothing movement of the ship under him, listening to the musical thrum of it. And it was pleasant to think of the fact that he was going home. How infernally long those seven months had been, down in the States! And how he had missed everyone he had ever known—even his enemies!

He closed his eyes and visualized the home that was still thousands of miles away—the endless tundras, the blue and purple foothills of the Endicott Mountains, and "Alan's Range" at the beginning of them. Spring was breaking up there, and it was warm on the tundras and the southern slopes, and the pussy-willow buds were popping out of their coats like corn from a hopper.

He prayed God the months had been kind to his people—the people of the range. It was a long time to be away from them, when one loved them as he did. He was sure that Tautuk and Amuk Toolik, his two chief herdsmen, would care for things as well as himself. But much could happen in seven months. Nawadlook, the little beauty of his distant kingdom, was not looking well when he left. He was worried about her. The pneumonia of the previous winters had left its mark. And Keok, her rival in prettiness! He smiled in the darkness, wondering how Tautuk's sometimes hopeless love affair had progressed. For Keok was a little heart-breaker and had long reveled in Tautuk's sufferings. An archangel of iniquity, Alan thought, as he grinned—but worth any man's risk of life, if he had but a drop of brown blood in him! As for his herds, they had undoubtedly fared well. Ten thousand head was something to be proud of—

Suddenly he drew in his breath and listened. Someone was at his door and had paused there. Twice he had heard footsteps outside, but each time they had passed. He sat up, and the springs of his berth made a sound under him. He heard movement then, a swift, running movement—and he switched on his light. A moment later he opened the door. No one was there. The long corridor was empty. And then—a distance away—he heard the soft opening and closing of another door.

It was then that his eyes saw a white, crumpled object on the floor. He picked it up and reentered his room. It was a woman's handkerchief. And he had seen it before. He had admired the pretty laciness of it that evening in the smoking-room. Rather curious, he thought, that he should now find it at his door.

* * * * *

CHAPTER IV

For a few minutes after finding the handkerchief at his door, Alan experienced a feeling of mingled curiosity and disappointment—also a certain resentment. The suspicion that he was becoming involved in spite of himself was not altogether pleasant. The evening, up to a certain point, had been fairly entertaining. It was true he might have passed a pleasanter hour recalling old times with Stampede Smith, or discussing Kadiak bears with the English earl, or striking up an acquaintance with the unknown graybeard who had voiced an opinion about John Graham. But he was not regretting lost hours, nor was he holding Mary Standish accountable for them. It was, last of all, the handkerchief that momentarily upset him.

Why had she dropped it at his door? It was not a dangerous-looking affair, to be sure, with its filmy lace edging and ridiculous diminutiveness. As the question came to him, he was wondering how even as dainty a nose as that possessed by Mary Standish could be much comforted by it. But it was pretty. And, like Mary Standish, there was something exquisitely quiet and perfect about it, like the simplicity of her hair. He was not analyzing the matter. It was a thought that came to him almost unconsciously, as he tossed the annoying bit of fabric on the little table at the head of his berth. Undoubtedly the dropping of it had been entirely unpremeditated and accidental. At least he told himself so. And he also assured himself, with an involuntary shrug of his shoulders, that any woman or girl had the right to pass his door if she so desired, and that he was an idiot for thinking otherwise. The argument was only slightly adequate. But Alan was not interested in mysteries, especially when they had to do with woman—and such an absurdly inconsequential thing as a handkerchief.

A second time he went to bed. He fell asleep thinking about Keok and Nawadlook and the people of his range. From somewhere he had been given the priceless heritage of dreaming pleasantly, and Keok was very real, with her swift smile and mischievous face, and Nawadlook's big, soft eyes were brighter than when he had gone away. He saw Tautuk, gloomy as usual over the heartlessness of Keok. He was beating a tom-tom that gave out the peculiar sound of bells, and to this Amuk Toolik was dancing the Bear Dance, while Keok clapped her hands in exaggerated admiration. Even in his dreams Alan chuckled. He knew what was happening, and that out of the corners of her laughing eyes Keok was enjoying Tautuk's jealousy. Tautuk was so stupid he would never understand. That was the funny part of it. And he beat his drum savagely, scowling so that he almost shut his eyes, while Keok laughed outright.

It was then that Alan opened his eyes and heard the last of the ship's bells. It was still dark. He turned on the light and looked at his watch. Tautuk's drum had tolled eight bells, aboard the ship, and it was four o'clock in the morning.

Through the open port came the smell of sea and land, and with it a chill air which Alan drank in deeply as he stretched himself for a few minutes after awakening. The tang of it was like wine in his blood, and he got up quietly and dressed while he smoked the stub-end of a cigar he had laid aside at midnight. Not until he had finished dressing did he notice the handkerchief on the table. If its presence had suggested a significance a few hours before, he no longer disturbed himself by thinking about it. A bit of carelessness on the girl's part, that was all. He would return it. Mechanically he put the crumpled bit of cambric in his coat pocket before going on deck.

He had guessed that he would be alone. The promenade was deserted. Through the ghost-white mist of morning he saw the rows of empty chairs, and lights burning dully in the wheel-house. Asian monsoon and the drifting warmth of the Japan current had brought an early spring to the Alexander Archipelago, and May had stolen much of the flowering softness of June. But the dawns of these days were chilly and gray. Mists and fogs settled in the valleys, and like thin smoke rolled down the sides of the mountains to the sea, so that a ship traveling the inner waters felt its way like a child creeping in darkness.

Alan loved this idiosyncrasy of the Alaskan coast. The phantom mystery of it was stimulating, and in the peril of it was a challenging lure. He could feel the care with which the *Nome* was picking her way northward. Her engines were thrumming softly, and her movement was a slow and cautious glide, catlike and slightly trembling, as if every pound of steel in her were a living nerve widely alert. He knew Captain Rifle would not be asleep and that straining eyes were peering into the white gloom from the wheel-house. Somewhere west of them, hazardously near, must lie the rocks of Admiralty Island; eastward were the still more pitiless glacial sandstones and granites of the coast, with that deadly finger of sea-washed reef between, along the lip of which they must creep to Juneau. And Juneau could not be far ahead.

He leaned over the rail, puffing at the stub of his cigar. He was eager for his work. Juneau, Skagway, and Cordova meant nothing to him, except that they were Alaska. He yearned for the still farther north, the wide tundras, and the mighty achievement that lay ahead of him there. His blood sang to the surety of it now, and for that reason he was not sorry he had spent seven months of loneliness in the States. He had proved with his own eyes that the day was near when Alaska would come into her own. Gold! He laughed. Gold had its lure, its romance, its thrill, but what was all the gold the mountains might possess compared with this greater thing he was helping to build! It seemed to him the people he had met in the south had thought only of gold when they learned he was from Alaska. Always gold—that first, and then ice, snow, endless nights, desolate barrens, and craggy mountains frowning everlastingly upon a blasted land in which men fought against odds and only the fittest survived. It was gold that had been Alaska's doom. When people thought of it, they visioned nothing beyond the old stampede days, the Chilkoot, White Horse, Dawson, and Circle City. Romance and glamor and the tragedies of dead men clung to their ribs. But they were beginning to believe now. Their eyes were opening. Even the Government was waking up, after proving there was something besides graft in railroad building north of Mount St. Elias. Senators and Congressmen at Washington had listened to him seriously, and especially to Carl Lomen. And the beef barons, wisest of all, had tried to buy him off and had offered a fortune for Lomen's forty thousand head of reindeer in the Seward Peninsula! That was proof of the awakening. Absolute proof.

He lighted a fresh cigar, and his mind shot through the dissolving mist into the vast land ahead of him. Some Alaskans had cursed Theodore Roosevelt for putting what they called "the conservation shackles" on their country. But he, for one, did not. Roosevelt's far-sightedness had kept the body-snatchers at bay, and because he had foreseen what money-power and greed would do, Alaska was not entirely stripped today, but lay ready to serve with all her mighty resources the mother who had neglected her for a generation. But it was going to be a struggle, this opening up of a great land. It must be done resourcefully and with intelligence. Once the bars were down, Roosevelt's shadow-hand could not hold back such desecrating forces as John Graham and the syndicate he represented.

Thought of Graham was an unpleasant reminder, and his face grew hard in the sea-mist. Alaskans themselves must fight against the licensed plunderers. And it would be a hard fight. He had seen the pillaging work of these financial brigands in a dozen states during the past winter— states raped of their forests, their lakes and streams robbed and polluted, their resources hewn down to naked skeletons. He had been horrified and a little frightened when he looked over the desolation of Michigan, once the richest timber state in America. What if the Government at Washington made it possible for such a thing to happen in Alaska? Politics—and money—were already fighting for just that thing.

He no longer heard the throb of the ship under his feet. It was *his* fight, and brain and muscle reacted to it almost as if it had been a physical thing. And his end of that fight he was determined to win, if it took every year of his life. He, with a few others, would prove to the world that the millions of acres of treeless tundras of the north were not the cast-off ends of the earth. They would populate them, and the so-called "barrens" would thunder to the innumerable hoofs of reindeer herds as the American plains had never thundered to the beat of cattle. He was not thinking of the treasure he would find at the end of this rainbow of success which he visioned. Money, simply as money, he hated. It was the achievement of the thing that gripped him; the passion to hew a trail through which his beloved land might come into its own, and the desire to see it achieve a final triumph by feeding a half of that America which had laughed at it and kicked it when it was down.

The tolling of the ship's bell roused him from the subconscious struggle into which he had allowed himself to be drawn. Ordinarily he had no sympathy with himself when he fell into one of these mental spasms, as he called them. Without knowing it, he was a little proud of a certain dispassionate tolerance which he possessed—a philosophical mastery of his emotions which at times was almost cold-blooded, and which made some people think he was a thing of stone instead of flesh and blood. His thrills he kept to himself. And a mildly disturbing sensation passed through him now, when he found that unconsciously his fingers had twined themselves about the little handkerchief in his pocket. He drew it out and made a sudden movement as if to toss it overboard. Then, with a grunt expressive of the absurdity of the thing, he replaced it in his pocket and began to walk slowly toward the bow of the ship.

He wondered, as he noted the lifting of the fog, what he would have been had he possessed a sister like Mary Standish. Or any family at all, for that matter—even an uncle or two who might have been interested in him. He remembered his father vividly, his mother a little less so, because his mother had died when he was six and his father when he was twenty.

It was his father who stood out above everything else, like the mountains he loved. The father would remain with him always, inspiring him, urging him, encouraging him to live like a gentleman, fight like a man, and die at last unafraid. In that fashion the older Alan Holt had lived and died. But his mother, her face and voice scarcely remembered in the passing of many years, was more a hallowed memory to him than a thing of flesh and blood. And there had been no sisters or brothers. Often he had regretted this lack of brotherhood. But a sister . . . He grunted his disapprobation of the thought. A sister would have meant enchainment to civilization. Cities, probably. Even the States. And slavery to a life he detested. He appreciated the immensity of his freedom. A Mary Standish, even though she were his sister, would be a catastrophe. He could not conceive of her, or any other woman like her, living with Keok and Nawadlook and the rest of his people in the heart of the tundras. And the tundras would always be his home, because his heart was there.

He had passed round the wheel-house and came suddenly upon an odd figure crumpled in a chair. It was Stampede Smith. In the clearer light that came with the dissolution of the sea-mist Alan saw that he was not asleep. He paused, unseen by the other. Stampede stretched himself, groaned, and stood up. He was a little man, and his fiercely bristling red whiskers, wet with dew, were luxuriant enough for a giant. His head of tawny hair, bristling like his whiskers, added to the piratical effect of him above the neck, but below that part of his anatomy there was little to strike fear into the hearts of humanity. Some people smiled when they looked at him. Others, not knowing their man, laughed outright. Whiskers could be funny. And they were undoubtedly funny on Stampede Smith. But Alan neither smiled nor laughed, for in his heart was something very near to the missing love of brotherhood for this little man who had written his name across so many pages of Alaskan history.

This morning, as Alan saw him, Stampede Smith was no longer the swiftest gunman between White Horse and Dawson City. He was a pathetic reminder of the old days when, single-handed, he had run down

Soapy Smith and his gang—days when the going of Stampede Smith to new fields meant a stampede behind him, and when his name was mentioned in the same breath with those of George Carmack, and Alex McDonald, and Jerome Chute, and a hundred men like Curley Monroe and Joe Barret set their compasses by his. To Alan there was tragedy in his aloneness as he stood in the gray of the morning. Twenty times a millionaire, he knew that Stampede Smith was broke again.

"Good morning," he said so unexpectedly that the little man jerked himself round like the lash of a whip, a trick of the old gun days. "Why so much loneliness, Stampede?"

Stampede grinned wryly. He had humorous, blue eyes, buried like an Airedale's under brows which bristled even more fiercely than his whiskers. "I'm thinkin'," said he, "what a fool thing is money. Good mornin', Alan!"

He nodded and chuckled, and continued to chuckle in the face of the lifting fog, and Alan saw the old humor which had always been Stampede's last asset when in trouble. He drew nearer and stood beside him, so that their shoulders touched as they leaned over the rail.

"Alan," said Stampede, "it ain't often I have a big thought, but I've been having one all night. Ain't forgot Bonanza, have you?"

Alan shook his head. "As long as there is an Alaska, we won't forget Bonanza, Stampede."

"I took a million out of it, next to Carmack's Discovery—an' went busted afterward, didn't I?"

Alan nodded without speaking.

"But that wasn't a circumstance to Gold Run Creek, over the Divide," Stampede continued ruminatively. "Ain't forgot old Aleck McDonald, the Scotchman, have you, Alan? In the 'wash' of Ninety-eight we took up seventy sacks to bring our gold back in and we lacked thirty of doin' the job. Nine hundred thousand dollars in a single clean-up, and that was only the beginning. Well, I went busted again. And old Aleck went busted later on. But he had a pretty wife left. A girl from Seattle. I had to grub-stake."

He was silent for a moment, caressing his damp whiskers, as he noted the first rose-flush of the sun breaking through the mist between them and the unseen mountain tops.

"Five times after that I made strikes and went busted," he said a little proudly. "And I'm busted again!"

"I know it," sympathized Alan.

"They took every cent away from me down in Seattle an' Frisco," chuckled Stampede, rubbing his hands together cheerfully, "an' then bought me a ticket to Nome. Mighty fine of them, don't you think? Couldn't have been more decent. I knew that fellow Kopf had a heart. That's why I trusted him with my money. It wasn't his fault he lost it."

"Of course not," agreed Alan.

"And I'm sort of sorry I shot him up for it. I am, for a fact."

"You killed him?"

"Not quite. I clipped one ear off as a reminder, down in Chink Holleran's place. Mighty sorry. Didn't think then how decent it was of him to buy me a ticket to Nome. I just let go in the heat of the moment. He did me a favor in cleanin' me, Alan. He did, so help me! You don't realize how free an' easy an' beautiful everything is until you're busted."

Smiling, his odd face almost boyish behind its ambush of hair, he saw the grim look in Alan's eyes and about his jaws. He caught hold of the other's arm and shook it.

"Alan, I mean it!" he declared. "That's why I think money is a fool thing. It ain't *spendin'* money that makes me happy. It's *findin'* it—the gold in the mountains—that makes the blood run fast through my gizzard. After I've found it, I can't find any use for it in particular. I want to go broke. If I didn't, I'd get lazy and fat, an' some newfangled doctor would operate on me, and I'd die. They're doing a lot of that operatin' down in Frisco, Alan. One day I had a pain, and they wanted to cut out something from inside me. Think what can happen to a man when he's got money!"

"You mean all that, Stampede?"

"On my life, I do. I'm just aching for the open skies, Alan. The mountains. And the yellow stuff that's going to be my playmate till I die. Somebody'll grub-stake me in Nome."

"They won't," said Alan suddenly. "Not if I can help it. Stampede, I want you. I want you with me up under the Endicott Mountains. I've got ten thousand reindeer up there. It's No Man's Land, and we can do as we please in it. I'm not after gold. I want another sort of thing. But I've fancied the Endicott ranges are full of that yellow playmate of yours. It's a new country. You've never seen it. God only knows what you may find. Will you come?"

The humorous twinkle had gone out of Stampede's eyes. He was staring at Alan.

"Will I *come?* Alan, will a cub nurse its mother? Try me. Ask me. Say it all over ag'in."

The two men gripped hands. Smiling, Alan nodded to the east. The last of the fog was clearing swiftly. The tips of the cragged Alaskan ranges rose up against the blue of a cloudless sky, and the morning sun was flashing in rose and gold at their snowy peaks. Stampede also nodded. Speech was unnecessary. They both understood, and the thrill of the life they loved passed from one to the other in the grip of their hands.

* * * * *

CHAPTER V

Breakfast hour was half over when Alan went into the dining-room. There were only two empty chairs at his table. One was his own. The other belonged to Mary Standish. There was something almost aggressively suggestive in their simultaneous vacancy, it struck him at first. He nodded as he sat down, a flash of amusement in his eyes when he observed the look in the young engineer's face. It was both envious and accusing, and yet Alan was sure the young man was unconscious of betraying an emotion. The fact lent to the eating of his grapefruit an accompaniment of pleasing and amusing thought. He recalled the young man's name. It was Tucker. He was a clean-faced, athletic, likable-looking chap. And an idiot would have guessed the truth, Alan told himself. The young engineer was more than casually interested in Mary Standish; he was in love. It was not a discovery which Alan made. It was a decision, and as soon as possible he would remedy the unfortunate omission of a general introduction at their table by bringing the two together. Such an introduction would undoubtedly relieve him of a certain responsibility which had persisted in attaching itself to him.

So he tried to think. But in spite of his resolution he could not get the empty chair opposite him out of his mind. It refused to be obliterated, and when other chairs became vacant as their owners left the table, this one straight across from him continued to thrust itself upon him. Until this morning it had been like other empty chairs. Now it was persistently annoying, inasmuch as he had no desire to be so constantly reminded of last night, and the twelve o'clock tryst of Mary Standish with Graham's agent, Rossland.

He was the last at the table. Tucker, remaining until his final hope of seeing Mary Standish was gone, rose with two others. The first two had made their exit through the door leading from the dining salon when the young engineer paused. Alan, watching him, saw a sudden change in his face. In a moment it was explained. Mary Standish came in. She passed Tucker without appearing to notice him, and gave Alan a cool little nod as she seated herself at the table. She was very pale. He could see nothing of the flush of color that had been in her cheeks last night. As she bowed her head a little, arranging her dress, a pool of sunlight played in her hair, and Alan was staring at it when she raised her eyes. They were coolly beautiful, very direct, and without embarrassment. Something inside him challenged their loveliness. It seemed inconceivable that such eyes could play a part in fraud and deception, yet he was in possession of quite conclusive proof of it. If they had lowered themselves an instant, if they had in any way betrayed a shadow of regret, he would have found an apology. Instead of that, his fingers touched the handkerchief in his pocket.

"Did you sleep well, Miss Standish?" he asked politely.

"Not at all," she replied, so frankly that his conviction was a bit unsettled. "I tried to powder away the dark rings under my eyes, but I am afraid I have failed. Is that why you ask?"

He was holding the handkerchief in his hand. "This is the first morning I have seen you at breakfast. I accepted it for granted you must have slept well. Is this yours, Miss Standish?"

He watched her face as she took the crumpled bit of cambric from his fingers. In a moment she was smiling. The smile was not forced. It was the quick response to a feminine instinct of pleasure, and he was disappointed not to catch in her face a betrayal of embarrassment.

"It is my handkerchief, Mr. Holt. Where did you find it?"

"In front of my cabin door a little after midnight."

He was almost brutal in the definiteness of detail. He expected some kind of result. But there was none, except that the smile remained on her lips a moment longer, and there was a laughing flash back in the clear depths of her eyes. Her level glance was as innocent as a child's and as he looked at her, he thought of a child—a most beautiful child—and so utterly did he feel the discomfiture of his mental analysis of her that he rose to his feet with a frigid bow.

"I thank you, Mr. Holt," she said. "You can imagine my sense of obligation when I tell you I have only three handkerchiefs aboard the ship with me. And this is my favorite."

She busied herself with the breakfast card, and as Alan left, he heard her give the waiter an order for fruit and cereal. His blood was hot, but the flush of it did not show in his face. He felt the uncomfortable sensation of her eyes following him as he stalked through the door. He did not look back. Something was wrong with him, and he knew it. This chit of a girl with her smooth hair and clear eyes had thrown a grain of dust into the satisfactory mechanism of his normal self, and the grind of it was upsetting certain specific formulae which made up his life. He was a fool. He lighted a cigar and called himself names.

Someone brushed against him, jarring the hand that held the burning match. He looked up. It was Rossland. The man had a mere twist of a smile on his lips. In his eyes was a coolly appraising look as he nodded.

"Beg pardon." The words were condescending, carelessly flung at him over Rossland's shoulder. He might as well have said, "I'm sorry, Boy, but you must keep out of my way."

Alan smiled back and returned the nod. Once, in a spirit of sauciness, Keok had told him his eyes were like purring cats when he was in a humor to kill. They were like that now as they flashed their smile at Rossland. The sneering twist left Rossland's lips as he entered the dining-room.

A rather obvious prearrangement between Mary Standish and John Graham's agent, Alan thought. There were not half a dozen people left at the tables, and the scheme was that Rossland should be served tête-à-tête with Miss Standish, of course. That, apparently, was why she had greeted him with such cool civility. Her anxiety for him to leave the table before

Rossland appeared upon the scene was evident, now that he understood the situation.

He puffed at his cigar. Rossland's interference had spoiled a perfect lighting of it, and he struck another match. This time he was successful, and he was about to extinguish the burning end when he hesitated and held it until the fire touched his flesh. Mary Standish was coming through the door. Amazed by the suddenness of her appearance, he made no movement except to drop the match. Her eyes were flaming, and two vivid spots burned in her cheeks. She saw him and gave the slightest inclination to her head as she passed. When she had gone, he could not resist looking into the salon. As he expected, Rossland was seated in a chair next to the one she had occupied, and was calmly engaged in looking over the breakfast card.

All this was rather interesting, Alan conceded, if one liked puzzles. Personally he had no desire to become an answerer of conundrums, and he was a little ashamed of the curiosity that had urged him to look in upon Rossland. At the same time he was mildly elated at the freezing reception which Miss Standish had evidently given to the dislikable individual who had jostled him in passing.

He went on deck. The sun was pouring in an iridescent splendor over the snowy peaks of the mountains, and it seemed as if he could almost reach out his arms and touch them. The *Nome* appeared to be drifting in the heart of a paradise of mountains. Eastward, very near, was the mainland; so close on the other hand that he could hear the shout of a man was Douglas Island, and ahead, reaching out like a silver-blue ribbon was Gastineau Channel. The mining towns of Treadwell and Douglas were in sight.

Someone nudged him, and he found Stampede Smith at his side.

"That's Bill Treadwell's place," he said. "Once the richest gold mines in Alaska. They're flooded now. I knew Bill when he was worrying about the price of a pair of boots. Had to buy a second-hand pair an' patched 'em himself. Then he struck it lucky, got four hundred dollars somewhere, and bought some claims over there from a man named French Pete. They called it Glory Hole. An' there was a time when there were nine hundred stamps at work. Take a look, Alan. It's worth it."

Somehow Stampede's voice and information lacked appeal. The decks were crowded with passengers as the ship picked her way into Juneau, and Alan wandered among them with a gathering sense of disillusionment pressing upon him. He knew that he was looking with more than casual interest for Mary Standish, and he was glad when Stampede bumped into an old acquaintance and permitted him to be alone. He was not pleased with the discovery, and yet he was compelled to acknowledge the truth of it. The grain of dust had become more than annoying. It did not wear away, as he had supposed it would, but was becoming an obsessive factor in his thoughts. And the half-desire it built up in him, while aggravatingly persistent, was less disturbing than before. The little drama in the dining-room had had its effect upon him in spite of himself. He liked fighters. And Mary Standish, intensely feminine in her quiet prettiness, had shown her mettle in those few moments when he had seen her flashing eyes and blazing cheeks after leaving Rossland. He began to look for Rossland, too. He was in a humor to meet him.

Not until Juneau hung before him in all its picturesque beauty, literally terraced against the green sweep of Mount Juneau, did he go down to the lower deck. The few passengers ready to leave the ship gathered near the gangway with their luggage. Alan was about to pass them when he suddenly stopped. A short distance from him, where he could see every person who disembarked, stood Rossland. There was something grimly unpleasant in his attitude as he fumbled his watch-fob and eyed the stair from above. His watchfulness sent an unexpected thrill through Alan. Like a shot his mind jumped to a conclusion. He stepped to Rossland's side and touched his arm.

"Watching for Miss Standish?" he asked.

"I am." There was no evasion in Rossland's words. They possessed the hard and definite quality of one who had an incontestable authority behind him.

"And if she goes ashore?"

"I am going too. Is it any affair of yours, Mr. Holt? Has she asked you to discuss the matter with me? If so——"

"No, Miss Standish hasn't done that."

"Then please attend to your own business. If you haven't enough to take up your time, I'll lend you some books. I have several in my cabin."

Without waiting for an answer Rossland coolly moved away. Alan did not follow. There was nothing for him to resent, nothing for him to imprecate but his own folly. Rossland's words were not an insult. They were truth. He had deliberately intruded in an affair which was undoubtedly of a highly private nature. Possibly it was a domestic tangle. He shuddered. A sense of humiliation swept over him, and he was glad that Rossland did not even look back at him. He tried to whistle as he climbed back to the main-deck; Rossland, even though he detested the man, had set him right. And he would lend him books, if he wanted to be amused! Egad, but the fellow had turned the trick nicely. And it was something to be remembered. He stiffened his shoulders and found old Donald Hardwick and Stampede Smith. He did not leave them until the *Nome* had landed her passengers and freight and was churning her way out of Gastineau Channel toward Skagway. Then he went to the smoking-room and remained there until luncheon hour.

Today Mary Standish was ahead of him at the table. She was seated with her back toward him as he entered, so she did not see him as he came up behind her, so near that his coat brushed her chair. He looked across at her and smiled as he seated himself. She returned the smile, but it seemed to him an apologetic little effort. She did not look well, and her presence at the table struck him as being a brave front to hide something from someone. Casually he looked over his left shoulder. Rossland was there, in his seat at the opposite side of the room. Indirect as his glance had been, Alan saw the girl understood the significance of it. She bowed her head a little, and her long lashes shaded her eyes for a moment. He wondered why he always looked at her hair first. It had a peculiarly pleasing effect on him. He had been observant enough to know that she had rearranged it since breakfast, and the smooth coils twisted in mysterious intricacy at the crown of her head were like softly glowing velvet. The ridiculous thought came to him that he would like to see them tumbling down about her. They must be even more beautiful when freed from their bondage.

The pallor of her face was unusual. Possibly it was the way the light fell upon her through the window. But when she looked across at him again, he caught for an instant the tiniest quiver about her mouth. He began telling her something about Skagway, quite carelessly, as if he had seen nothing which she might want to conceal. The light in her eyes changed, and it was almost a glow of gratitude he caught in them. He had broken a tension, relieved her of some unaccountable strain she was under. He noticed that her ordering of food was merely a pretense. She scarcely touched it, and yet he was sure no other person at the table had discovered the insincerity of her effort, not even Tucker, the enamored engineer. It was likely Tucker placed a delicate halo about her lack of appetite, accepting daintiness of that sort as an angelic virtue.

Only Alan, sitting opposite her, guessed the truth. She was making a splendid effort, but he felt that every nerve in her body was at the breaking-point. When she arose from her seat, he thrust back his own chair. At the same time he saw Rossland get up and advance rather hurriedly from the opposite side of the room. The girl passed through the door first, Rossland followed a dozen steps behind, and Alan came last, almost shoulder to shoulder with Tucker. It was amusing in a way, yet beyond the humor of it was something that drew a grim line about the corners of his mouth.

At the foot of the luxuriously carpeted stair leading from the dining salon to the main deck Miss Standish suddenly stopped and turned upon

Rossland. For only an instant her eyes were leveled at him. Then they flashed past him, and with a swift movement she came toward Alan. A flush had leaped into her cheeks, but there was no excitement in her voice when she spoke. Yet it was distinct, and clearly heard by Rossland.

"I understand we are approaching Skagway, Mr. Holt," she said. "Will you take me on deck, and tell me about it?"

Graham's agent had paused at the foot of the stair and was slowly preparing to light a cigarette. Recalling his humiliation of a few hours before at Juneau, when the other had very clearly proved him a meddler, words refused to form quickly on Alan's lips. Before he was ready with an answer Mary Standish had confidently taken his arm. He could see the red flush deepening in her upturned face. She was amazingly unexpected, bewilderingly pretty, and as cool as ice except for the softly glowing fire in her cheeks. He saw Rossland staring with his cigarette half poised. It was instinctive for him to smile in the face of danger, and he smiled now, without speaking. The girl laughed softly. She gave his arm a gentle tug, and he found himself moving past Rossland, amazed but obedient, her eyes looking at him in a way that sent a gentle thrill through him.

At the head of the wide stair she whispered, with her lips close to his shoulder: "You are splendid! I thank you, Mr. Holt."

Her words, along with the decisive relaxing of her hand upon his arm, were like a dash of cold water in his face. Rossland could no longer see them, unless he had followed. The girl had played her part, and a second time he had accepted the role of a slow-witted fool. But the thought did not anger him. There was a remarkable element of humor about it for him, viewing himself in the matter, and Mary Standish heard him chuckling as they came out on deck.

Her fingers tightened resentfully upon his arm. "It isn't funny," she reproved. "It is tragic to be bored by a man like that."

He knew she was politely lying to anticipate the question he might ask, and he wondered what would happen if he embarrassed her by letting her know he had seen her alone with Rossland at midnight. He looked down at her, and she met his scrutiny unflinchingly. She even smiled at him, and her eyes, he thought, were the loveliest liars he had ever looked into. He felt the stir of an unusual sentiment—a sort of pride in her, and he made up his mind to say nothing about Rossland. He was still absurdly convinced that he had not the smallest interest in affairs which were not entirely his own. Mary Standish evidently believed he was blind, and he would make no effort to spoil her illusion. Such a course would undoubtedly be most satisfactory in the end.

Even now she seemed to have forgotten the incident at the foot of the stair. A softer light was in her eyes when they came to the bow of the ship, and Alan fancied he heard a strange little cry on her lips as she looked about her upon the paradise of Taiya Inlet. Straight ahead, like a lilac ribbon, ran the narrow waterway to Skagway's door, while on both sides rose high mountains, covered with green forests to the snowy crests that gleamed like white blankets near the clouds. In this melting season there came to them above the slow throb of the ship's engines the liquid music of innumerable cascades, and from a mountain that seemed to float almost directly over their heads fell a stream of water a sheer thousand feet to the sea, smoking and twisting in the sunshine like a living thing at play. And then a miracle happened which even Alan wondered at, for the ship seemed to stand still and the mountain to swing slowly, as if some unseen and mighty force were opening a guarded door, and green foothills with glistening white cottages floated into the picture, and Skagway, heart of romance, monument to brave men and thrilling deeds, drifted out slowly from its hiding-place. Alan turned to speak, but what he saw in the girl's face held him silent. Her lips were parted, and she was staring as if an unexpected thing had risen before her eyes, something that bewildered her and even startled her.

And then, as if speaking to herself and not to Alan Holt, she said in a tense whisper: "I have seen this place before. It was a long time ago. Maybe it was a hundred years or a thousand. But I have been here. I have lived under that mountain with the waterfall creeping down it—"

A tremor ran through her, and she remembered Alan. She looked up at him, and he was puzzled. A weirdly beautiful mystery lay in her eyes.

"I must go ashore here," she said. "I didn't know I would find it so soon. Please—"

With her hand touching his arm she turned. He was looking at her and saw the strange light fade swiftly out of her eyes. Following her glance he saw Rossland standing half a dozen paces behind them.

In another moment Mary Standish was facing the sea, and again her hand was resting confidently in the crook of Alan's arm. "Did you ever feel like killing a man, Mr. Holt?" she asked with an icy little laugh.

"Yes," he answered rather unexpectedly. "And some day, if the right opportunity comes, I am going to kill a certain man—the man who murdered my father."

She gave a little gasp of horror. "Your father—was—murdered—"

"Indirectly—yes. It wasn't done with knife or gun, Miss Standish. Money was the weapon. Somebody's money. And John Graham was the man who struck the blow. Some day, if there is justice, I shall kill him. And right now, if you will allow me to demand an explanation of this man Rossland—"

"*No.*" Her hand tightened on his arm. Then, slowly, she drew it away. "I don't want you to ask an explanation of him," she said. "If he should make it, you would hate me. Tell me about Skagway, Mr. Holt. That will be pleasanter."

* * * * *

CHAPTER VI

Not until early twilight came with the deep shadows of the western mountains, and the *Nome* was churning slowly back through the narrow water-trails to the open Pacific, did the significance of that afternoon fully impress itself upon Alan. For hours he had surrendered himself to an impulse which he could not understand, and which in ordinary moments he would not have excused. He had taken Mary Standish ashore. For two hours she had walked at his side, asking him questions and listening to him as no other had ever questioned him or listened to him before. He had shown her Skagway. Between the mountains he pictured the wind-racked cañon where Skagway grew from one tent to hundreds in a day, from hundreds to thousands in a week; he visioned for her the old days of romance, adventure, and death; he told her of Soapy Smith and his gang of outlaws, and side by side they stood over Soapy's sunken grave as the first somber shadows of the mountains grew upon them.

But among it all, and through it all, she had asked him about *himself*. And he had responded. Until now he did not realize how much he had confided in her. It seemed to him that the very soul of this slim and beautiful girl who had walked at his side had urged him on to the indiscretion of personal confidence. He had seemed to feel her heart beating with his own as he described his beloved land under the Endicott Mountains, with its vast tundras, his herds, and his people. There, he had told her, a new world was in the making, and the glow in her eyes and the thrilling something in her voice had urged him on until he forgot that Rossland was waiting at the ship's gangway to see when they returned. He had built up for her his castles in the air, and the miracle of it was that she had helped him to build them. He had described for her the change that was creeping slowly over Alaska, the replacement of mountain trails by stage and automobile highways, the building of railroads, the growth of cities where tents had stood a few years before. It was then, when he had pictured progress and civilization and the breaking down of nature's last barriers before science and invention, that he had seen a cloud of doubt in her gray eyes.

And now, as they stood on the deck of the *Nome* looking at the white peaks of the mountains dissolving into the lavender mist of twilight, doubt and perplexity were still deeper in her eyes, and she said:

"I would always love tents and old trails and nature's barriers. I envy Belinda Mulrooney, whom you told me about this afternoon. I hate cities and railroads and automobiles, and all that goes with them, and I am sorry to see those things come to Alaska. And I, too, hate this man—John Graham!"

Her words startled him.

"And I want you to tell me what he is doing—with his money—now." Her voice was cold, and one little hand, he noticed, was clenched at the edge of the rail.

"He has stripped Alaskan waters of fish resources which will never be replaced, Miss Standish. But that is not all. I believe I state the case well within fact when I say he has killed many women and little children by robbing the inland waters of the food supplies upon which the natives have subsisted for centuries. I know. I have seen them die."

It seemed to him that she swayed against him for an instant.

"And that—is all?"

He laughed grimly. "Possibly some people would think it enough, Miss Standish. But the tentacles of his power are reaching everywhere in Alaska. His agents swarm throughout the territory, and Soapy Smith was a gentleman outlaw compared with these men and their master. If men like John Graham are allowed to have their way, in ten years greed and graft will despoil what two hundred years of Rooseveltian conservation would not be able to replace."

She raised her head, and in the dusk her pale face looked up at the ghost-peaks of the mountains still visible through the thickening gloom of evening. "I am glad you told me about Belinda Mulrooney," she said. "I am beginning to understand, and it gives me courage to think of a woman like her. She could fight, couldn't she? She could make a man's fight?"

"Yes, and did make it."

"And she had no money to give her power. Her last dollar, you told me, she flung into the Yukon for luck."

"Yes, at Dawson. It was the one thing between her and hunger."

She raised her hand, and on it he saw gleaming faintly the single ring which she wore. Slowly she drew it from her finger.

"Then this, too, for luck—the luck of Mary Standish," she laughed softly, and flung the ring into the sea.

She faced him, as if expecting the necessity of defending what she had done. "It isn't melodrama," she said. "I mean it. And I believe in it. I want something of mine to lie at the bottom of the sea in this gateway to Skagway, just as Belinda Mulrooney wanted her dollar to rest forever at the bottom of the Yukon."

She gave him the hand from which she had taken the ring, and for a moment the warm thrill of it lay in his own. "Thank you for the wonderful afternoon you have given me, Mr. Holt. I shall never forget it. It is dinner time. I must say good night."

He followed her slim figure with his eyes until she disappeared. In returning to his cabin he almost bumped into Rossland. The incident was irritating. Neither of the men spoke or nodded, but Rossland met Alan's look squarely, his face rock-like in its repression of emotion. Alan's impression of the man was changing in spite of his prejudice. There was a growing something about him which commanded attention, a certainty of poise which could not be mistaken for sham. A scoundrel he might be, but a cool brain was at work inside his head—a brain not easily disturbed by unimportant things, he decided. He disliked the man. As an agent of John Graham Alan looked upon him as an enemy, and as an acquaintance of Mary Standish he was as much of a mystery as the girl herself. And only now, in his cabin, was Alan beginning to sense the presence of a real authority behind Rossland's attitude.

He was not curious. All his life he had lived too near the raw edge of practical things to dissipate in gossipy conjecture. He cared nothing about the relationship between Mary Standish and Rossland except as it involved himself, and the situation had become a trifle too delicate to please him. He could see no sport in an adventure of the kind it suggested, and the possibility that he had been misjudged by both Rossland and Mary Standish sent a flush of anger into his cheeks. He cared nothing for Rossland, except that he would like to wipe him out of existence with all other Graham agents. And he persisted in the conviction that he thought of the girl only in a most casual sort of way. He had made no effort to discover her history. He had not questioned her. At no time had he intimated a desire to intrude upon her personal affairs, and at no time had she offered information about herself, or an explanation of the singular espionage which Rossland had presumed to take upon himself. He grimaced as he reflected how dangerously near that hazard he had been—and he admired her for the splendid judgment she had shown in the matter. She had saved him the possible alternative of apologizing to Rossland or throwing him overboard!

There was a certain bellicose twist to his mind as he went down to the dining salon, an obstinate determination to hold himself aloof from any increasing intimacy with Mary Standish. No matter how pleasing his experience had been, he resented the idea of being commandeered at unexpected moments. Had Mary Standish read his thoughts, her bearing toward him during the dinner hour could not have been more satisfying. There was, in a way, something seductively provocative about it. She greeted him with the slightest inclination of her head and a cool little smile. Her attitude did not invite spoken words, either from him or from his neighbors, yet no one would have accused her of deliberate reserve.

Her demure unapproachableness was a growing revelation to him, and he found himself interested in spite of the new law of self-preservation he had set down for himself. He could not keep his eyes from stealing glimpses at her hair when her head was bowed a little. She had smoothed it tonight until it was like softest velvet, with rich glints in it, and the amazing thought came to him that it would be sweetly pleasant to touch with one's hand. The discovery was almost a shock. Keok and Nawadlook had beautiful hair, but he had never thought of it in this way. And he had never thought of Keok's pretty mouth as he was thinking of the girl's opposite him. He shifted uneasily and was glad Mary Standish did not look at him in these moments of mental unbalance.

When he left the table, the girl scarcely noticed his going. It was as if she had used him and then calmly shuttled him out of the way. He tried to laugh as he hunted up Stampede Smith. He found him, half an hour later, feeding a captive bear on the lower deck. It was odd, he thought, that a captive bear should be going north. Stampede explained. The animal was a pet and belonged to the Thlinkit Indians. There were seven, getting off at Cordova. Alan observed that the two girls watched him closely and whispered together. They were very pretty, with large, dark eyes and pink in their cheeks. One of the men did not look at him at all, but sat cross-legged on the deck, with his face turned away.

With Stampede he went to the smoking-room, and until a late hour they discussed the big range up under the Endicott Mountains, and Alan's plans for the future. Once, early in the evening, Alan went to his cabin to get maps and photographs. Stampede's eyes glistened as his mind seized upon the possibilities of the new adventure. It was a vast land. An unknown country. And Alan was its first pioneer. The old thrill ran in Stampede's blood, and its infectiousness caught Alan, so that he forgot Mary Standish, and all else but the miles that lay between them and the mighty tundras beyond the Seward Peninsula. It was midnight when Alan went to his cabin.

He was happy. Love of life swept in an irresistible surge through his body, and he breathed in deeply of the soft sea air that came in through his open port from the west. In Stampede Smith he had at last found the comradeship which he had missed, and the responsive note to the wild and half-savage desires always smoldering in his heart. He looked out at the stars and smiled up at them, and his soul was filled with an unspoken thankfulness that he was not born too late. Another generation and there would be no last frontier. Twenty-five years more and the world would lie utterly in the shackles of science and invention and what the human race called progress.

So God had been good to him. He was helping to write the last page in that history which would go down through the eons of time, written in the red blood of men who had cut the first trails into the unknown. After him, there would be no more frontiers. No more mysteries of unknown lands to solve. No more pioneering hazards to make. The earth would be tamed. And suddenly he thought of Mary Standish and of what she had said to him in the dusk of evening. Strange that it had been *her* thought, too—that she would always love tents and old trails and nature's barriers, and hated to see cities and railroads and automobiles come to Alaska. He shrugged his shoulders. Probably she had guessed what was in his own mind, for she was clever, very clever.

A tap at his door drew his eyes from the open watch in his hand. It was a quarter after twelve o'clock, an unusual hour for someone to be tapping at his door.

It was repeated—a bit hesitatingly, he thought. Then it came again, quick and decisive. Replacing his watch in his pocket, he opened the door.

It was Mary Standish who stood facing him.

He saw only her eyes at first, wide-open, strange, frightened eyes. And then he saw the pallor of her face as she came slowly in, without waiting for him to speak or give her permission to enter. And it was Mary Standish herself who closed the door, while he stared at her in stupid wonderment—and stood there with her back against it, straight and slim and deathly pale.

"May I come in?" she asked.

"My God, you're in!" gasped Alan. "*You're in.*"

* * * * *

CHAPTER VII

That it was past midnight, and Mary Standish had deliberately come to his room, entering it and closing the door without a word or a nod of invitation from him, seemed incredible to Alan. After his first explosion of astonishment he stood mute, while the girl looked at him steadily and her breath came a little quickly. But she was not excited. Even in his amazement he could see that. What he had thought was fright had gone out of her eyes. But he had never seen her so white, and never had she appeared quite so slim and childish-looking as while she stood there in these astounding moments with her back against the door.

The pallor of her face accentuated the rich darkness of her hair. Even her lips were pale. But she was not embarrassed. Her eyes were clear and unafraid now, and in the poise of her head and body was a sureness of purpose that staggered him. A feeling of anger, almost of personal resentment, began to possess him as he waited for her to speak. This, at last, was the cost of his courtesies to her, The advantage she was taking of him was an indignity and an outrage, and his mind flashed to the suspicion that Rossland was standing just outside the door.

In another moment he would have brushed her aside and opened it, but her quiet face held him. The tenseness was fading out of it. He saw her lips tremble, and then a miracle happened. In her wide-open, beautiful eyes tears were gathering. Even then she did not lower her glance or bury her face in her hands, but looked at him bravely while the tear-drops glistened like diamonds on her cheeks. He felt his heart give way. She read his thoughts, had guessed his suspicion, and he was wrong.

"You—you will have a seat, Miss Standish?" he asked lamely, inclining his head toward the cabin chair.

"No. Please let me stand." She drew in a deep breath. "It is late, Mr. Holt?"

"Rather an irregular hour for a visit such as this," he assured her. "Half an hour after midnight, to be exact. It must be very important business that has urged you to make such a hazard aboard ship, Miss Standish."

For a moment she did not answer him, and he saw the little heart-throb in her white throat.

"Would Belinda Mulrooney have considered this a very great hazard, Mr. Holt? In a matter of life and death, do you not think she would have come to your cabin at midnight—even aboard ship? And it is that with me—a matter of life and death. Less than an hour ago I came to that decision. I could not wait until morning. I had to see you tonight."

"And why me?" he asked. "Why not Rossland, or Captain Rifle, or some other? Is it because—"

He did not finish. He saw the shadow of something gather in her eyes, as if for an instant she had felt a stab of humiliation or of pain, but it was gone as quickly as it came. And very quietly, almost without emotion, she answered him.

"I know how you feel. I have tried to place myself in your position. It is all very irregular, as you say. But I am not ashamed. I have come to you as I would want anyone to come to me under similar circumstances, if I were a man. If watching you, thinking about you, making up my mind about you is taking an advantage—then I have been unfair, Mr. Holt. But I am not sorry. I trust you. I know you will believe me good until I am proved bad. I have come to ask you to help me. Would you make it possible for another human being to avert a great tragedy if you found it in your power to do so?"

He felt his sense of judgment wavering. Had he been coolly analyzing such a situation in the detached environment of the smoking-room, he would have called any man a fool who hesitated to open his cabin door and show his visitor out. But such a thought did not occur to him now. He was thinking of the handkerchief he had found the preceding midnight. Twice she had come to his cabin at a late hour.

"It would be my inclination to make such a thing possible," he said, answering her question. "Tragedy is a nasty thing."

She caught the hint of irony in his voice. If anything, it added to her calmness. He was to suffer no weeping entreaties, no feminine play of helplessness and beauty. Her pretty mouth was a little firmer and the tilt of her dainty chin a bit higher.

"Of course, I can't pay you," she said. "You are the sort of man who would resent an offer of payment for what I am about to ask you to do. But I must have help. If I don't have it, and quickly"—she shuddered slightly and tried to smile—"something very unpleasant will happen, Mr. Holt," she finished.

"If you will permit me to take you to Captain Rifle—"

"No. Captain Rifle would question me. He would demand explanations. You will understand when I tell you what I want. And I will do that if I may have your word of honor to hold in confidence what I tell you, whether you help me or not. Will you give me that pledge?"

"Yes, if such a pledge will relieve your mind, Miss Standish."

He was almost brutally incurious. As he reached for a cigar, he did not see the sudden movement she made, as if about to fly from his room, or the quicker throb that came in her throat. When he turned, a faint flush was gathering in her cheeks.

"I want to leave the ship," she said.

The simplicity of her desire held him silent.

"And I must leave it tonight, or tomorrow night—before we reach Cordova."

"Is that—your problem?" he demanded, astonished.

"No. I must leave it in such a way that the world will believe I am dead. I can not reach Cordova alive."

At last she struck home and he stared at her, wondering if she were insane. Her quiet, beautiful eyes met his own with unflinching steadiness. His brain all at once was crowded with questioning, but no word of it came to his lips.

"You can help me," he heard her saying in the same quiet, calm voice, softened so that one could not have heard it beyond the cabin door. "I haven't a plan. But I know you can arrange one—if you will. It must appear to be an accident. I must disappear, fall overboard, anything, just so the world will believe I am dead. It is necessary. And I can not tell you why. I can not. Oh, I *can not*."

A note of passion crept into her voice, but it was gone in an instant, leaving it cold and steady again. A second time she tried to smile. He could see courage, and a bit of defiance, shining in her eyes.

"I know what you are thinking, Mr. Holt. You are asking yourself if I am mad, if I am a criminal, what my reason can be, and why I haven't gone to Rossland, or Captain Rifle, or some one else. And the only answer I can make is that I have come to you because you are the only man in the world—in this hour—that I have faith in. Some day you will understand, if you help me. If you do not care to help me—"

She stopped, and he made a gesture.

"Yes, if I don't? What will happen then?"

"I shall be forced to the inevitable," she said. "It is rather unusual, isn't it, to be asking for one's life? But that is what I mean."

"I'm afraid—I don't quite understand."

"Isn't it clear, Mr. Holt? I don't like to appear spectacular, and I don't want you to think of me as theatrical—even now. I hate that sort of thing. You must simply believe me when I tell you it is impossible for me to reach Cordova alive. If you do not help me to disappear, help me to live—and at the same time give all others the impression that I am dead—then I must do the other thing. I must really die."

For a moment his eyes blazed angrily. He felt like taking her by the shoulders and shaking her, as he would have shaken the truth out of a child.

"You come to me with a silly threat like that, Miss Standish? A threat of suicide?"

"If you want to call it that—yes."

"And you expect me to believe you?"

"I had hoped you would."

She had his nerves going. There was no doubt of that. He half believed her and half disbelieved. If she had cried, if she had made the smallest effort to work upon his sentiment, he would have disbelieved utterly. But he was not blind to the fact that she was making a brave fight, even though a lie was behind it, and with a consciousness of pride that bewildered him.

She was not humiliating herself. Even when she saw the struggle going on within him she made no effort to turn the balance in her favor. She had stated the facts, as she claimed them to be. Now she waited. Her long lashes glistened a little. But her eyes were clear, and her hair glowed softly, so softly that he would never forget it, as she stood there with her back against the door, nor the strange desire that came to him—even then—to touch it with his hand.

He nipped off the end of his cigar and lighted a match. "It is Rossland," he said. "You're afraid of Rossland?"

"In a way, yes; in a large way, no. I would laugh at Rossland if it were not for the other."

The *other*! Why the deuce was she so provokingly ambiguous? And she had no intention of explaining. She simply waited for him to decide.

"What other?" he demanded.

"I can not tell you. I don't want you to hate me. And you would hate me if I told you the truth."

"Then you confess you are lying," he suggested brutally.

Even this did not stir her as he had expected it might. It did not anger her or shame her. But she raised a pale hand and a little handkerchief to her eyes, and he turned toward the open port, puffing at his cigar, knowing she was fighting to keep the tears back. And she succeeded.

"No, I am not lying. What I have told you is true. It is because I will not lie that I have not told you more. And I thank you for the time you have given me, Mr. Holt. That you have not driven me from your cabin is a kindness which I appreciate. I have made a mistake, that is all. I thought—"

"How could I bring about what you ask?" he interrupted.

"I don't know. You are a man. I believed you could plan a way, but I see now how foolish I have been. It is impossible." Her hand reached slowly for the knob of the door.

"Yes, you are foolish," he agreed, and his voice was softer. "Don't let such thoughts overcome you, Miss Standish. Go back to your cabin and get a night's sleep. Don't let Rossland worry you. If you want me to settle with that man—"

"Good night, Mr. Holt."

She was opening the door. And as she went out she turned a little and looked at him, and now she was smiling, and there were tears in her eyes.

"Good night."

"Good night."

The door closed behind her. He heard her retreating footsteps. In half a minute he would have called her back. But it was too late.

* * * * *

CHAPTER VIII

For half an hour Alan sat smoking his cigar. Mentally he was not at ease. Mary Standish had come to him like a soldier, and she had left him like a soldier. But in that last glimpse of her face he had caught for an instant something which she had not betrayed in his cabin—a stab of what he thought was pain in her tear-wet eyes as she smiled, a proud regret, possibly a shadow of humiliation at last—or it may have been a pity for him. He was not sure. But it was not despair. Not once had she whimpered in look or word, even when the tears were in her eyes, and the thought was beginning to impress itself upon him that it was he—and not Mary Standish—who had shown a yellow streak this night. A half shame fell upon him as he smoked. For it was clear he had not come up to her judgment of him, or else he was not so big a fool as she had hoped he might be. In his own mind, for a time, he was at a loss to decide.

It was possibly the first time he had ever deeply absorbed himself in the analysis of a woman. It was outside his business. But, born and bred of the open country, it was as natural for him to recognize courage as it was for him to breathe. And the girl's courage was unusual, now that he had time to think about it. It was this thought of her coolness and her calm refusal to impose her case upon him with greater warmth that comforted him after a little. A young and beautiful woman who was actually facing death would have urged her necessity with more enthusiasm, it seemed to him. Her threat, when he debated it intelligently, was merely thrown in, possibly on the spur of the moment, to give impetus to his decision. She had not meant it. The idea of a girl like Mary Standish committing suicide was stupendously impossible. Her quiet and wonderful eyes, her beauty and the exquisite care which she gave to herself emphasized the absurdity of such a supposition. She had come to him bravely. There was no doubt of that. She had merely exaggerated the importance of her visit.

Even after he had turned many things over in his mind to bolster up this conclusion, he was still not at ease. Against his will he recalled certain unpleasant things which had happened within his knowledge under sudden and unexpected stress of emotion. He tried to laugh the absurd stuff out of his thoughts and to the end that he might add a new color to his visionings he exchanged his half-burned cigar for a black-bowled pipe, which he filled and lighted. Then he began walking back and forth in his cabin, like a big animal in a small cage, until at last he stood with his head half out of the open port, looking at the clear stars and setting the perfume of his tobacco adrift with the soft sea wind.

He felt himself growing comforted. Reason seated itself within him again, with sentiment shuttled under his feet. If he had been a little harsh with Miss Standish tonight, he would make up for it by apologizing tomorrow. She would probably have recovered her balance by that time, and they would laugh over her excitement and their little adventure. That is, he would. "I'm not at all curious in the matter," some persistent voice kept telling him, "and I haven't any interest in knowing what irrational whim drove her to my cabin." But he smoked viciously and smiled grimly as the voice kept at him. He would have liked to obliterate Rossland from his mind. But Rossland persisted in bobbing up, and with him Mary Standish's words, "If I should make an explanation, you would hate me," or something to that effect. He couldn't remember exactly. And he didn't want to remember exactly, for it was none of his business.

In this humor, with half of his thoughts on one side of the fence and half on the other, he put out his light and went to bed. And he began thinking of the Range. That was pleasanter. For the tenth time he figured out how long it would be before the glacial-twisted ramparts of the Endicott Mountains rose up in first welcome to his home-coming.

Carl Lomen, following on the next ship, would join him at Unalaska. They would go on to Nome together. After that he would spend a week or so in the Peninsula, then go up the Kobuk, across the big portage to the Koyukuk and the far headwaters of the north, and still farther— beyond the last trails of civilized men—to his herds and his people. And Stampede Smith would be with him. After a long winter of homesickness it was all a comforting inducement to sleep and pleasant dreams. But somewhere there was a wrong note in his anticipations tonight. Stampede Smith slipped away from him, and Rossland took his place. And Keok, laughing, changed into Mary Standish with tantalizing deviltry. It was like Keok, Alan thought drowsily—she was always tormenting someone.

He felt better in the morning. The sun was up, flooding the wall of his cabin, when he awoke, and under him he could feel the roll of the open sea. Eastward the Alaskan coast was a deep blue haze, but the white peaks of the St. Elias Range flung themselves high up against the sun-filled sky behind it, like snowy banners. The *Nome* was pounding ahead at full speed, and Alan's blood responded suddenly to the impelling thrill of her engines, beating like twin hearts with the mighty force that was speeding them on. This was business. It meant miles foaming away behind them and a swift biting off of space between him and Unalaska, midway of the Aleutians. He was sorry they were losing time by making the swing up the coast to Cordova. And with Cordova he thought of Mary Standish.

He dressed and shaved and went down to breakfast, still thinking of her. The thought of meeting her again was rather discomforting, now that the time of that possibility was actually at hand, for he dreaded moments of embarrassment even when he was not directly accountable for them. But Mary Standish saved him any qualms of conscience which he might have had because of his lack of chivalry the preceding night. She was at the table. And she was not at all disturbed when he seated himself opposite her. There was color in her cheeks, a fragile touch of that warm glow in the heart of the wild rose of the tundras. And it seemed to him there was a deeper, more beautiful light in her eyes than he had ever seen before.

She nodded, smiled at him, and resumed a conversation which she had evidently broken for a moment with a lady who sat next to her. It was the first time Alan had seen her interested in this way. He had no intention of listening, but something perverse and compelling overcame his will. He discovered the lady was going up to teach in a native school at Noorvik, on the Kobuk River, and that for many years she had taught in Dawson and knew well the story of Belinda Mulrooney. He gathered that Mary Standish had shown a great interest, for Miss Robson, the teacher, was offering to send her a photograph she possessed of Belinda Mulrooney; if Miss Standish would give her an address. The girl hesitated, then said she was not certain of her destination, but would write Miss Robson at Noorvik.

"You will surely keep your promise?" urged Miss Robson.

"Yes, I will keep my promise."

A sense of relief swept over Alan. The words were spoken so softly that he thought she had not wanted him to hear. It was evident that a few hours' sleep and the beauty of the morning had completely changed her mental attitude, and he no longer felt the suspicion of responsibility which had persisted in attaching itself to him. Only a fool, he assured himself, could possibly see a note of tragedy in her appearance now. Nor was she different at luncheon or at dinner. During the day he saw nothing of her, and he was growing conscious of the fact that she was purposely avoiding contact with him. This did not displease him. It allowed him to pick up the threads of other interests in a normal sort of way. He discussed Alaskan politics in the smoking-room, smoked his black pipe without fear of giving offense, and listened to the talk of the ship with a freedom of mind which he had not experienced since his first meeting with Miss Standish. Yet, as night drew on, and he walked his two-mile promenade about the deck, he felt gathering about him a peculiar impression of aloneness. Something was missing. He did not acknowledge to himself what it was until, as if to convict him, he saw Mary Standish come out of the door leading from her cabin passageway, and stand alone at the rail of the ship. For a moment he hesitated, then quietly he came up beside her.

"It has been a wonderful day, Miss Standish," he said, "and Cordova is only a few hours ahead of us."

She scarcely turned her face and continued to look off into the shrouding darkness of the sea. "Yes, a wonderful day, Mr. Holt," she repeated after him, "and Cordova is only a few hours ahead." Then, in the same soft, unemotional voice, she added: "I want to thank you for last night. You brought me to a great decision."

"I fear I did not help you."

It may have been fancy of the gathering dusk, that made him believe he caught a shuddering movement of her slim shoulders.

"I thought there were two ways," she said, "but you made me see there was only *one*." She emphasized that word. It seemed to come with a little tremble in her voice. "I was foolish. But please let us forget. I want to think of pleasanter things. I am about to make a great experiment, and it takes all my courage."

"You will win, Miss Standish," he said in a sure voice. "In whatever you undertake you will win. I know it. If this experiment you speak of is the adventure of coming to Alaska—seeking your fortune—finding your life here—it will be glorious. I can assure you of that."

She was quiet for a moment, and then said:

"The unknown has always held a fascination for me. When we were under the mountains in Skagway yesterday, I almost told you of an odd faith which I have. I believe I have lived before, a long time ago, when America was very young. At times the feeling is so strong that I must have faith in it. Possibly I am foolish. But when the mountain swung back, like a great door, and we saw Skagway, I knew that sometime—somewhere— I had seen a thing like that before. And I have had strange visions of it.

Maybe it is a touch of madness in me. But it is that faith which gives me courage to go on with my experiment. That—and *you*!"

Suddenly she faced him, her eyes flaming.

"You—and your suspicions and your brutality," she went on, her voice trembling a little as she drew herself up straight and tense before him. "I wasn't going to tell you, Mr. Holt. But you have given me the opportunity, and it may do you good—after tomorrow. I came to you because I foolishly misjudged you. I thought you were different, like your mountains. I made a great gamble, and set you up on a pedestal as clean and unafraid and believing all things good until you found them bad—and I lost. I was terribly mistaken. Your first thoughts of me when I came to your cabin were suspicious. You were angry and afraid. Yes, *afraid*—fearful of something happening which you didn't want to happen. You thought, almost, that I was unclean. And you believed I was a liar, and told me so. It wasn't fair, Mr. Holt. It wasn't *fair*. There were things which I couldn't explain to you, but I told you Rossland knew. I didn't keep everything back. And I believed you were big enough to think that I was not dishonoring you with my—friendship, even though I came to your cabin. Oh, I had that much faith in myself—I didn't think I would be mistaken for something unclean and lying!"

"Good God!" he cried. "Listen to me—Miss Standish—"

She was gone, so suddenly that his movement to intercept her was futile, and she passed through the door before he could reach her. Again he called her name, but her footsteps were almost running up the passageway. He dropped back, his blood cold, his hands clenched in the darkness, and his face as white as the girl's had been. Her words had held him stunned and mute. He saw himself stripped naked, as she believed him to be, and the thing gripped him with a sort of horror. And she was wrong. He had followed what he believed to be good judgment and common sense. If, in doing that, he had been an accursed fool—

Determinedly he started for her cabin, his mind set upon correcting her malformed judgment of him. There was no light coming under her door. When he knocked, there was no answer from within. He waited, and tried again, listening for a sound of movement. And each moment he waited he was readjusting himself. He was half glad, in the end, that the door did not open. He believed Miss Standish was inside, and she would undoubtedly accept the reason for his coming without an apology in words.

He went to his cabin, and his mind became increasingly persistent in its disapproval of the wrong viewpoint she had taken of him. He was not comfortable, no matter how he looked at the thing. For her clear eyes, her smoothly glorious hair, and the pride and courage with which she had faced him remained with him overpoweringly. He could not get away from the vision of her as she had stood against the door with tears like diamonds on her cheeks. Somewhere he had missed fire. He knew it. Something had escaped him which he could not understand. And she was holding him accountable.

The talk of the smoking-room did not interest him tonight. His efforts to become a part of it were forced. A jazzy concert of piano and string music in the social hall annoyed him, and a little later he watched the dancing with such grimness that someone remarked about it. He saw Rossland whirling round the floor with a handsome, young blonde in his arms. The girl was looking up into his eyes, smiling, and her cheek lay unashamed against his shoulder, while Rossland's face rested against her fluffy hair when they mingled closely with the other dancers. Alan turned away, an unpleasant thought of Rossland's association with Mary Standish in his mind. He strolled down into the steerage. The Thlinkit people had shut themselves in with a curtain of blankets, and from the stillness he judged they were asleep. The evening passed slowly for him after that, until at last he went to his cabin and tried to interest himself in a book. It was something he had anticipated reading, but after a little he wondered if the writing was stupid, or if it was himself. The thrill he had always experienced with this particular writer was missing. There was no inspiration. The words were dead. Even the tobacco in his pipe seemed to lack something, and he changed it for a cigar—and chose another book. The result was the same. His mind refused to function, and there was no comfort in his cigar.

He knew he was fighting against a new thing, even as he subconsciously lied to himself. And he was obstinately determined to win. It was a fight between himself and Mary Standish as she had stood against his door. Mary Standish—the slim beauty of her—her courage—a score of things that had never touched his life before. He undressed and put on his smoking-gown and slippers, repudiating the honesty of the emotions that were struggling for acknowledgment within him. He was a bit mad and entirely a fool, he told himself. But the assurance did him no good.

He went to bed, propped himself up against his pillows, and made another effort to read. He half-heartedly succeeded. At ten o'clock music and dancing ceased, and stillness fell over the ship. After that he found himself becoming more interested in the first book he had started to read. His old satisfaction slowly returned to him. He relighted his cigar and enjoyed it. Distantly he heard the ship's bells, eleven o'clock, and after that the half-hour and midnight. The printed pages were growing dim, and drowsily he marked his book, placed it on the table, and yawned. They must be nearing Cordova. He could feel the slackened speed of the *Nome* and the softer throb of her engines. Probably they had passed Cape St. Elias and were drawing inshore.

And then, sudden and thrilling, came a woman's scream. A piercing cry of terror, of agony—and of something else that froze the blood in his veins as he sprang from his berth. Twice it came, the second time ending in a moaning wail and a man's husky shout. Feet ran swiftly past his window. He heard another shout and then a voice of command. He could not distinguish the words, but the ship herself seemed to respond. There came the sudden smoothness of dead engines, followed by the pounding shock of reverse and the clanging alarm of a bell calling boats' crews to quarters.

Alan faced his cabin door. He knew what had happened. Someone was overboard. And in this moment all life and strength were gone out of his body, for the pale face of Mary Standish seemed to rise for an instant before him, and in her quiet voice she was telling him again that *this was the other way*. His face went white as he caught up his smoking-gown, flung open his door, and ran down the dimly lighted corridor.

* * * * *

CHAPTER IX

The reversing of the engines had not stopped the momentum of the ship when Alan reached the open deck. She was fighting, but still swept slowly ahead against the force struggling to hold her back. He heard running feet, voices, and the rattle of davit blocks, and came up as the starboard boat aft began swinging over the smooth sea. Captain Rifle was ahead of him, half-dressed, and the second officer was giving swift commands. A dozen passengers had come from the smoking-room. There was only one woman. She stood a little back, partly supported in a man's arms, her face buried in her hands. Alan looked at the man, and he knew from his appearance that she was the woman who had screamed.

He heard the splash of the boat as it struck water, and the rattle of oars, but the sound seemed a long distance away. Only one thing came to him distinctly in the sudden sickness that gripped him, and that was the terrible sobbing of the woman. He went to them, and the deck seemed to sway under his feet. He was conscious of a crowd gathering about the empty davits, but he had eyes only for these two.

"Was it a man—or a woman?" he asked.

It did not seem to him it was his voice speaking. The words were forced from his lips. And the other man, with the woman's head crumpled against his shoulder, looked into a face as emotionless as stone.

"A woman," he replied. "This is my wife. We were sitting here when she climbed upon the rail and leaped in. My wife screamed when she saw her going."

The woman raised her head. She was still sobbing, with no tears in her eyes, but only horror. Her hands were clenched about her husband's arm. She struggled to speak and failed, and the man bowed his head to comfort her. And then Captain Rifle stood at their side. His face was haggard, and a glance told Alan that he knew.

"Who was it?" he demanded.

"This lady thinks it was Miss Standish."

Alan did not move or speak. Something seemed to have gone wrong for a moment in his head. He could not hear distinctly the excitement behind him, and before him things were a blur. The sensation came and passed swiftly, with no sign of it in the immobility of his pale face.

"Yes, the girl at your table. The pretty girl. I saw her clearly, and then—then—"

It was the woman. The captain broke in, as she caught herself with a choking breath:

"It is possible you are mistaken. I can not believe Miss Standish would do that. We shall soon know. Two boats are gone, and a third lowering." He was hurrying away, throwing the last words over his shoulder.

Alan made no movement to follow. His brain cleared itself of shock, and a strange calmness began to possess him. "You are quite sure it was the girl at my table?" he found himself saying. "Is it possible you might be mistaken?"

"No," said the woman. "She was so quiet and pretty that I have noticed her often. I saw her clearly in the starlight. And she saw me just before she climbed to the rail and jumped. I'm almost sure she smiled at me and was going to speak. And then—then—she was gone!"

"I didn't know until my wife screamed," added the man. "I was seated facing her at the time. I ran to the rail and could see nothing behind but the wash of the ship. I think she went down instantly."

Alan turned. He thrust himself silently through a crowd of excited and questioning people, but he did not hear their questions and scarcely sensed the presence of their voices. His desire to make great haste had left him, and he walked calmly and deliberately to the cabin where Mary Standish would be if the woman was mistaken, and it was not she who had leaped into the sea. He knocked at the door only once. Then he opened it. There was no cry of fear or protest from within, and he knew the room was empty before he turned on the electric light. He had known it from the beginning, from the moment he heard the woman's scream. Mary Standish was gone.

He looked at her bed. There was the depression made by her head in the pillow. A little handkerchief lay on the coverlet, crumpled and twisted. Her few possessions were arranged neatly on the reading table. Then he saw her shoes and her stockings, and a dress on the bed, and he picked up one of the shoes and held it in a cold, steady hand. It was a little shoe. His fingers closed about it until it crushed like paper.

He was holding it when he heard someone behind him, and he turned slowly to confront Captain Rifle. The little man's face was like gray wax. For a moment neither of them spoke. Captain Rifle looked at the shoe crumpled in Alan's hand.

"The boats got away quickly," he said in a husky voice. "We stopped inside the third-mile. If she can swim—there is a chance."

"She won't swim," replied Alan. "She didn't jump in for that. She is gone."

In a vague and detached sort of way he was surprised at the calmness of his own voice. Captain Rifle saw the veins standing out on his clenched hands and in his forehead. Through many years he had witnessed tragedy of one kind and another. It was not strange to him. But a look of wonderment shot into his eyes at Alan's words. It took only a few seconds to tell what had happened the preceding night, without going into details. The captain's hand was on Alan's arm when he finished, and the flesh under his fingers was rigid and hard as steel.

"We'll talk with Rossland after the boats return," he said.

He drew Alan from the room and closed the door.

Not until he had reentered his own cabin did Alan realize he still held the crushed shoe in his hand. He placed it on his bed and dressed. It took him only a few minutes. Then he went aft and found the captain. Half an hour later the first boat returned. Five minutes after that, a second came in. And then a third. Alan stood back, alone, while the passengers crowded the rail. He knew what to expect. And the murmur of it came to him—failure! It was like a sob rising softly out of the throats of many people. He drew away. He did not want to meet their eyes, or talk with them, or hear the things they would be saying. And as he went, a moan came to his lips, a strangled cry filled with an agony which told him he was breaking down. He dreaded that. It was the first law of his kind to stand up under blows, and he fought against the desire to reach out his arms to the sea and entreat Mary Standish to rise up out of it and forgive him.

He drove himself on like a mechanical thing. His white face was a mask through which burned no sign of his grief, and in his eyes was a deadly coldness. Heartless, the woman who had screamed might have said. And she would have been right. His heart was gone.

Two people were at Rossland's door when he came up. One was Captain Rifle, the other Marston, the ship's doctor. The captain was knocking when Alan joined them. He tried the door. It was locked.

"I can't rouse him," he said. "And I did not see him among the passengers."

"Nor did I," said Alan.

Captain Rifle fumbled with his master key.

"I think the circumstances permit," he explained. In a moment he looked up, puzzled. "The door is locked on the inside, and the key is in the lock."

He pounded with his fist on the panel. He continued to pound until his knuckles were red. There was still no response.

"Odd," he muttered.

"Very odd," agreed Alan.

His shoulder was against the door. He drew back and with a single crash sent it in. A pale light filtered into the room from a corridor lamp, and the men stared. Rossland was in bed. They could see his face dimly, upturned, as if staring at the ceiling. But even now he made no movement and spoke no word. Marston entered and turned on the light.

After that, for ten seconds, no man moved. Then Alan heard Captain Rifle close the door behind them, and from Marston's lips came a startled whisper:

"Good God!"

Rossland was not covered. He was undressed and flat on his back. His arms were stretched out, his head thrown back, his mouth agape. And the white sheet under him was red with blood. It had trickled over the edges and to the floor. His eyes were loosely closed. After the first shock Doctor Marston reacted swiftly. He bent over Rossland, and in that moment, when his back was toward them, Captain Rifle's eyes met Alan's. The same thought—and in another instant disbelief—flashed from one to the other.

Marston was speaking, professionally cool now. "A knife stab, close to the right lung, if not in it. And an ugly bruise over his eye. He is not dead. Let him lie as he is until I return with instruments and dressing."

"The door was locked on the inside," said Alan, as soon as the doctor was gone. "And the window is closed. It looks like—suicide. It is possible—there was an understanding between them—and Rossland chose this way instead of the sea?"

Captain Rifle was on his knees. He looked under the berth, peered into the corners, and pulled back the blanket and sheet. "There is no knife," he said stonily. And in a moment he added: "There are red stains on the window. It was not attempted suicide. It was—"

"Murder."

"Yes, if Rossland dies. It was done through the open window. Someone called Rossland to the window, struck him, and then closed the window. Or it is possible, if he were sitting or standing here, that a long-armed man might have reached him. It was a man, Alan. We've got to believe that. It was a *man*."

"Of course, a man," Alan nodded.

They could hear Marston returning, and he was not alone. Captain Rifle made a gesture toward the door. "Better go," he advised. "This is a ship's matter, and you won't want to be unnecessarily mixed up in it. Come to my cabin in half an hour. I shall want to see you."

The second officer and the purser were with Doctor Marston when Alan passed them, and he heard the door of Rossland's room close behind him. The ship was trembling under his feet again. They were moving away. He went to Mary Standish's cabin and deliberately gathered her belongings and put them in the small hand-bag with which she had come aboard. Without any effort at concealment he carried the bag to his room and packed his own dunnage. After that he hunted up Stampede Smith and explained to him that an unexpected change in his plans compelled them to stop at Cordova. He was five minutes late in his appointment with the captain.

Captain Rifle was seated at his desk when Alan entered his cabin. He nodded toward a chair.

"We'll reach Cordova inside of an hour," he said. "Doctor Marston says Rossland will live, but of course we can not hold the *Nome* in port until he is able to talk. He was struck through the window. I will make oath to that. Have you anything—in mind?"

"Only one thing," replied Alan, "a determination to go ashore as soon as I can. If it is possible, I shall recover her body and care for it. As for Rossland, it is not a matter of importance to me whether he lives or dies. Mary Standish had nothing to do with the assault upon him. It was merely coincident with her own act and nothing more. Will you tell me our location when she leaped into the sea."

He was fighting to retain his calmness, his resolution not to let Captain Rifle see clearly what the tragedy of her death had meant to him.

"We were seven miles off the Eyak River coast, a little south and west. If her body goes ashore, it will be on the island, or the mainland east of Eyak River. I am glad you are going to make an effort. There is a chance. And I hope you will find her."

Captain Rifle rose from his chair and walked nervously back and forth. "It's a bad blow for the ship—her first trip," he said. "But I'm not thinking of the *Nome*. I'm thinking of Mary Standish. My God, it is terrible! If it had been anyone else—*anyone*—" His words seemed to choke him, and he made a despairing gesture with his hands. "It is hard to believe—almost impossible to believe she would deliberately kill herself. Tell me again what happened in your cabin."

Crushing all emotion out of his voice, Alan repeated briefly certain details of the girl's visit. But a number of things which she had trusted to his confidence he did not betray. He did not dwell upon Rossland's influence or her fear of him. Captain Rifle saw his effort, and when he had finished, he gripped his hand, understanding in his eyes.

"You're not responsible—not so much as you believe," he said. "Don't take it too much to heart, Alan. But find her. Find her if you can, and let me know. You will do that—you will let me know?"

"Yes, I shall let you know."

"And Rossland. He is a man with many enemies. I am positive his assailant is still on board."

"Undoubtedly."

The captain hesitated. He did not look at Alan as he said: "There is nothing in Miss Standish's room. Even her bag is gone. I thought I saw things in there when I was with you. I thought I saw something in your hand. But I must have been mistaken. She probably flung everything into the sea—before she went."

"Such a thought is possible," agreed Alan evasively.

Captain Rifle drummed the top of his desk with his finger-tips. His face looked haggard and old in the shaded light of the cabin. "That's all, Alan. God knows I'd give this old life of mine to bring her back if I could. To me she was much like—someone—a long time dead. That's why I broke ship's regulations when she came aboard so strangely at Seattle, without reservation. I'm sorry now. I should have sent her ashore. But she is gone, and it is best that you and I keep to ourselves a little of what we guess. I hope you will find her, and if you do——"

"I shall send you word."

They shook hands, and Captain Rifle's fingers still held to Alan's as they went to the door and opened it. A swift change had come in the sky. The stars were gone, and a moaning whisper hovered over the darkened sea.

"A thunder-storm," said the captain.

His mastery was gone, his shoulders bent, and there was a tremulous note in his voice that compelled Alan to look straight out into darkness. And then he said,

"Rossland will be sent to the hospital in Cordova, if he lives."

Alan made no answer. The door closed softly behind him, and slowly he went through gloom to the rail of the ship, and stood there, with the whispered moaning of the sea coming to him out of a pit of darkness. A vast distance away he heard a low intonation of thunder.

He struggled to keep hold of himself as he returned to his cabin. Stampede Smith was waiting for him, his dunnage packed in an oilskin bag. Alan explained the unexpected change in his plans. Business in Cordova would make him miss a boat and would delay him at least a month in reaching the tundras. It was necessary for Stampede to go on to the range alone. He could make a quick trip by way of the Government railroad to Tanana. After that he would go to Allakakat, and thence still farther north into the Endicott country. It would be easy for a man like Stampede to find the range. He drew a map, gave him certain written instructions, money, and a final warning not to lose his head and take up gold-hunting on the way. While it was necessary for him to go ashore at once, he advised Stampede not to leave the ship until morning. And Stampede swore on oath he would not fail him.

Alan did not explain his own haste and was glad Captain Rifle had not questioned him too closely. He was not analyzing the reasonableness of his action. He only knew that every muscle in his body was aching for physical action and that he must have it immediately or break. The desire was a touch of madness in his blood, a thing which he was holding back by sheer force of will. He tried to shut out the vision of a pale face floating in the sea; he fought to keep a grip on the dispassionate calmness which was a part of him. But the ship itself was battering down his stoic resistance. In an hour—since he had heard the scream of the woman—he had come to hate it. He wanted the feel of solid earth under his feet. He wanted, with all his soul, to reach that narrow strip of coast where Mary Standish was drifting in.

But even Stampede saw no sign of the fire that was consuming him. And not until Alan's feet touched land, and Cordova lay before him like a great hole in the mountains, did the strain give way within him. After he had left the wharf, he stood alone in the darkness, breathing deeply of the mountain smell and getting his bearings. It was more than darkness about him. An occasional light burning dimly here and there gave to it the appearance of a sea of ink threatening to inundate him. The storm had not broken, but it was close, and the air was filled with a creeping warning. The moaning of thunder was low, and yet very near, as if smothered by the hand of a mighty force preparing to take the earth unaware.

Through the pit of gloom Alan made his way. He was not lost. Three years ago he had walked a score of times to the cabin of old Olaf Ericksen, half a mile up the shore, and he knew Ericksen would still be there, where he had squatted for twenty years, and where he had sworn to stay until the sea itself was ready to claim him. So he felt his way instinctively, while a crash of thunder broke over his head. The forces of the night were unleashing. He could hear a gathering tumult in the mountains hidden beyond the wall of blackness, and there came a sudden glare of lightning that illumined his way. It helped him. He saw a white reach of sand ahead and quickened his steps. And out of the sea he heard more distinctly an increasing sound. It was as if he walked between two great armies that were setting earth and sea atremble as they advanced to deadly combat.

The lightning came again, and after it followed a discharge of thunder that gave to the ground under his feet a shuddering tremor. It rolled away, echo upon echo, through the mountains, like the booming of signal-guns, each more distant than the other. A cold breath of air struck Alan in the face, and something inside him rose up to meet the thrill of storm.

He had always loved the rolling echoes of thunder in the mountains and the fire of lightning among their peaks. On such a night, with the crash of the elements about his father's cabin and the roaring voices of the ranges filling the darkness with tumult, his mother had brought him into the world. Love of it was in his blood, a part of his soul, and there were times when he yearned for this "talk of the mountains" as others yearn for the coming of spring. He welcomed it now as his eyes sought through the darkness for a glimmer of the light that always burned from dusk until dawn in Olaf Ericksen's cabin.

He saw it at last, a yellow eye peering at him through a slit in an inky wall. A moment later the darker shadow of the cabin rose up in his face, and a flash of lightning showed him the door. In a moment of silence he could hear the patter of huge raindrops on the roof as he dropped his bags and began hammering with his fist to arouse the Swede. Then he flung open the unlocked door and entered, tossing his dunnage to the floor, and shouted the old greeting that Ericksen would not have forgotten, though nearly a quarter of a century had passed since he and Alan's father had tramped the mountains together.

The long, black launch nosed its way out to sea.

He had turned up the wick of the oil lamp on the table when into the frame of an inner door came Ericksen himself, with his huge, bent shoulders, his massive head, his fierce eyes, and a great gray beard streaming over his naked chest. He stared for a moment, and Alan flung off his hat, and as the storm broke, beating upon the cabin in a mighty shock of thunder and wind and rain, a bellow of recognition came from Ericksen. They gripped hands.

The Swede's voice rose above wind and rain and the rattle of loose windows, and he was saying something about three years ago and rubbing the sleep from his eyes, when the strange look in Alan's face made him pause to hear other words than his own.

Five minutes later he opened a door looking out over the black sea, bracing his arm against it. The wind tore in, beating his whitening beard over his shoulders, and with it came a deluge of rain that drenched him as he stood there. He forced the door shut and faced Alan, a great, gray ghost of a man in the yellow glow of the oil lamp.

From then until dawn they waited. And in the first break of that dawn the long, black launch of Olaf, the Swede, nosed its way steadily out to sea.

* * * * *

CHAPTER X

The wind had died away, but the rain continued, torrential in its downpour, and the mountains grumbled with dying thunder. The town was blotted out, and fifty feet ahead of the hissing nose of the launch Alan could see only a gray wall. Water ran in streams from his rubber slicker, and Olaf's great beard was dripping like a wet rag. He was like a huge gargoyle at the wheel, and in the face of impenetrable gloom he opened speed until the *Norden* was shooting with the swiftness of a torpedo through the sea.

In Olaf's cabin Alan had listened to the folly of expecting to find Mary Standish. Between Eyak River and Katalla was a mainland of battered reefs and rocks and an archipelago of islands in which a pirate fleet might have found a hundred hiding-places. In his experience of twenty years Ericksen had never known of the finding of a body washed ashore, and he stated firmly his belief that the girl was at the bottom of the sea. But the impulse to go on grew no less in Alan. It quickened with the straining eagerness of the *Norden* as the slim craft leaped through the water.

Even the drone of thunder and the beat of rain urged him on. To him there was nothing absurd in the quest he was about to make. It was the least he could do, and the only honest thing he could do, he kept telling himself. And there was a chance that he would find her. All through his life had run that element of chance; usually it was against odds he had won, and there rode with him in the gray dawn a conviction he was going to win now—that he would find Mary Standish somewhere in the sea or along the coast between Eyak River and the first of the islands against which the shoreward current drifted. And when he found her—

He had not gone beyond that. But it pressed upon him now, and in moments it overcame him, and he saw her in a way which he was fighting to keep out of his mind. Death had given a vivid clearness to his mental pictures of her. A strip of white beach persisted in his mind, and waiting for him on this beach was the slim body of the girl, her pale face turned up to the morning sun, her long hair streaming over the sand. It was a vision that choked him, and he struggled to keep away from it. If he found her like that, he knew, at last, what he would do. It was the final crumbling away of something inside him, the breaking down of that other Alan Holt whose negative laws and self-imposed blindness had sent Mary Standish to her death.

Truth seemed to mock at him, flaying him for that invulnerable poise in which he had taken such an egotistical pride. For she had come to *him* in her hour of trouble, and there were five hundred others aboard the *Nome*. She had believed in him, had given him her friendship and her confidence, and at the last had placed her life in his hands. And when he had failed her, she had not gone to another. She had kept her word, proving to him she was not a liar and a fraud, and he knew at last the courage of womanhood and the truth of her words, "You will understand—tomorrow."

He kept the fight within himself. Olaf did not see it as the dawn lightened swiftly into the beginning of day. There was no change in the tense lines of his face and the grim resolution in his eyes. And Olaf did not press his folly upon him, but kept the *Norden* pointed seaward, adding still greater speed as the huge shadow of the headland loomed up in the direction of Hinchinbrook Island. With increasing day the rain subsided; it fell in a drizzle for a time and then stopped. Alan threw off his slicker and wiped the water from his eyes and hair. White mists began to rise, and through them shot faint rose-gleams of light. Olaf grunted approbation as he wrung water from his beard. The sun was breaking through over the mountain tops, and straight above, as the mist dissolved, was radiant blue sky.

The miracle of change came swiftly in the next half-hour. Storm had washed the air until it was like tonic; a salty perfume rose from the sea; and Olaf stood up and stretched himself and shook the wet from his body as he drank the sweetness into his lungs. Shoreward Alan saw the mountains taking form, and one after another they rose up like living things, their crests catching the fire of the sun. Dark inundations of forest took up the shimmering gleam, green slopes rolled out from behind veils of smoking vapor, and suddenly—in a final triumph of the sun—the Alaskan coast lay before him in all its glory.

The Swede made a great gesture of exultation with his free arm, grinning at his companion, pride and the joy of living in his bearded face. But in Alan's there was no change. Dully he sensed the wonder of day and of sunlight breaking over the mighty ranges to the sea, but something was missing. The soul of it was gone, and the old thrill was dead. He felt the tragedy of it, and his lips tightened even as he met the other's smile, for he no longer made an effort to blind himself to the truth.

Olaf began to guess deeply at that truth, now that he could see Alan's face in the pitiless light of the day, and after a little the thing lay naked in his mind. The quest was not a matter of duty, nor was it inspired by the captain of the *Nome*, as Alan had given him reason to believe. There was more than grimness in the other's face, and a strange sort of sickness lay in his eyes. A little later he observed the straining eagerness with which those eyes scanned the softly undulating surface of the sea.

At last he said, "If Captain Rifle was right, the girl went overboard *out there*," and he pointed.

Alan stood up.

"But she wouldn't be there now," Olaf added.

In his heart he believed she was, straight down—at the bottom. He turned his boat shoreward. Creeping out from the shadow of the mountains was the white sand of the beach three or four miles away. A quarter of an hour later a spiral of smoke detached itself from the rocks and timber that came down close to the sea.

"That's McCormick's," he said.

Alan made no answer. Through Olaf's binoculars he picked out the Scotchman's cabin. It was Sandy McCormick, Olaf had assured him, who knew every eddy and drift in fifty miles of coast, and with his eyes shut could find Mary Standish if she came ashore. And it was Sandy who came down to greet them when Ericksen dropped his anchor in shallow water.

They leaped out, thigh-deep, and waded to the beach, and in the door of the cabin beyond Alan saw a woman looking down at them wonderingly. Sandy himself was young and ruddy-faced, more like a boy than a man. They shook hands. Then Alan told of the tragedy aboard the *Nome* and what his mission was. He made a great effort to speak calmly, and believed that he succeeded. Certainly there was no break of emotion in his cold, even voice, and at the same time no possibility of evading its deadly earnestness. McCormick, whose means of livelihood were frequently more unsubstantial than real, listened to the offer of pecuniary reward for his services with something like shock. Fifty dollars a day for his time, and an additional five thousand dollars if he found the girl's body.

To Alan the sums meant nothing. He was not measuring dollars, and if he had said ten thousand or twenty thousand, the detail of price would not have impressed him as important. He possessed as much money as that in the Nome banks, and a little more, and had the thing been practicable he would as willingly have offered his reindeer herds could they have guaranteed him the possession of what he sought. In Olaf's face McCormick caught a look which explained the situation a little. Alan Holt was not mad. He was as any other man might be who had lost the most precious thing in the world. And unconsciously, as he pledged his services in acceptance of the offer, he glanced in the direction of the little woman standing in the doorway of the cabin.

Alan met her. She was a quiet, sweet-looking girl-woman. She smiled gravely at Olaf, gave her hand to Alan, and her blue eyes dilated when she heard what had happened aboard the *Nome*. Alan left the three together and returned to the beach, while between the loading and the lighting of his pipe the Swede told what he had guessed—that this girl whose body would never be washed ashore was the beginning and the end of the world to Alan Holt.

For many miles they searched the beach that day, while Sandy McCormick skirmished among the islands south and eastward in a light shore-launch. He was, in a way, a Paul Revere spreading intelligence, and with Scotch canniness made a good bargain for himself. In a dozen cabins he left details of the drowning and offered a reward of five hundred dollars for the finding of the body, so that twenty men and boys and half as many women were seeking before nightfall.

"And remember," Sandy told each of them, "the chances are she'll wash ashore sometime between tomorrow and three days later, if she comes ashore at all."

In the dusk of that first day Alan found himself ten miles up the coast. He was alone, for Olaf Ericksen had gone in the opposite direction. It was a different Alan who watched the setting sun dipping into the western sea, with the golden slopes of the mountains reflecting its glory behind him. It was as if he had passed through a great sickness, and up from the earth of his own beloved land had crept slowly into his body and soul a new understanding of life. There was despair in his face, but it was a gentler thing now. The harsh lines of an obstinate will were gone from about his mouth, his eyes no longer concealed their grief, and there was something in his attitude of a man chastened by a consuming fire. He retraced his steps through deepening twilight, and with each mile of his questing return there grew in him that something which had come to him out of death, and which he knew would never leave him. And with this change the droning softness of the night itself seemed to whisper that the sea would not give up its dead.

Olaf and Sandy McCormick and Sandy's wife were in the cabin when he returned at midnight. He was exhausted. Seven months in the

States had softened him, he explained. He did not inquire how successful the others had been. He knew. The woman's eyes told him, the almost mothering eagerness in them when he came through the door. She had coffee and food ready for him, and he forced himself to eat. Sandy gave a report of what he had done, and Olaf smoked his pipe and tried to speak cheerfully of the splendid weather that was coming tomorrow. Not one of them spoke of Mary Standish.

Alan felt the strain they were under and knew his presence was the cause of it, so he lighted his own pipe after eating and talked to Ellen McCormick about the splendor of the mountains back of Eyak River, and how fortunate she was to have her home in this little corner of paradise. He caught a flash of something unspoken in her eyes. It was a lonely place for a woman, alone, without children, and he spoke about children to Sandy, smiling. They should have children—a lot of them. Sandy blushed, and Olaf let out a boom of laughter. But the woman's face was unflushed and serious; only her eyes betrayed her, something wistful and appealing in them as she looked at Sandy.

"We're building a new cabin," he said, "and there's two rooms in it specially for kids."

There was pride in his voice as he made pretense to light a pipe that was already lighted, and pride in the look he gave his young wife. A moment later Ellen McCormick deftly covered with her apron something which lay on a little table near the door through which Alan had to pass to enter his sleeping-room. Olaf's eyes twinkled. But Alan did not see. Only he knew there should be children here, where there was surely love. It did not occur to him as being strange that he, Alan Holt, should think of such a matter at all.

The next morning the search was resumed. Sandy drew a crude map of certain hidden places up the east coast where drifts and cross-currents tossed the flotsam of the sea, and Alan set out for these shores with Olaf at the wheel of the *Norden*. It was sunset when they returned, and in the calm of a wonderful evening, with the comforting peace of the mountains smiling down at them, Olaf believed the time had come to speak what was in his mind. He spoke first of the weird tricks of the Alaskan waters, and of strange forces deep down under the surface which he had never had explained to him, and of how he had lost a cask once upon a time, and a week later had run upon it well upon its way to Japan. He emphasized the hide-and-seek playfulness of the undertows and the treachery of them.

Then he came bluntly to the point of the matter. It would be better if Mary Standish never did come ashore. It would be days—probably weeks—if it ever happened at all, and there would be nothing about her for Alan to recognize. Better a peaceful resting-place at the bottom of the sea. That was what he called it—"a peaceful resting-place"—and in his earnestness to soothe another's grief he blundered still more deeply into the horror of it all, describing certain details of what flesh and bone could and could not stand, until Alan felt like clubbing him beyond the power of speech. He was glad when he saw the McCormick cabin.

Sandy was waiting for them when they waded ashore. Something unusual was in his face, Alan thought, and for a moment his heart waited in suspense. But the Scotchman shook his head negatively and went close to Olaf Ericksen. Alan did not see the look that passed between them. He went to the cabin, and Ellen McCormick put a hand on his arm when he entered. It was an unusual thing for her to do. And there was a glow in her eyes which had not been there last night, and a flush in her cheeks, and a new, strange note in her voice when she spoke to him. It was almost exultation, something she was trying to keep back.

"You—you didn't find her?" she asked.

"No." His voice was tired and a little old. "Do you think I shall ever find her?"

"Not as you have expected," she answered quietly. "She will never come like that." She seemed to be making an effort. "You—you would give a great deal to have her back, Mr. Holt?"

Her question was childish in its absurdity, and she was like a child looking at him as she did in this moment. He forced a smile to his lips and nodded.

"Of course. Everything I possess."

"You—you—loved her—"

Her voice trembled. It was odd she should ask these questions. But the probing did not sting him; it was not a woman's curiosity that inspired them, and the comforting softness in her voice did him good. He had not realized before how much he wanted to answer that question, not only for himself, but for someone else—aloud.

"Yes, I did."

The confession almost startled him. It seemed an amazing confidence to be making under any circumstances, and especially upon such brief acquaintance. But he said no more, though in Ellen McCormick's face and eyes was a tremulous expectancy. He stepped into the little room which had been his sleeping place, and returned with his dunnage-sack. Out of this he took the bag in which were Mary Standish's belongings, and gave it to Sandy's wife. It was a matter of business now, and he tried to speak in a businesslike way.

"Her things are inside. I got them in her cabin. If you find her, after I am gone, you will need them. You understand, of course. And if you don't find her, keep them for me. I shall return some day." It seemed hard for him to give his simple instructions. He went on: "I don't think I shall stay any longer, but I will leave a certified check at Cordova, and it will be turned over to your husband when she is found. And if you do find her, you will look after her yourself, won't you, Mrs. McCormick?"

Ellen McCormick choked a little as she answered him, promising to do what he asked. He would always remember her as a sympathetic little thing, and half an hour later, after he had explained everything to Sandy, he wished her happiness when he took her hand in saying good-by. Her hand was trembling. He wondered at it and said something to Sandy about the priceless value of a happiness such as his, as they went down to the beach.

The velvety darkness of the sky was athrob with the heart-beat of stars, when the *Norden's* shimmering trail led once more out to sea. Alan looked up at them, and his mind groped strangely in the infinity that lay above him. He had never measured it before. Life had been too full. But now it seemed so vast, and his range in the tundras so far away, that a great loneliness seized upon him as he turned his eyes to look back at the dimly white shore-line dissolving swiftly in the gloom that lay beneath the mountains.

* * * *

CHAPTER XI

That night, in Olaf's cabin, Alan put himself back on the old track again. He made no effort to minimize the tragedy that had come into his life, and he knew its effect upon him would never be wiped away, and that Mary Standish would always live in his thoughts, no matter what happened in the years to come. But he was not the sort to let any part of himself wither up and die because of a blow that had darkened his mental visions of things. His plans lay ahead of him, his old ambitions and his dreams of achievement. They seemed pulseless and dead now, but he knew it was because his own fire had temporarily burned out. And he realized the vital necessity of building it up again. So he first wrote a letter to Ellen McCormick, and in this placed a second letter—carefully sealed—which was not to be opened unless they found Mary Standish, and which contained something he had found impossible to put into words in Sandy's cabin. It was trivial and embarrassing when spoken to others, but it meant a great deal to him. Then he made the final arrangements for Olaf to carry him to Seward in the *Norden*, for Captain Rifle's ship was well on her way to Unalaska. Thought of Captain Rifle urged him to write another letter in which he told briefly the disappointing details of his search.

He was rather surprised the next morning to find he had entirely forgotten Rossland. While he was attending to his affairs at the bank, Olaf secured information that Rossland was resting comfortably in the hospital and had not one chance in ten of dying. It was not Alan's intention to see him. He wanted to hear nothing he might have to say about Mary Standish. To associate them in any way, as he thought of her now, was little short of sacrilege. He was conscious of the change in himself, for it was rather an amazing upsetting of the original Alan Holt. That person would have gone to Rossland with the deliberate and businesslike intention of sifting the matter to the bottom that he might disprove his own responsibility and set himself right in his own eyes. In self-defense he would have given Rossland an opportunity to break down with cold facts the disturbing something which his mind had unconsciously built up. But the new Alan revolted. He wanted to carry the thing away with him, he wanted it to live, and so it went with him, uncontaminated by any truths or lies which Rossland might have told him.

They left Cordova early in the afternoon, and at sunset that evening camped on the tip of a wooded island a mile or two from the mainland. Olaf knew the island and had chosen it for reasons of his own. It was primitive and alive with birds. Olaf loved the birds, and the cheer of their vesper song and bedtime twitter comforted Alan. He seized an ax, and for the first time in seven months his muscles responded to the swing of it. And Ericksen, old as his years in the way of the north, whistled loudly and rumbled a bit of crude song through his beard as he lighted a fire, knowing the medicine of the big open was getting its hold on Alan again. To Alan it was like coming to the edge of home once more. It seemed an age, an infinity, since he had heard the sputtering of bacon in an open skillet and the bubbling of coffee over a bed of coals with the mysterious darkness of the timber gathering in about him. He loaded his pipe after his chopping, and sat watching Olaf as he mothered the half-baked bannock loaf. It made him think of his father. A thousand times the two must have camped like this in the days when Alaska was new and there were no maps to tell them what lay beyond the next range.

Olaf felt resting upon him something of the responsibility of a doctor, and after supper he sat with his back to a tree and talked of the old days as if they were yesterday and the day before, with tomorrow always the pot of gold at the end of the rainbow which he had pursued for thirty years. He was sixty just a week ago this evening, he said, and he was beginning to doubt if he would remain on the beach at Cordova much longer. Siberia was dragging him—that forbidden world of adventure and mystery and monumental opportunity which lay only a few miles across the strait from the Seward Peninsula. In his enthusiasm he forgot Alan's tragedy. He cursed Cossack law and the prohibitory measures to keep Americans out. More gold was over there than had ever been dreamed of in Alaska; even the mountains and rivers were unnamed; and he was going if he lived another year or two—going to find his fortune or his end in the Stanovoi Mountains and among the Chukchi tribes. Twice he had tried it since his old comrade had died, and twice he had been driven out. The next time he would know how to go about it, and he invited Alan to go with him.

There was a thrill in this talk of a land so near, scarcely a night ride across the neck of Bering Sea, and yet as proscribed as the sacred plains of Tibet. It stirred old desires in Alan's blood, for he knew that of all frontiers the Siberian would be the last and the greatest, and that not only men, but nations, would play their part in the breaking of it. He saw the red gleam of firelight in Olaf's eyes.

"And if we don't go in first from *this side*, Alan, the yellow fellows will come out some day from *that*," rumbled the old sour-dough, striking his pipe in the hollow of his hand. "And when they do, they won't come over to us in ones an' twos an' threes, but in millions. That's what the yellow fellows will do when they once get started, an' it's up to a few Alaska Jacks an' Tough-Nut Bills to get their feet planted first on the other side. Will you go?"

Alan shook his head. "Some day—but not now." The old flash was in his eyes and he was seeing the fight ahead of him again—the fight to do his bit in striking the shackles of misgovernment from Alaska and rousing the world to an understanding of the menace which hung over her like a smoldering cloud. "But you're right about the danger," he said. "It won't come from Japan to California. It will pour like a flood through Siberia and jump to Alaska in a night. It isn't the danger of the yellow man alone, Olaf. You've got to combine that with Bolshevism, the menace of blackest Russia. A disease which, if it crosses the little neck of water and gets hold of Alaska, will shake the American continent to bed-rock. It may be a generation from now, maybe a century, but it's coming sure as God makes light—if we let Alaska go down and out. And my way of preventing it is different from yours."

He stared into the fire, watching the embers flare up and die. "I'm not proud of the States," he went on, as if speaking to something which he saw in the flames. "I can't be, after the ruin their unintelligent propaganda and legislation have brought upon Alaska. But they're our salvation and conditions are improving. I concede we have factions in Alaska and we are not at all unanimous in what we want. It's going to be largely a matter of education. We can't take Alaska down to the States—we've got to bring them up to us. We must make a large part of a hundred and ten million Americans understand. We must bring a million of them up here before that danger-flood we speak of comes beyond the Gulf of Anadyr. It's God's own country we have north of Fifty-eight, Olaf. And we have ten times the wealth of California. We can care for a million people easily. But bad politics and bad judgment both here in Alaska and at Washington won't let them come. With coal enough under our feet to last a thousand years, we are buying fuel from the States. We've got billions in copper and oil, but can't touch them. We should have some of the world's greatest manufacturing plants, but we can not, because everything up here is locked away from us. I repeat that isn't conservation. If they had applied a little of it to the salmon industry—but they didn't. And the salmon are going, like the buffalo of the plains.

"The destruction of the salmon shows what will happen to us if the bars are let down all at once to the financial banditti. Understanding and common sense must guard the gates. The fight we must win is to bring about an honest and reasonable adjustment, Olaf. And that fight will take place right here—in Alaska—and not in Siberia. And if we don't win—"

He raised his eyes from the fire and smiled grimly into Olaf's bearded face.

"Then we can count on that thing coming across the neck of sea from the Gulf of Anadyr," he finished. "And if it ever does come, the people of the States will at last face the tragic realization of what Alaska could have meant to the nation."

The force of the old spirit surged uppermost in Alan again, and after that, for an hour or more, something lived for him in the glow of the fire which Olaf kept burning. It was the memory of Mary Standish, her quiet, beautiful eyes gazing at him, her pale face taking form in the lacy wisps of birch-smoke. His mind pictured her in the flame-glow as she had listened to him that day in Skagway, when he had told her of this fight that was ahead. And it pleased him to think she would have made this same fight for Alaska if she had lived. It was a thought which brought a painful thickening in his breath, for always these visions which Olaf could not see ended with Mary Standish as she had faced him in his cabin, her back against the door, her lips trembling, and her eyes softly radiant with tears in the broken pride of that last moment of her plea for life.

He could not have told how long he slept that night. Dreams came to him in his restless slumber, and always they awakened him, so that he was looking at the stars again and trying not to think. In spite of the grief in his soul they were pleasant dreams, as though some gentle force were at work in him subconsciously to wipe away the shadows of tragedy. Mary Standish was with him again, between the mountains at Skagway; she was at his side in the heart of the tundras, the sun in her shining hair and eyes, and all about them the wonder of wild roses and purple iris and white seas of sedge-cotton and yellow-eyed daisies, and birds singing in the gladness of summer. He heard the birds. And he heard the girl's voice, answering them in her happiness and turning that happiness from the radiance of her eyes upon him. When he awoke, it was with a little cry, as if someone had stabbed him; and Olaf was building a fire, and dawn was breaking in rose-gleams over the mountains.

* * * * *

CHAPTER XII

This first night and dawn in the heard of his wilderness, with the new import of life gleaming down at him from the mighty peaks of the Chugach and Kenai ranges, marked the beginning of that uplift which drew Alan out of the pit into which he had fallen. He understood, now, how it was that through many long years his father had worshiped the memory of a woman who had died, it seemed to him, an infinity ago. Unnumbered times he had seen the miracle of her presence in his father's eyes, and once, when they had stood overlooking a sun-filled valley back in the mountains, the elder Holt had said:

"Twenty-seven years ago the twelfth day of last month, mother went with me through this valley, Alan. Do you see the little bend in the creek, with the great rock in the sun? We rested there—before you were born!"

He had spoken of that day as if it had been but yesterday. And Alan recalled the strange happiness in his father's face as he had looked down upon something in the valley which no other but himself could see.

And it was happiness, the same strange, soul-aching happiness, that began to build itself a house close up against the grief in Alan's heart. It would never be a house quite empty. Never again would he be alone. He knew at last it was an undying part of him, as it had been a part of his father, clinging to him in sweet pain, encouraging him, pressing gently upon him the beginning of a great faith that somewhere beyond was a place to meet again. In the many days that followed, it grew in him, but in a way no man or woman could see. It was a secret about which he built a wall, setting it apart from that stoical placidity of his nature which some people called indifference. Olaf could see farther than others, because he had known Alan's father as a brother. It had always been that way with the elder Holt—straight, clean, deep-breathing, and with a smile on his lips in times of hurt. Olaf had seen him face death like that. He had seen him rise up with awesome courage from the beautiful form that had turned to clay under his eyes, and fight forth again into a world burned to ashes. Something of that look which he had seen in the eyes of the father he saw in Alan's, in these days when they nosed their way up the Alaskan coast together. Only to himself did Alan speak the name of Mary Standish, just as his father had kept Elizabeth Holt's name sacred in his own heart. Olaf, with mildly casual eyes and strong in the possession of memories, observed how much alike they were, but discretion held his tongue, and he said nothing to Alan of many things that ran in his mind.

He talked of Siberia—always of Siberia, and did not hurry on the way to Seward. Alan himself felt no great urge to make haste. The days were soft with the premature breath of summer. The nights were cold, and filled with stars. Day after day mountains hung about them like mighty castles whose battlements reached up into the cloud-draperies of the sky. They kept close to the mainland and among the islands, camping early each evening. Birds were coming northward by the thousand, and each night Olaf's camp-fire sent up the delicious aroma of flesh-pots and roasts. When at last they reached Seward, and the time came for Olaf to turn back, there was an odd blinking in the old Swede's eyes, and as a final comfort Alan told him again that the day would probably come when he would go to Siberia with him. After that, he watched the *Norden* until the little boat was lost in the distance of the sea.

Alone, Alan felt once more a greater desire to reach his own country. And he was fortunate. Two days after his arrival at Seward the steamer which carried mail and the necessities of life to the string of settlements reaching a thousand miles out into the Pacific left Resurrection Bay, and he was given passage. Thereafter the countless islands of the North

Pacific drifted behind, while always northward were the gray cliffs of the Alaskan Peninsula, with the ramparted ranges beyond, glistening with glaciers, smoking with occasional volcanoes, and at times so high their snowy peaks were lost in the clouds. First touching the hatchery at Karluk and then the canneries at Uyak and Chignik, the mail boat visited the settlements on the Island of Unga, and thence covered swiftly the three hundred miles to Dutch Harbor and Unalaska. Again he was fortunate. Within a week he was berthed on a freighter, and on the twelfth day of June set foot in Nome.

His home-coming was unheralded, but the little, gray town, with its peculiar, black shadowings, its sea of stove-pipes, and its two solitary brick chimneys, brought a lump of joy into his throat as he watched its growing outlines from the small boat that brought him ashore. He could see one of the only two brick chimneys in northern Alaska gleaming in the sun; beyond it, fifty miles away, were the ragged peaks of the Saw-Tooth Range, looking as if one might walk to them in half an hour, and over all the world between seemed to hover a misty gloom. But it was where he had lived, where happiness and tragedy and unforgetable memories had come to him, and the welcoming of its frame buildings, its crooked streets, and what to others might have been ugliness, was a warm and thrilling thing. For here were his *people*. Here were the men and women who were guarding the northern door of the world, an epic place, filled with strong hearts, courage, and a love of country as inextinguishable as one's love of life. From this drab little place, shut out from all the world for half the year, young men and women went down to southern universities, to big cities, to the glamor and lure of "outside." But they always came back. Nome called them. Its loneliness in winter. Its gray gloom in springtime. Its glory in summer and autumn. It was the breeding-place of a new race of men, and they loved it as Alan loved it. To him the black wireless tower meant more than the Statue of Liberty, the three weather-beaten church spires more than the architectural colossi of New York and Washington. Beside one of the churches he had played as a boy. He had seen the steeples painted. He had helped make the crooked streets. And his mother had laughed and lived and died here, and his father's footprints had been in the white sands of the beach when tents dotted the shore like gulls.

When he stepped ashore, people stared at him and then greeted him. He was unexpected. And the surprise of his arrival added strength to the grip which men's hands gave him. He had not heard voices like theirs down in the States, with a gladness in them that was almost excitement. Small boys ran up to his side, and with white men came the Eskimo, grinning and shaking his hands. Word traveled swiftly that Alan Holt had come back from the States. Before the day was over, it was on its way to Shelton and Candle and Keewalik and Kotzebue Sound. Such was the beginning of his home-coming. But ahead of the news of his arrival Alan walked up Front Street, stopped at Bahlke's restaurant for a cup of coffee, and then dropped casually into Lomen's offices in the Tin Bank Building.

For a week Alan remained in Nome. Carl Lomen had arrived a few days before, and his brothers were "in" from the big ranges over on the Choris Peninsula. It had been a good winter and promised to be a tremendously successful summer. The Lomen herds would exceed forty thousand head, when the final figures were in. A hundred other herds were prospering, and the Eskimo and Lapps were full-cheeked and plump with good feeding and prosperity. A third of a million reindeer were on the hoof in Alaska, and the breeders were exultant. Pretty good, when compared with the fact that in 1902 there were less than five thousand! In another twenty years there would be ten million.

But with this prosperity of the present and still greater promise for the future Alan sensed the undercurrent of unrest and suspicion in Nome. After waiting and hoping through another long winter, with their best men fighting for Alaska's salvation at Washington, word was traveling from mouth to mouth, from settlement to settlement, and from range to range, that the Bureaucracy which misgoverned them from thousands of miles away was not lifting a hand to relieve them. Federal office-holders refused to surrender their deadly power, and their strangling methods were to continue. Coal, which should cost ten dollars a ton if dug from Alaskan mines, would continue to cost forty dollars; cold storage from Nome would continue to be fifty-two dollars a ton, when it should be twenty. Commercial brigandage was still given letters of marque. Bureaus were fighting among themselves for greater power, and in the turmoil Alaska was still chained like a starving man just outside the reach of all the milk and honey in a wonderful land. Pauperizing, degrading, actually killing, the political misrule that had already driven 25 per cent of Alaska's population from their homes was to continue indefinitely. A President of the United States had promised to visit the mighty land of the north and see with his own eyes. But would he come? There had been other promises, many of them, and promises had always been futile. But it was a hope that crept through Alaska, and upon this hope men whose courage never died began to build. Freedom was on its way, even if slowly. Justice must triumph ultimately, as it always triumphed. Rusty keys would at last be turned in the locks which had kept from Alaskans all the riches and resources of their country, and these men were determined to go on building against odds that they might be better prepared for that freedom of human endeavor when it came.

In these days, when the fires of achievement needed to be encouraged, and not smothered, neither Alan nor Carl Lomen emphasized the menace of gigantic financial interests like that controlled by John Graham—interests fighting to do away with the best friend Alaska ever had, the Biological Survey, and backing with all their power the ruinous legislation to put Alaska in the control of a group of five men that an aggrandizement even more deadly than a suffocating policy of conservation might be more easily accomplished. Instead, they spread the optimism of men possessed of inextinguishable faith. The blackest days were gone. Rifts were breaking in the clouds. Intelligence was creeping through, like rays of sunshine. The end of Alaska's serfdom was near at hand. So they preached, and knew they were preaching truth, for what remained of Alaska's men after years of hopelessness and distress were fighting men. And the women who had remained with them were the mothers and wives of a new nation in the making.

These mothers and wives Alan met during his week in Nome. He would have given his life if a few million people in the States could have known these women. Something would have happened then, and the sisterhood of half a continent—possessing the power of the ballot— would have opened their arms to them. Men like John Graham would have gone out of existence; Alaska would have received her birthright. For these women were of the kind who greeted the sun each day, and the gloom of winter, with something greater than hope in their hearts. They, too, were builders. Fear of God and love of land lay deep in their souls, and side by side with their men-folk they went on in this epic struggle for the building of a nation at the top of the world.

Many times during this week Alan felt it in his heart to speak of Mary Standish. But in the end, not even to Carl Lomen did word of her escape his lips. The passing of each day had made her more intimately a part of him, and a secret part. He could not tell people about her. He even made evasions when questioned about his business and experiences at Cordova and up the coast. Curiously, she seemed nearer to him when he was away from other men and women. He remembered it had been that way with his father, who was always happiest when in the deep mountains or the unending tundras. And so Alan thrilled with an inner gladness when his business was finished and the day came for him to leave Nome.

Carl Lomen went with him as far as the big herd on Choris Peninsula. For one hundred miles, up to Shelton, they rode over a narrow-gauge, four-foot railway on a hand-car drawn by dogs. And it seemed to Alan, at times, as though Mary Standish were with him, riding in this strange way through a great wilderness. He could *see* her. That was the strange thing which began to possess him. There were moments when her eyes were shining softly upon him, her lips smiling, her presence so real he might have spoken to her if Lomen had not been at his side. He did not fight against these visionings. It pleased him to think of her going with him into the heart of Alaska, riding the picturesque "pup-mobile," losing herself in the mountains and in his tundras, with all the wonder and glory of a new world breaking upon her a little at a time, like the unfolding of a great mystery. For there was both wonder and glory in these countless miles running ahead and drifting behind, and the miracle of northward-sweeping life. The days were long. Night, as Mary Standish had always known night, was gone. On the twentieth of June there were twenty hours of day, with a dim and beautiful twilight between the hours of eleven and one. Sleep was no longer a matter of the rising and setting of the sun, but was regulated by the hands of the watch. A world frozen to the core for seven months was bursting open like a great flower.

From Shelton, Alan and his companion visited the eighty or ninety people at Candle, and thence continued down the Keewalik River to Keewalik, on Kotzebue Sound. A Lomen power-boat, run by Lapps, carried them to Choris Peninsula, where for a week Alan remained with Lomen and his huge herd of fifteen thousand reindeer. He was eager to go on, but tried to hide his impatience. Something was urging him, whipping him on to greater haste. For the first time in months he heard the crackling thunder of reindeer hoofs, and the music of it was like a wild call from his own herds hurrying him home. He was glad when the week-end came and his business was done. The power-boat took him to Kotzebue. It was night, as his watch went, when Paul Davidovich started up the delta of the Kobuk River with him in a lighterage company's boat. But there was no darkness. In the afternoon of the fourth day they came to the Redstone, two hundred miles above the mouth of the Kobuk as the river winds. They had supper together on the shore. After that Paul Davidovich turned back with the slow sweep of the current, waving his hand until he was out of sight.

Not until the sound of the Russian's motor-boat was lost in distance did Alan sense fully the immensity of the freedom that swept upon him. At last, after months that had seemed like so many years, he was *alone*. North and eastward stretched the unmarked trail which he knew so well, a hundred and fifty miles straight as a bird might fly, almost unmapped, unpeopled, right up to the doors of his range in the slopes of the Endicott Mountains. A little cry from his own lips gave him a start. It was as if he had called out aloud to Tautuk and Amuk Toolik, and to Keok and Nawadlook, telling them he was on his way home and would soon be there. Never had this hidden land which he had found for himself seemed so desirable as it did in this hour. There was something about it that was all-mothering, all-good, all-sweetly-comforting to that other thing which had become a part of him now. It was holding out its arms to him, understanding, welcoming, inspiring him to travel strongly and swiftly the space between. And he was ready to answer its call.

He looked at his watch. It was five o'clock in the afternoon. He had spent a long day with the Russian, but he felt no desire for rest or sleep. The musk-tang of the tundras, coming to him through the thin timber of the river-courses, worked like an intoxicant in his blood. It was the tundra he wanted, before he lay down upon his back with his face to the stars. He was eager to get away from timber and to feel the immeasurable space of the big country, the open country, about him. What fool had given to it the name of *Barren Lands*? What idiots people were to lie about it in that way on the maps! He strapped his pack over his shoulders and seized his rifle. Barren Lands!

He set out, walking like a man in a race. And long before the twilight hours of sleep they were sweeping out ahead of him in all their glory— the Barren Lands of the map-makers, *his* paradise. On a knoll he stood in the golden sun and looked about him. He set his pack down and stood with bared head, a whispering of cool wind in his hair. If Mary Standish could have lived to see *this*! He stretched out his arms, as if pointing for her eyes to follow, and her name was in his heart and whispering on his silent lips. Immeasurable the tundras reached ahead of him—rolling, sweeping, treeless, green and golden and a glory of flowers, athrill with a life no forest land had ever known. Under his feet was a crush of forget-me-nots and of white and purple violets, their sweet perfume filling his lungs as he breathed. Ahead of him lay a white sea of yellow-eyed daisies, with purple iris high as his knees in between, and as far as he could see, waving softly in the breeze, was the cotton-tufted sedge he loved. The pods were green. In a few days they would be opening, and the tundras would be white carpets.

He listened to the call of life. It was about him everywhere, a melody of bird-life subdued and sleepy even though the sun was still warmly aglow in the sky. A hundred times he had watched this miracle of bird instinct, the going-to-bed of feathered creatures in the weeks and months when there was no real night. He picked up his pack and went on. From a pool hidden in the lush grasses of a distant hollow came to him the twilight honking of nesting geese and the quacking content of wild ducks. He heard the reed-like, musical notes of a lone "organ-duck" and the plaintive cries of plover, and farther out, where the shadows seemed deepening against the rim of the horizon, rose the harsh, rolling notes of cranes and the raucous cries of the loons. And then, from a clump of willows near him, came the chirping twitter of a thrush whose throat was tired for the day, and the sweet, sleepy evening song of a robin. *Night!* Alan laughed softly, the pale flush of the sun in his face. *Bedtime!* He looked at his watch.

It was nine o'clock. Nine o'clock, and the flowers still answering to the glow of the sun! And the people down there—in the States—called it a frozen land, a hell of ice and snow at the end of the earth, a place of the survival of the fittest! Well, to just such extremes had stupidity and ignorance gone through all the years of history, even though men called themselves super-creatures of intelligence and knowledge. It was humorous. And it was tragic.

At last he came to a shining pool between two tufted ridges, and in this velvety hollow the twilight was gathering like a shadow in a cup. A little creek ran out of the pool, and here Alan gathered soft grass and spread out his blankets. A great stillness drew in about him, broken only by the old squaws and the loons. At eleven o'clock he could still see clearly the sleeping water-fowl on the surface of the pool. But the stars were appearing. It grew duskier, and the rose-tint of the sun faded into purple gloom as pale night drew near—four hours of rest that was neither darkness nor day. With a pillow of sedge and grass under his head he slept.

The song and cry of bird-life wakened him, and at dawn he bathed in the pool, with dozens of fluffy, new-born ducks dodging away from him among the grasses and reeds. That day, and the next, and the day after that he traveled steadily into the heart of the tundra country, swiftly and almost without rest. It seemed to him, at last, that he must be in that country where all the bird-life of the world was born, for wherever there was water, in the pools and little streams and the hollows between the ridges, the voice of it in the morning was a babel of sound. Out of the sweet breast of the earth he could feel the irresistible pulse of motherhood filling him with its strength and its courage, and whispering to him its everlasting message that because of the glory and need and faith of life had God created this land of twenty-hour day and four-hour twilight. In it, in these days of summer, was no abiding place for gloom; yet in his own heart, as he drew nearer to his home, was a place of darkness which its light could not quite enter.

The tundras had made Mary Standish more real to him. In the treeless spaces, in the vast reaches with only the sky shutting out his vision, she seemed to be walking nearer to him, almost with her hand in his. At times it was like a torture inflicted upon him for his folly, and when he visioned what might have been, and recalled too vividly that it was he who had stilled with death that living glory which dwelt with him in spirit now, a crying sob of which he was not ashamed came from his lips. For when he thought too deeply, he knew that Mary Standish would have lived if he had said other things to her that night aboard the ship. She had died, not for him, but *because* of him—because, in his failure to live up to what she believed she had found in him, he had broken down what must have been her last hope and her final faith. If he had been less blind, and God had given him the inspiration of a greater wisdom, she would have been walking with him now, laughing in the rose-tinted dawn, growing tired amid the flowers, sleeping under the clear stars—happy and unafraid, and looking to him for all things. At least so he dreamed, in his immeasurable loneliness.

He did not tolerate the thought that other forces might have called her even had she lived, and that she might not have been his to hold and to fight for. He did not question the possibility of shackles and chains that might have bound her, or other inclinations that might have led her. He claimed her, now that she was dead, and knew that living he would have possessed her. Nothing could have kept him from that. But she was gone. And for that he was accountable, and the fifth night he lay sleepless under the stars, and like a boy he cried for her with his face upon his arm, and when morning came, and he went on, never had the world seemed so vast and empty.

His face was gray and haggard, a face grown suddenly old, and he traveled slowly, for the desire to reach his people was dying within him. He could not laugh with Keok and Nawadlook, or give the old tundra call to Amuk Toolik and his people, who would be riotous in their happiness at his return. They loved him. He knew that. Their love had been a part of his life, and the knowledge that his response to this love would be at best a poor and broken thing filled him with dread. A strange sickness crept through his blood; it grew in his head, so that when noon came, he did not trouble himself to eat.

It was late in the afternoon when he saw far ahead of him the clump of cottonwoods near the warm springs, very near his home. Often he had come to these old cottonwoods, an oasis of timber lost in the great tundras, and he had built himself a little camp among them. He loved the place. It had seemed to him that now and then he must visit the forlorn trees to give them cheer and comradeship. His father's name was carved in the bole of the greatest of them all, and under it the date and day when the elder Holt had discovered them in a land where no man had gone before. And under his father's name was his mother's, and under that, his own. He had made of the place a sort of shrine, a green and sweet-flowered tabernacle of memories, and its bird-song and peace in summer and the weird aloneness of it in winter had played their parts in the making of his soul. Through many months he had anticipated this hour of his home-coming, when in the distance he would see the beckoning welcome of the old cottonwoods, with the rolling foothills and frosted peaks of the Endicott Mountains beyond. And now he was looking at the trees and the mountains, and something was lacking in the thrill of them. He came up from the west, between two willow ridges through which ran the little creek from the warm springs, and he was within a quarter of a mile of them when something stopped him in his tracks.

At first he thought the sound was the popping of guns, but in a moment he knew it could not be so, and the truth flashed suddenly upon him. This day was the Fourth of July, and someone in the cottonwoods was shooting firecrackers!

A smile softened his lips. He recalled Keok's mischievous habit of lighting a whole bunch at one time, for which apparent wastefulness Nawadlook never failed to scold her. They had prepared for his home-coming with a celebration, and Tautuk and Amuk Toolik had probably imported a supply of "bing-bangs" from Allakakat or Tanana. The oppressive weight inside him lifted, and the smile remained on his lips. And then as if commanded by a voice, his eyes turned to the dead cottonwood stub which had sentineled the little oasis of trees for many years. At the very crest of it, floating bravely in the breeze that came with the evening sun, was an American flag!

He laughed softly. These were the people who loved him, who thought of him, who wanted him back. His heart beat faster, stirred by the old happiness, and he drew himself quickly into a strip of willows that grew almost up to the cottonwoods. He would surprise them! He would walk suddenly in among them, unseen and unheard. That was the sort of thing that would amaze and delight them.

He came to the first of the trees and concealed himself carefully. He heard the popping of individual firecrackers and the louder bang of one of the "giants" that always made Nawadlook put her fingers in her pretty ears. He crept stealthily over a knoll, down through a hollow, and then up again to the opposite crest. It was as he had thought. He could see Keok a hundred yards away, standing on the trunk of a fallen tree, and as he looked, she tossed another bunch of sputtering crackers away from her. The others were probably circled about her, out of his sight, watching her performance. He continued cautiously, making his way so that he could come up behind a thick growth of bush unseen, within a dozen paces of them. At last he was as near as that to her, and Keok was still standing on the log with her back toward him.

It puzzled him that he could not see or hear the others. And something about Keok puzzled him, too. And then his heart gave a sudden throb and seemed to stop its beating. It was not Keok on the log. And it was not Nawadlook! He stood up and stepped out from his hiding-place. The slender figure of the girl on the log turned a little, and he saw the glint of golden sunshine in her hair. He called out.

"Keok!"

Was he mad? Had the sickness in his head turned his brain?

And then:

"Mary!" he called. "*Mary Standish*!"

She turned. And in that moment Alan Holt's face was the color of gray rock. It was the dead he had been thinking of, and it was the dead that had risen before him now. For it was Mary Standish who stood there on the old cottonwood log, shooting firecrackers in this evening of his home-coming.

* * * *

116

CHAPTER XIII

After that one calling of her name Alan's voice was dead, and he made no movement. He could not disbelieve. It was not a mental illusion or a temporary upsetting of his sanity. It was truth. The shock of it was rending every nerve in his body, even as he stood as if carved out of wood. And then a strange relaxation swept over him. Some force seemed to pass out of his flesh, and his arms hung limp. She was there, *alive!* He could see the whiteness leave her face and a flush of color come into it, and he heard a little cry as she jumped down from the log and came toward him. It had all happened in a few seconds, but it seemed a long time to Alan.

He saw nothing about her or beyond her. It was as if she were floating up to him out of the cold mists of the sea. And she stopped only a step away from him, when she saw more clearly what was in his face. It must have been something that startled her. Vaguely he realized this and made an effort to recover himself.

"You almost frightened me," she said. "We have been expecting you and watching for you, and I was out there a few minutes ago looking back over the tundra. The sun was in my eyes, and I didn't see you."

It seemed incredible that he should be hearing her voice, the same voice, unexcited, sweet, and thrilling, speaking as if she had seen him yesterday and with a certain reserved gladness was welcoming him again today. It was impossible for him to realize in these moments the immeasurable distance that lay between their viewpoints. He was simply Alan Holt—she was the dead risen to life. Many times in his grief he had visualized what he would do if some miracle could bring her back to him like this; he had thought of taking her in his arms and never letting her go. But now that the miracle had come to pass, and she was within his reach, he stood without moving, trying only to speak.

"You—Mary Standish!" he said at last. "I thought—"

He did not finish. It was not himself speaking. It was another individual within him, a detached individual trying to explain his lack of physical expression. He wanted to cry out his gladness, to shout with joy, yet the directing soul of action in him was stricken. She touched his arm hesitatingly.

"I didn't think you would care," she said. "I thought you wouldn't mind—if I came up here."

Care! The word was like an explosion setting things loose in his brain, and the touch of her hand sent a sweep of fire through him. He heard himself cry out, a strange, unhuman sort of cry, as he swept her to his breast. He held her close, crushing kisses upon her mouth, his fingers buried in her hair, her slender body almost broken in his arms. She was alive—she had come back to him—and he forgot everything in these blind moments but that great truth which was sweeping over him in a glorious inundation. Then, suddenly, he found that she was fighting him, struggling to free herself and putting her hands against his face in her efforts. She was so close that he seemed to see nothing but her eyes, and in them he did not see what he had dreamed of finding—but horror. It was a stab that went into his heart, and his arms relaxed. She staggered back, trembling and swaying a little as she got her breath, her face very white.

He had hurt her. The hurt was in her eyes, in the way she looked at him, as if he had become a menace from which she would run if he had not taken the strength from her. As she stood there, her parted lips showing the red of his kisses, her shining hair almost undone, he held out his hands mutely.

"You think—I came here for *that?*" she panted.

"No," he said. "Forgive me. I am sorry."

It was not anger that he saw in her face. It was, instead, a mingling of shock and physical hurt; a measurement of him now, as she looked at him, which recalled her to him as she had stood that night with her back against his cabin door. Yet he was not trying to piece things together. Even subconsciously that was impossible, for all life in him was centered in the one stupendous thought that she was not dead, but living, and he did not wonder why. There was no question in his mind as to the manner in which she had been saved from the sea. He felt a weakness in his limbs; he wanted to laugh, to cry out, to give himself up to strange inclinations for a moment or two, like a woman. Such was the shock of his happiness. It crept in a living fluid through his flesh. She saw it in the swift change of the rock-like color in his face, and his quicker breathing, and was a little amazed, but Alan was too completely possessed by the one great thing to discover the astonishment growing in her eyes.

"You are alive," he said, giving voice again to the one thought pounding in his brain. "*Alive!*"

It seemed to him that word wanted to utter itself an impossible number of times. Then the truth that was partly dawning came entirely to the girl.

"Mr. Holt, you did not receive my letter at Nome?" she asked.

"Your letter? At Nome?" He repeated the words, shaking his head. "No."

"And all this time—you have been thinking—I was dead?"

He nodded, because the thickness in his throat made it the easier form of speech.

"I wrote you there," she said. "I wrote the letter before I jumped into the sea. It went to Nome with Captain Rifle's ship."

"I didn't get it."

"You didn't get it?" There was wonderment in her voice, and then, if he had observed it, understanding.

"Then you didn't mean that just now? You didn't intend to do it? It was because you had blamed yourself for my death, and it was a great relief to find me alive. That was it, wasn't it?"

Stupidly he nodded again. "Yes, it was a great relief."

"You see, I had faith in you even when you wouldn't help me," she went on. "So much faith that I trusted you with my secret in the letter I wrote. To all the world but you I am dead—to Rossland, Captain Rifle, everyone. In my letter I told you I had arranged with the young Thlinkit Indian. He smuggled the canoe over the side just before I leaped in, and picked me up. I am a good swimmer. Then he paddled me ashore while the boats were making their search."

In a moment she had placed a gulf between them again, on the other side of which she stood unattainable. It was inconceivable that only a few moments ago he had crushed her in his arms. The knowledge that he had done this thing, and that she was looking at him now as if it had never happened, filled him with a smothering sense of humiliation. She made it impossible for him to speak about it, even to apologize more fully.

"Now I am here," she was saying in a quiet, possessive sort of way. "I didn't think of coming when I jumped into the sea. I made up my mind afterward. I think it was because I met a little man with red whiskers whom you once pointed out to me in the smoking salon on the *Nome*. And so—I am your guest, Mr. Holt."

There was not the slightest suspicion of apology in her voice as she smoothed back her hair where he had crumpled it. It was as if she belonged here, and had always belonged here, and was giving him permission to enter her domain. Shock was beginning to pass away from him, and he could feel his feet upon the earth once more. His spirit-visions of her as she had walked hand in hand with him during the past weeks, her soft eyes filled with love, faded away before the reality of Mary Standish in flesh and blood, her quiet mastery of things, her almost omniscient unapproachableness. He reached out his hands, but there was a different light in his eyes, and she placed her own in them confidently.

"It was like a bolt of lightning," he said, his voice free at last and trembling. "Day and night I have been thinking of you, dreaming of you, and cursing myself because I believed I had killed you. And now I find you alive. And *here!*"

She was so near that the hands he clasped lay against his breast. But reason had returned to him, and he saw the folly of dreams.

"It is difficult to believe. Out there I thought I was sick. Perhaps I am. But if I am not sick, and you are really you, I am glad. If I wake up and find I have imagined it all, as I imagined so many of the other things—"

He laughed, freeing her hands and looking into eyes shining half out of tears at him. But he did not finish. She drew away from him, with a lingering of her finger-tips on his arm, and the little heart-beat in her throat revealed itself clearly again as on that night in his cabin.

"I have been thinking of you back there, every hour, every step," he said, making a gesture toward the tundras over which he had come. "Then I heard the firecrackers and saw the flag. It is almost as if I had created you!"

A quick answer was on her lips, but she stopped it.

"And when I found you here, and you didn't fade away like a ghost, I thought something was wrong with my head. Something must have been wrong, I guess, or I wouldn't have done *that*. You see, it puzzled me that a ghost should be setting off firecrackers—and I suppose that was the first impulse I had of making sure you were real."

A voice came from the edge of the cottonwoods beyond them. It was a clear, wild voice with a sweet trill in it. "*Maa-rie!*" it called. "*Maa-rie!*"

"Supper," nodded the girl. "You are just in time. And then we are going home in the twilight."

It made his heart thump, that casual way in which she spoke of his place as home. She went ahead of him, with the sun glinting in the soft coils of her hair, and he picked up his rifle and followed, eyes and soul filled only with the beauty of her slim figure—a glory of life where for a long time he had fashioned a spirit of the dead. They came into an open, soft with grass and strewn with flowers, and in this open a man was kneeling beside a fire no larger than his two hands, and at his side, watching him, stood a girl with two braids of black hair rippling down her back. It was Nawadlook who turned first and saw who it was with Mary Standish, and from his right came an odd little screech that only one person in the world could make, and that was Keok. She dropped the armful of sticks she had gathered for the fire and made straight for him, while Nawadlook, taller and less like a wild creature in the manner of her coming, was only a moment behind. And then he was shaking hands with Stampede, and Keok had slipped down among the flowers and was crying. That was like Keok. She always cried when he went away, and cried when he returned; and then, in another moment, it was Keok who was laughing first, and Alan noticed she no longer wore her hair in braids, as the quieter Nawadlook persisted in doing, but had it coiled about her head just as Mary Standish wore her own.

These details pressed themselves upon him in a vague and unreal sort of way. No one, not even Mary Standish, could understand how his mind and nerves were fighting to recover themselves. His senses were swimming back one by one to a vital point from which they had been swept by an unexpected sea, gripping rather incoherently at unimportant realities as they assembled themselves. In the edge of the tundra beyond the cottonwoods he noticed three saddle-deer grazing at the ends of ropes which were fastened to cotton-tufted nigger-heads. He drew off his pack as Mary Standish went to help Keok pick up the fallen sticks. Nawadlook was pulling a coffee-pot from the tiny fire. Stampede began to fill a pipe. He realized that because they had expected him, if not today then tomorrow or the next day or a day soon after that, no one had experienced shock but himself, and with a mighty effort he reached back and dragged the old Alan Holt into existence again. It was like bringing an intelligence out of darkness into light.

It was difficult for him—afterward—to remember just what happened during the next half-hour. The amazing thing was that Mary Standish sat opposite him, with the cloth on which Nawadlook had spread the supper things between them, and that she was the same clear-eyed, beautiful Mary Standish who had sat across the table from him in the dining-salon of the *Nome*.

Not until later, when he stood alone with Stampede Smith in the edge of the cottonwoods, and the three girls were riding deer back over the tundra in the direction of the Range, did the sea of questions which had been gathering begin to sweep upon him. It had been Keok's suggestion that she and Mary and Nawadlook ride on ahead, and he had noticed how quickly Mary Standish had caught at the idea. She had smiled at him as she left, and a little farther out had waved her hand at him, as Keok and Nawadlook both had done, but not another word had passed between them alone. And as they rode off in the warm glow of sunset Alan stood watching them, and would have stared without speech until they were out of sight, if Stampede's fingers had not gripped his arm.

"Now, go to it, Alan," he said. "I'm ready. Give me hell!"

* * * * *

CHAPTER XIV

It was thus, with a note of something inevitable in his voice, that Stampede brought Alan back solidly to earth. There was a practical and awakening inspiration in the manner of the little red-whiskered man's invitation.

"I've been a damn fool," he confessed. "And I'm waiting."

The word was like a key opening a door through which a flood of things began to rush in upon Alan. There were other fools, and evidently he had been one. His mind went back to the *Nome*. It seemed only a few hours ago—only yesterday—that the girl had so artfully deceived them all, and he had gone through hell because of that deception. The trickery had been simple, and exceedingly clever because of its simplicity; it must have taken a tremendous amount of courage, now that he clearly understood that at no time had she wanted to die.

"I wonder," he said, "why she did a thing like that?"

Stampede shook his head, misunderstanding what was in Alan's mind. "I couldn't keep her back, not unless I tied her to a tree." And he added, "The little witch even threatened to shoot me!"

A flash of exultant humor filled his eyes. "Begin, Alan. I'm waiting. Go the limit."

"For what?"

"For letting her ride over me, of course. For bringing her up. For not shufflin' her in the bush. You can't take it out of *her* hide, can you?"

He twisted his red whiskers, waiting for an answer. Alan was silent. Mary Standish was leading the way up out of a dip in the tundra a quarter of a mile away, with Nawadlook and Keok close behind her. They trotted up a low ridge and disappeared.

"It's none of my business," persisted Stampede, "but you didn't seem to expect her—"

"You're right," interrupted Alan, turning toward his pack. "I didn't expect her. I thought she was dead."

A low whistle escaped Stampede's lips. He opened his mouth to speak and closed it again. Alan observed him as he slipped the pack over his shoulders. Evidently his companion did not know Mary Standish was the girl who had jumped overboard from the *Nome*, and if she had kept her secret, it was not his business just now to explain, even though he guessed that Stampede's quick wits would readily jump at the truth. A light was beginning to dispel the little man's bewilderment as they started toward the Range. He had seen Mary Standish frequently aboard the *Nome*; a number of times he had observed her in Alan's company, and he knew of the hours they had spent together in Skagway. Therefore, if Alan had believed her dead when they went ashore at Cordova, a few hours after the supposed tragedy, it must have been she who jumped into the sea. He shrugged his shoulders in deprecation of his failure to discover this amazing fact in his association with Mary Standish.

"It beats the devil!" he exclaimed suddenly.

"It does," agreed Alan.

Cold, hard reason began to shoulder itself inevitably against the happiness that possessed him, and questions which he had found no interest in asking when aboard ship leaped upon him with compelling force. Why was it so tragically important to Mary Standish that the world should believe her dead? What was it that had driven her to appeal to him and afterward to jump into the sea? What was her mysterious association with Rossland, an agent of Alaska's deadliest enemy, John Graham— the one man upon whom he had sworn vengeance if opportunity ever came his way? Over him, clubbing other emotions with its insistence, rode a demand for explanations which it was impossible for him to make. Stampede saw the tense lines in his face and remained silent in the lengthening twilight, while Alan's mind struggled to bring coherence and reason out of a tidal wave of mystery and doubt. Why had she come to *his* cabin aboard the *Nome*? Why had she played him with such conspicuous intent against Rossland, and why—in the end—had she preceded him to his home in the tundras? It was this question which persisted, never for an instant swept aside by the others. She had not come because of love for him. In a brutal sort of way he had proved that, for when he had taken her in his arms, he had seen distress and fear and a flash of horror in her face. Another and more mysterious force had driven her.

The joy in him was a living flame even as this realization pressed upon him. He was like a man who had found life after a period of something that was worse than death, and with his happiness he felt himself twisted upon an upheaval of conflicting sensations and half convictions out of which, in spite of his effort to hold it back, suspicion began to creep like a shadow. But it was not the sort of suspicion to cool the thrill in his blood or frighten him, for he was quite ready to concede that Mary Standish was a fugitive, and that her flight from Seattle had been in the face of a desperate necessity. What had happened aboard ship was further proof, and her presence at his range a final one. Forces had driven her which it had been impossible for her to combat, and in desperation she had come to him for refuge. She had chosen him out of all the world to help her; she believed in him; she had faith that with him no harm could come, and his muscles tightened with sudden desire to fight for her.

In these moments he became conscious of the evening song of the tundras and the soft splendor of the miles reaching out ahead of them. He strained his eyes to catch another glimpse of the mounted figures when they came up out of hollows to the clough-tops, but the lacy veils of evening were drawing closer, and he looked in vain. Bird-song grew softer; sleepy cries rose from the grasses and pools; the fire of the sun itself died out, leaving its radiance in a mingling of vivid rose and mellow gold over the edge of the world. It was night and yet day, and Alan wondered what thoughts were in the heart of Mary Standish. What had driven her to the Range was of small importance compared with the thrilling fact that she was just ahead of him. The mystery of her would be explained tomorrow. He was sure of that. She would confide in him. Now that she had so utterly placed herself under his protection, she would tell him what she had not dared to disclose aboard the *Nome*. So he thought only of the silvery distance of twilight that separated them, and spoke at last to Stampede.

"I'm rather glad you brought her," he said.

"I didn't bring her," protested Stampede. "She *came*." He shrugged his shoulders with a grunt. "And furthermore I didn't manage it. She did that herself. She didn't come with me. I came with *her*."

He stopped and struck a match to light his pipe. Over the tiny flame he glared fiercely at Alan, but in his eyes was something that betrayed him. Alan saw it and felt a desire to laugh out of sheer happiness. His keen vision and sense of humor were returning.

"How did it happen?"

Stampede puffed loudly at his pipe, then took it from his mouth and drew in a deep breath.

"First I remember was the fourth night after we landed at Cordova. Couldn't get a train on the new line until then. Somewhere up near Chitina we came to a washout. It didn't rain. You couldn't call it that, Alan. It was the Pacific Ocean falling on us, with two or three other oceans backing it up. The stage came along, horses swimming, coach floating, driver half drowned in his seat. I was that hungry I got in for Chitina. There was one other climbed in after me, and I wondered what sort of fool he was. I said something about being starved or I'd have hung to the train. The other didn't answer. Then I began to swear. I did, Alan. I cursed terrible. Swore at the Government for building such a road, swore at the rain, an' I swore at myself for not bringin' along grub. I said my belly was as empty as a shot-off cartridge, and I said it good an' loud. I was mad. Then a big flash of lightning lit up the coach. Alan, it was *her* sittin' there with a box in her lap, facing me, drippin' wet, her eyes shining—and she was smiling at me! Yessir, *smiling*."

Stampede paused to let the shock sink in. He was not disappointed.

Alan stared at him in amazement. "The fourth night—after—" He caught himself. "Go on, Stampede!"

"I began hunting for the latch on the door, Alan. I was goin' to sneak out, drop in the mud, disappear before the lightnin' come again. But it caught me. An' there she was, undoing the box, and I heard her saying she had plenty of good stuff to eat. An' she called me Stampede, like she'd known me all her life, and with that coach rolling an' rocking and the thunder an' lightning an' rain piling up against each other like sin, she came over and sat down beside me and began to feed me. She did that, Alan—*fed* me. When the lightning fired up, I could see her eyes shining and her lips smilin' as if all that hell about us made her happy, and I thought she was plumb crazy. Before I knew it she was telling me how you pointed me out to her in the smoking-room, and how happy she was that I was goin' her way. *Her* way, mind you, Alan, not *mine*. And that's just the way she's kept me goin' up to the minute you hove in sight back there in the cottonwoods!"

He lighted his pipe again. "Alan, how the devil did she know I was hitting the trail for your place?"

"She didn't," replied Alan.

"But she did. She said that meeting with me in the coach was the happiest moment of her life, because *she* was on her way up to your range, and I'd be such jolly good company for her. 'Jolly good'—them were the words she used! When I asked her if you knew she was coming up, she said no, of course not, and that it was going to be a grand surprise. Said it was possible she'd buy your range, and she wanted to look it over before you arrived. An' it seems queer I can't remember anything more about the thunder and lightning between there and Chitina. When we took the train again, she began askin' a million questions about you and the Range and Alaska. Soak me if you want to, Alan—but everything I knew she got out of me between Chitina and Fairbanks, and she got it in such a sure-fire nice way that I'd have eat soap out of her hand if she'd offered it to me. Then, sort of sly and soft-like, she began asking questions about John Graham—and I woke up."

"John Graham!" Alan repeated the name.

"Yes, John Graham. And I had a lot to tell. After that I tried to get away from her. But she caught me just as I was sneakin' aboard a down-river boat, and cool as you please—with her hand on my arm—she said she wasn't quite ready to go yet, and would I please come and help her carry some stuff she was going to buy. Alan, it ain't a lie what I'm going to tell you! She led me up the street, telling me what a wonderful idea she had for surprisin' *you*. Said she knew you would return to the Range by the Fourth of July and we sure must have some fireworks. Said you was such a good American you'd be disappointed if you didn't have 'em. So she took me in a store an' bought it out. Asked the man what he'd take for everything in his joint that had powder in it. Five hundred dollars, that was what she paid. She pulled a silk something out of the front of her dress with a pad of hundred-dollar bills in it an inch think. Then she asked *me* to get them firecrackers 'n' wheels 'n' skyrockets 'n' balloons 'n' other stuff down to the boat, and she asked me just as if I was a sweet little boy who'd be tickled to death to do it!"

In the excitement of unburdening himself of a matter which he had borne in secret for many days, Stampede did not observe the effect of his words upon his companion. Incredulity shot into Alan's eyes, and the humorous lines about his mouth vanished when he saw clearly that Stampede was not drawing upon his imagination. Yet what he had told him seemed impossible. Mary Standish had come aboard the *Nome* a fugitive. All her possessions she had brought with her in a small hand-bag, and these things she had left in her cabin when she leaped into the sea. How, then, could she logically have had such a sum of money at Fairbanks as Stampede described? Was it possible the Thlinkit Indian had also become her agent in transporting the money ashore on the night she played her desperate game by making the world believe she had died? And was this money—possibly the manner in which she had secured it in Seattle—the cause of her flight and the clever scheme she had put into execution a little later?

He had been thinking crime, and his face grew hot at the sin of it. It was like thinking it of another woman, who was dead, and whose name was cut under his father's in the old cottonwood tree.

Stampede, having gained his wind, was saying: "You don't seem interested, Alan. But I'm going on, or I'll bust. I've got to tell you what happened, and then if you want to lead me out and shoot me, I won't say a word. I say, curse a firecracker anyway!"

"Go on," urged Alan. "I'm interested."

"I got 'em on the boat," continued Stampede viciously. "And she with me every minute, smiling in that angel way of hers, and not letting me out of her sight a flick of her eyelash, unless there was only one hole to go in an' come out at. And then she said she wanted to do a little shopping, which meant going into every shack in town and buyin' something, an' I did the lugging. At last she bought a gun, and when I asked her what she was goin' to do with it, she said, 'Stampede, that's for you,' an' when I went to thank her, she said: 'No, I don't mean it that way. I mean that if you try to run away from me again I'm going to fill you full of holes.' She said that! Threatened me. Then she bought me a new outfit from toe to summit—boots, pants, shirt, hat *and* a necktie! And I didn't say a word, not a word. She just led me in an' bought what she wanted and made me put 'em on."

Stampede drew in a mighty breath, and a fourth time wasted a match on his pipe. "I was getting used to it by the time we reached Tanana," he half groaned. "Then the hell of it begun. She hired six Indians to tote the luggage, and we set out over the trail for your place. 'You're goin' to have a rest, Stampede,' she says to me, smiling so cool and sweet like you wanted to eat her alive. 'All you've got to do is show us the way and carry the bums.' 'Carry the what?' I asks. 'The bums,' she says, an' then she explains that a bum is a thing filled with powder which makes a terrible racket when it goes off. So I took the bums, and the next day one of the Indians sprained a leg, and dropped out. He had the firecrackers, pretty near a hundred pounds, and we whacked up his load among us. I couldn't stand up straight when we camped. We had crooks in our backs every inch of the way to the Range. And *would* she let us cache some of that junk? Not on your life she wouldn't! And all the time while they was puffing an' panting them Indians was worshipin' her with their eyes. The last day, when we camped with the Range almost in sight, she drew 'em all up in a circle about her and gave 'em each a handful of money above their pay. 'That's because I love you,' she says, and then she begins asking them funny questions. Did they have wives and children? Were they ever hungry? Did they ever know about any of their people starving to death? And just *why* did they starve? And, Alan, so help me thunder if them Indians didn't talk! Never heard Indians tell so much. And in the end she asked them the funniest question of all, asked them if they'd heard of a man named John Graham. One of them had, and afterward I saw her talking a long time with him alone, and when she come back to me, her eyes were sort of burning up, and she didn't say good night when she went into her tent. That's all, Alan, except—"

"Except what, Stampede?" said Alan, his heart throbbing like a drum inside him.

Stampede took his time to answer, and Alan heard him chuckling and saw a flash of humor in the little man's eyes.

"Except that she's done with everyone on the Range just what she did with me between Chitina and here," he said. "Alan, if she wants to say the word, why, *you* ain't boss any more, that's all. She's been there ten days, and you won't know the place. It's all done up in flags, waiting for you. She an' Nawadlook and Keok are running everything but the deer. The kids would leave their mothers for her, and the men—" He chuckled again. "Why, the men even go to the Sunday school she's started! I went. Nawadlook sings."

For a moment he was silent. Then he said in a subdued voice, "Alan, you've been a big fool."

"I know it, Stampede."

"She's a—a flower, Alan. She's worth more than all the gold in the world. And you could have married her. I know it. But it's too late now. I'm warnin' you."

"I don't quite understand, Stampede. Why is it too late?"

"Because she likes me," declared Stampede a bit fiercely. "I'm after her myself, Alan. You can't butt in now."

"Great Scott!" gasped Alan. "You mean that Mary Standish—"

"I'm not talking about Mary Standish," said Stampede. "It's Nawadlook. If it wasn't for my whiskers—"

His words were broken by a sudden detonation which came out of the pale gloom ahead of them. It was like the explosion of a cannon a long distance away.

"One of them cussed bums," he explained. "That's why they hurried on ahead of us, Alan. *She* says this Fourth of July celebration is going to mean a lot for Alaska. Wonder what she means?"

"I wonder," said Alan.

* * * * *

CHAPTER XV

Half an hour more of the tundra and they came to what Alan had named Ghost Kloof, a deep and jagged scar in the face of the earth, running down from the foothills of the mountains. It was a sinister thing, and in the depths lay abysmal darkness as they descended a rocky path worn smooth by reindeer and caribou hoofs. At the bottom, a hundred feet below the twilight of the plains, Alan dropped on his knees beside a little spring that he groped for among the stones, and as he drank he could hear the weird whispering and gurgling of water up and down the kloof, choked and smothered in the moss of the rock walls and eternally dripping from the crevices. Then he saw Stampede's face in the glow of another match, and the little man's eyes were staring into the black chasm that reached for miles up into the mountains.

"Alan, you've been up this gorge?"

"It's a favorite runway for the lynx and big brown bears that kill our fawns," replied Alan. "I hunt alone, Stampede. The place is supposed to be haunted, you know. Ghost Kloof, I call it, and no Eskimo will enter it. The bones of dead men lie up there."

"Never prospected it?" persisted Stampede.

"Never."

Alan heard the other's grunt of disgust.

"You're reindeer-crazy," he grumbled. "There's gold in this canyon. Twice I've found it where there were dead men's bones. They bring me good luck."

"But these were Eskimos. They didn't come for gold."

"I know it. The Boss settled that for me. When she heard what was the matter with this place, she made me take her into it. Nerve? Say, I'm telling you there wasn't any of it left out of her when she was born!" He was silent for a moment, and then added: "When we came to that dripping, slimy rock with the big yellow skull layin' there like a poison toadstool, she didn't screech and pull back, but just gave a little gasp and stared at it hard, and her fingers pinched my arm until it hurt. It was a devilish-looking thing, yellow as a sick orange and soppy with the drip of the wet moss over it. I wanted to blow it to pieces, and I guess I would if she hadn't put a hand on my gun. An' with a funny little smile she says: 'Don't do it, Stampede. It makes me think of someone I know—and I wouldn't want you to shoot him.' Darned funny thing to say, wasn't it? Made her think of someone she knew! Now, who the devil could look like a rotten skull?"

Alan made no effort to reply, except to shrug his shoulders. They climbed up out of gloom into the light of the plain. Smoothness of the tundra was gone on this side of the crevasse. Ahead of them rolled up a low hill, and mountainward hills piled one upon another until they were lost in misty distance. From the crest of the ridge they looked out into a vast sweep of tundra which ran in among the out-guarding billows and hills of the Endicott Mountains in the form of a wide, semicircular bay. Beyond the next swell in the tundra lay the range, and scarcely had they reached this when Stampede drew his big gun from its holster. Twice he blazed in the air.

"Orders," he said a little sheepishly. "Orders, Alan!"

Scarcely were the words out of his mouth when a yell came to them from beyond the light-mists that hovered like floating lace over the tundra. It was joined by another, and still another, until there was such a sound that Alan knew Tautuk and Amuk Toolik and Topkok and Tatpan and all the others were splitting their throats in welcome, and with it very soon came a series of explosions that set the earth athrill under their feet.

134

"Bums!" growled Stampede. "She's got Chink lanterns hanging up all about, too. You should have seen her face, Alan, when she found there was sunlight all night up here on July Fourth!"

From the range a pale streak went sizzling into the air, mounting until it seemed to pause for a moment to look down upon the gray world, then burst into innumerable little balls of puffy smoke. Stampede blazed away with his forty-five, and Alan felt the thrill of it and emptied the magazine of his gun, the detonations of revolver and rifle drowning the chorus of sound that came from the range. A second rocket answered them. Two columns of flame leaped up from the earth as huge fires gained headway, and Alan could hear the shrill chorus of children's voices mingling with the vocal tumult of men. All the people of his range were there. They had come in from the timber-naked plateaux and high ranges where the herds were feeding, and from the outlying shacks of the tundras to greet him. Never had there been such a concentration of effort on the part of his people. And Mary Standish was behind it all! He knew he was fighting against odds when he tried to keep that fact from choking up his heart a little.

He had not heard what Stampede was saying—that he and Amuk Toolik and forty kids had labored a week gathering dry moss and timber fuel for the big fires. There were three of these fires now, and the tom-toms were booming their hollow notes over the tundra as Alan quickened his steps. Over a little knoll, and he was looking at the buildings of the range, wildly excited figures running about, women and children flinging moss on the fires, the tom-tom beaters squatted in a half-circle facing the direction from which he would come, and fifty Chinese lanterns swinging in the soft night-breeze.

He knew what they were expecting of him, for they were children, all of them. Even Tautuk and Amuk Toolik, his chief herdsmen, were children. Nawadlook and Keok were children. Strong and loyal and ready to die for him in any fight or stress, they were still children. He gave Stampede his rifle and hastened on, determined to keep his eyes from questing for Mary Standish in these first minutes of his return. He sounded the tundra call, and men, women, and little children came running to meet him. The drumming of the tom-toms ceased, and the beaters leaped to their feet. He was inundated. There was a shrill crackling of voice, laughter, children's squeals, a babel of delight. He gripped hands with both his own—hard, thick, brown hands of men; little, softer, brown hands of women; he lifted children up in his arms, slapped his palm affectionately against the men's shoulders, and talked, talked, talked, calling each by name without a slip of memory, though there were fifty around him counting the children. First, last, and always these were *his people*. The old pride swept over him, a compelling sense of power and possession. They loved him, crowding in about him like a great family, and he shook hands twice and three times with the same men and women, and lifted the same children from the arms of delighted mothers, and cried out greetings and familiarities with an abandon which a few minutes ago knowledge of Mary Standish's presence would have tempered. Then, suddenly, he saw her under the Chinese lanterns in front of his cabin. Sokwenna, so old that he hobbled double and looked like a witch, stood beside her. In a moment Sokwenna's head disappeared, and there came the booming of a tom-tom. As quickly as the crowd had gathered about him, it fell away. The beaters squatted themselves in their semicircle again. Fireworks began to go off. Dancers assembled. Rockets hissed through the air. Roman candles popped. From the open door of his cabin came the sound of a phonograph. It was aimed directly at him, the one thing intended for his understanding alone. It was playing "When Johnny Comes Marching Home."

Mary Standish had not moved. He saw her laughing at him, and she was alone. She was not the Mary Standish he had known aboard ship. Fear, the quiet pallor of her face, and the strain and repression which had seemed to be a part of her were gone. She was aflame with life, yet it was not with voice or action that she revealed herself. It was in her eyes, the flush of her cheeks and lips, the poise of her slim body as she waited for him. A thought flashed upon him that for a space she had forgotten herself and the shadow which had driven her to leap into the sea.

"It is splendid!" she said when he came up to her, and her voice trembled a little. "I didn't guess how badly they wanted you back. It must be a great happiness to have people think of you like that."

"And I thank you for your part," he replied. "Stampede has told me. It was quite a bit of trouble, wasn't it, with nothing more than the hope of Americanizing a pagan to inspire you?" He nodded at the half-dozen flags over his cabin. "They're rather pretty."

"It was no trouble. And I hope you don't mind. It has been great fun."

He tried to look casually out upon his people as he answered her. It seemed to him there was only one thing to say, and that it was a duty to speak what was in his mind calmly and without emotion.

"Yes, I do mind," he said. "I mind so much that I wouldn't trade what has happened for all the gold in these mountains. I'm sorry because of what happened back in the cottonwoods, but I wouldn't trade that, either. I'm glad you're alive. I'm glad you're here. But something is missing. You know what it is. You must tell me about yourself. It is the only fair thing for you to do now."

She touched his arm with her hand. "Let us wait for tomorrow. Please—let us wait."

"And then—tomorrow—"

"It is your right to question me and send me back if I am not welcome. But not tonight. All this is too fine—just you—and your people—and their happiness." He bent his head to catch her words, almost drowned by the hissing of a sky-rocket and the popping of firecrackers. She nodded toward the buildings beyond his cabin. "I am with Keok and Nawadlook. They have given me a home." And then swiftly she added, "I don't think you love your people more than I do, Alan Holt!"

Nawadlook was approaching, and with a lingering touch of her fingers on his arm she drew away from him. His face did not show his disappointment, nor did he make a movement to keep her with him.

"Your people are expecting things of you," she said. "A little later, if you ask me, I may dance with you to the music of the tom-toms."

He watched her as she went away with Nawadlook. She looked back at him and smiled, and there was something in her face which set his heart beating faster. She had been afraid aboard the ship, but she was not afraid of tomorrow. Thought of it and the questions he would ask did not frighten her, and a happiness which he had persistently held away from himself triumphed in a sudden, submerging flood. It was as if something in her eyes and voice had promised him that the dreams he had dreamed through weeks of torture and living death were coming true, and that possibly in her ride over the tundra that night she had come a little nearer to the truth of what those weeks had meant to him. Surely he would never quite be able to tell her. And what she said to him tomorrow would, in the end, make little difference. She was alive, and he could not let her go away from him again.

He joined the tom-tom beaters and the dancers. It rather amazed him to discover himself doing things which he had never done before. His nature was an aloof one, observing and sympathetic, but always more or less detached. At his people's dances it was his habit to stand on the side-line, smiling and nodding encouragement, but never taking a part. His habit of reserve fell from him now, and he seemed possessed of a new sense of freedom and a new desire to give physical expression to something within him. Stampede was dancing. He was kicking his feet and howling with the men, while the women dancers went through the muscular movements of arms and bodies. A chorus of voices invited Alan. They had always invited him. And tonight he accepted, and took his place between Stampede and Amuk Toolik and the tom-tom beaters almost burst their instruments in their excitement. Not until he dropped out, half breathless, did he see Mary Standish and Keok in the outer circle. Keok was frankly amazed. Mary Standish's eyes were shining, and she clapped her hands when she saw that he had observed her. He tried to laugh, and waved his hand, but he felt too foolish to go to her. And then the balloon went up, a big, six-foot balloon, and with all its fire made only a pale glow in the sky, and after another hour of hand-shaking, shoulder-clapping, and asking of questions about health and domestic matters, Alan went to his cabin.

He looked about the one big room that was his living-room, and it never had seemed quite so comforting as now. At first he thought it was as he had left it, for there was his desk where it should be, the big table in the middle of the room, the same pictures on the walls, his gun-rack filled with polished weapons, his pipes, the rugs on the floor—and then, one at a time, he began to observe things that were different. In place of dark shades there were soft curtains at his windows, and new covers on his table and the home-made couch in the corner. On his desk were two pictures in copper-colored frames, one of George Washington and the other of Abraham Lincoln, and behind them crisscrossed against the wall just over the top of the desk, were four tiny American flags. They recalled Alan's mind to the evening aboard the *Nome* when Mary Standish had challenged his assertion that he was an Alaskan and not an American. Only she would have thought of those two pictures and the little flags. There were flowers in his room, and she had placed them there. She must have picked fresh flowers each day and kept them waiting the hour of his coming, and she had thought of him in Tanana, where she had purchased the cloth for the curtains and the covers. He went into his bedroom and found new curtains at the window, a new coverlet on his bed, and a pair of red morocco slippers that he had never seen before. He took them up in his hands and laughed when he saw how she had misjudged the size of his feet.

In the living-room he sat down and lighted his pipe, observing that Keok's phonograph, which had been there earlier in the evening, was gone. Outside, the noise of the celebration died away, and the growing stillness drew him to the window from which he could see the cabin where lived Keok and Nawadlook with their foster-father, the old and shriveled Sokwenna. It was there Mary Standish had said she was staying.

For a long time Alan watched it while the final sounds of the night drifted away into utter silence.

It was a knock at his door that turned him about at last, and in answer to his invitation Stampede came in. He nodded and sat down. Shiftingly his eyes traveled about the room.

"Been a fine night, Alan. Everybody glad to see you."

"They seemed to be. I'm happy to be home again."

"Mary Standish did a lot. She fixed up this room."

"I guessed as much," replied Alan. "Of course Keok and Nawadlook helped her."

"Not very much. She did it. Made the curtains. Put them pictures and flags there. Picked the flowers. Been nice an' thoughtful, hasn't she?"

"And somewhat unusual," added Alan.

"And she is pretty."

"Most decidedly so."

There was a puzzling look in Stampede's eyes. He twisted nervously in his chair and waited for words. Alan sat down opposite him.

"What's on your mind, Stampede?"

"Hell, mostly," shot back Stampede with sudden desperation. "I've come loaded down with a dirty job, and I've kept it back this long because I didn't want to spoil your fun tonight. I guess a man ought to keep to himself what he knows about a woman, but I'm thinking this is a little different. I hate to do it. I'd rather take the chance of a snake-bite. But you'd shoot me if you knew I was keeping it to myself."

"Keeping what to yourself?"

"The truth, Alan. It's up to me to tell you what I know about this young woman who calls herself Mary Standish."

* * * * *

CHAPTER XVI

The physical sign of strain in Stampede's face, and the stolid effort he was making to say something which it was difficult for him to put into words, did not excite Alan as he waited for his companion's promised disclosure. Instead of suspense he felt rather a sense of anticipation and relief. What he had passed through recently had burned out of him a certain demand upon human ethics which had been almost callous in its insistence, and while he believed that something very real and very stern in the way of necessity had driven Mary Standish north, he was now anxious to be given the privilege of gripping with any force of circumstance that had turned against her. He wanted to know the truth, yet he had dreaded the moment when the girl herself must tell it to him, and the fact that Stampede had in some way discovered this truth, and was about to make disclosure of it, was a tremendous lightening of the situation.

"Go on," he said at last. "What do you know about Mary Standish?"

Stampede leaned over the table, a gleam of distress in his eyes. "It's rotten. I know it. A man who backslides on a woman the way I'm goin' to oughta be shot, and if it was anything else—*anything*—I'd keep it to myself. But you've got to know. And you can't understand just how rotten it is, either; you haven't ridden in a coach with her during a storm that was blowing the Pacific outa bed, an' you haven't hit the trail with her all the way from Chitina to the Range as I did. If you'd done that, Alan, you'd feel like killing a man who said anything against her."

"I'm not inquiring into your personal affairs," reminded Alan. "It's your own business."

"That's the trouble," protested Stampede. "It's not my business. It's yours. If I'd guessed the truth before we hit the Range, everything would have been different. I'd have rid myself of her some way. But I didn't find out what she was until this evening, when I returned Keok's music machine to their cabin. I've been trying to make up my mind what to do ever since. If she was only making her get-away from the States, a pickpocket, a coiner, somebody's bunco pigeon chased by the police—almost anything—we could forgive her. Even if she'd shot up somebody—" He made a gesture of despair. "But she didn't. She's worse than that!"

He leaned a little nearer to Alan.

"She's one of John Graham's tools sent up here to sneak and spy on you," he finished desperately. "I'm sorry—but I've got the proof."

His hand crept over the top of the table; slowly the closed palm opened, and when he drew it back, a crumpled paper lay between them. "Found it on the floor when I took the phonograph back," he explained. "It was twisted up hard. Don't know why I unrolled it. Just chance."

He waited until Alan had read the few words on the bit of paper, watching closely the slight tensing of the other's face. After a moment Alan dropped the paper, rose to his feet, and went to the window. There was no longer a light in the cabin where Mary Standish had been accepted as a guest. Stampede, too, had risen from his seat. He saw the sudden and almost imperceptible shrug of Alan's shoulders.

It was Alan who spoke, after a half-mixture of silence. "Rather a missing link, isn't it? Adds up a number of things fairly well. And I'm grateful to you, Stampede. Almost—you didn't tell me."

"Almost," admitted Stampede.

"And I wouldn't have blamed you. She's that kind—the kind that makes you feel anything said against her is a lie. And I'm going to believe that paper is a lie—until tomorrow. Will you take a message to Tautuk and Amuk Toolik when you go out? I'm having breakfast at seven. Tell them to come to my cabin with their reports and records at eight. Later I'm going up into the foothills to look over the herds."

Stampede nodded. It was a good fight on Alan's part, and it was just the way he had expected him to take the matter. It made him rather ashamed of the weakness and uncertainty to which he had confessed. Of course they could do nothing with a woman; it wasn't a shooting business—yet. But there was a debatable future, if the gist of the note on the table ran true to their unspoken analysis of it. Promise of something like that was in Alan's eyes.

He opened the door. "I'll have Tautuk and Amuk Toolik here at eight. Good night, Alan!"

"Good night!"

Alan watched Stampede's figure until it had disappeared before he closed the door.

Now that he was alone, he no longer made an effort to restrain the anxiety which the prospector's unexpected revealment had aroused in him. The other's footsteps were scarcely gone when he again had the paper in his hand. It was clearly the lower part of a letter sheet of ordinary business size and had been carelessly torn from the larger part of the page, so that nothing more than the signature and half a dozen lines of writing in a man's heavy script remained.

What was left of the letter which Alan would have given much to have possessed, read as follows:

"—*If you work carefully and guard your real identity in securing facts and information, we should have the entire industry in our hands within a year.*"

Under these words was the strong and unmistakable signature of John Graham.

A score of times Alan had seen that signature, and the hatred he bore for its maker, and the desire for vengeance which had entwined itself like a fibrous plant through all his plans for the future, had made of it an unforgetable writing in his brain. Now that he held in his hand words written by his enemy, and the man who had been his father's enemy, all that he had kept away from Stampede's sharp eyes blazed in a sudden fury in his face. He dropped the paper as if it had been a thing unclean, and his hands clenched until his knuckles snapped in the stillness of the room, as he slowly faced the window through which a few moments ago he had looked in the direction of Mary Standish's cabin.

So John Graham was keeping his promise, the deadly promise he had made in the one hour of his father's triumph—that hour in which the elder Holt might have rid the earth of a serpent if his hands had not revolted in the last of those terrific minutes which he as a youth had witnessed. And Mary Standish was the instrument he had chosen to work his ends!

In these first minutes Alan could not find a doubt with which to fend the absoluteness of the convictions which were raging in his head, or still the tumult that was in his heart and blood. He made no pretense to deny the fact that John Graham must have written this letter to Mary Standish; inadvertently she had kept it, had finally attempted to destroy it, and Stampede, by chance, had discovered a small but convincing remnant of it. In a whirlwind of thought he pieced together things that had happened: her efforts to interest him from the beginning, the determination with which she had held to her purpose, her boldness in following him to the Range, and her apparent endeavor to work herself into his confidence—and with John Graham's signature staring at him from the table these things seemed conclusive and irrefutable evidence. The "industry" which Graham had referred to could mean only his own and Carl Lomen's, the reindeer industry which they had built up and were fighting to perpetuate, and which Graham and his beef-baron friends were combining to handicap and destroy. And in this game of destruction clever Mary Standish had come to play a part!

But why had she leaped into the sea?

It was as if a new voice had made itself heard in Alan's brain, a voice that rose insistently over a vast tumult of things, crying out against his arguments and demanding order and reason in place of the mad convictions that possessed him. If Mary Standish's mission was to pave the way for his ruin, and if she was John Graham's agent sent for that purpose, what reason could she have had for so dramatically attempting to give the world the impression that she had ended her life at sea? Surely such an act could in no way have been related with any plot which she might have had against him! In building up this structure of her defense he made no effort to sever her relationship with John Graham; that, he knew, was impossible. The note, her actions, and many of the things she had said were links inevitably associating her with his enemy, but these same things, now that they came pressing one upon another in his memory, gave to their collusion a new significance.

Was it conceivable that Mary Standish, instead of working for John Graham, was working *against* him? Could some conflict between them have been the reason for her flight aboard the *Nome*, and was it because she discovered Rossland there—John Graham's most trusted servant— that she formed her desperate scheme of leaping into the sea?

Between the two oppositions of his thought a sickening burden of what he knew to be true settled upon him. Mary Standish, even if she hated John Graham now, had at one time—and not very long ago—been an instrument of his trust; the letter he had written to her was positive proof of that. What it was that had caused a possible split between them and had inspired her flight from Seattle, and, later, her effort to bury a past under the fraud of a make-believe death, he might never learn, and just now he had no very great desire to look entirely into the whole truth of the matter. It was enough to know that of the past, and of the things that happened, she had been afraid, and it was in the desperation of this fear, with Graham's cleverest agent at her heels, that she had appealed to him in his cabin, and, failing to win him to her assistance, had taken the matter so dramatically into her own hands. And within that same hour a nearly successful attempt had been made upon Rossland's life. Of course the facts had shown that she could not have been directly responsible for his injury, but it was a haunting thing to remember as happening almost simultaneously with her disappearance into the sea.

He drew away from the window and, opening the door, went out into the night. Cool breaths of air gave a crinkly rattle to the swinging paper lanterns, and he could hear the soft whipping of the flags which Mary Standish had placed over his cabin. There was something comforting in the sound, a solace to the dishevelment of nerves he had suffered, a reminder of their day in Skagway when she had walked at his side with her hand resting warmly in his arm and her eyes and face filled with the inspiration of the mountains.

No matter what she was, or had been, there was something tenaciously admirable about her, a quality which had risen even above her feminine loveliness. She had proved herself not only clever; she was inspired by courage—a courage which he would have been compelled to respect even in a man like John Graham, and in this slim and fragile girl it appealed to him as a virtue to be laid up apart and aside from any of the motives which might be directing it. From the beginning it had been a bewildering part of her—a clean, swift, unhesitating courage that had leaped bounds where his own volition and judgment would have hung waveringly; that one courage in all the world—a woman's courage—which finds in the effort of its achievement no obstacle too high and no abyss too wide though death waits with outreaching arms on the other side. And, surely, where there had been all this, there must also have been some deeper and finer impulse than one of destruction, of physical gain, or of mere duty in the weaving of a human scheme.

The thought and the desire to believe brought words half aloud from Alan's lips, as he looked up again at the flags beating softly above his cabin. Mary Standish was not what Stampede's discovery had proclaimed her to be; there was some mistake, a monumental stupidity of reasoning on their part, and tomorrow would reveal the littleness and the injustice of their suspicions. He tried to force the conviction upon himself, and reentering the cabin he went to bed, still telling himself that a great lie had built itself up out of nothing, and that the God of all things was good to him because Mary Standish was alive, and not dead.

* * * * *

CHAPTER XVII

Alan slept soundly for several hours, but the long strain of the preceding day did not make him overreach the time he had set for himself, and he was up at six o'clock. Wegaruk had not forgotten her old habits, and a tub filled with cold water was waiting for him. He bathed, shaved himself, put on fresh clothes, and promptly at seven was at breakfast. The table at which he ordinarily sat alone was in a little room with double windows, through which, as he enjoyed his meals, he could see most of the habitations of the range. Unlike the average Eskimo dwellings they were neatly built of small timber brought down from the mountains, and were arranged in orderly fashion like the cottages of a village, strung out prettily on a single street. A sea of flowers lay in front of them, and at the end of the row, built on a little knoll that looked down into one of the watered hollows of the tundra, was Sokwenna's cabin. Because Sokwenna was the "old man" of the community and therefore the wisest—and because with him lived his foster-daughters, Keok and Nawadlook, the loveliest of Alan's tribal colony—Sokwenna's cabin was next to Alan's in size. And Alan, looking at it now and then as he ate his breakfast, saw a thin spiral of smoke rising from the chimney, but no other sign of life.

The sun was already up almost to its highest point, a little more than half-way between the horizon and the zenith, performing the apparent miracle of rising in the north and traveling east instead of west. Alan knew the men-folk of the village had departed hours ago for the distant herds. Always, when the reindeer drifted into the higher and cooler feeding-grounds of the foothills, there was this apparent abandonment, and after last night's celebration the women and children were not yet awake to the activities of the long day, where the rising and setting of the sun meant so little.

As he rose from the table, he glanced again toward Sokwenna's cabin. A solitary figure had climbed up out of the ravine and stood against the sun on the clough-top. Even at that distance, with the sun in his eyes, he knew it was Mary Standish.

He turned his back stoically to the window and lighted his pipe. For half an hour after that he sorted out his papers and range-books in preparation for the coming of Tautuk and Amuk Toolik, and when they arrived, the minute hand of his watch was at the hour of eight.

That the months of his absence had been prosperous ones he perceived by the smiling eagerness in the brown faces of his companions as they spread out the papers on which they had, in their own crude fashion, set down a record of the winter's happenings. Tautuk's voice, slow and very deliberate in its unfailing effort to master English without a slip, had in it a subdued note of satisfaction and triumph, while Amuk Toolik, who was quick and staccato in his manner of speech, using sentences seldom of greater length than three or four words, and who picked up slang and swear-words like a parrot, swelled with pride as he lighted his pipe, and then rubbed his hands with a rasping sound that always sent a chill up Alan's back.

"A ver' fine and prosper' year," said Tautuk in response to Alan's first question as to general conditions. "We bean ver' fortunate."

"One hell-good year," backed up Amuk Toolik with the quickness of a gun. "Plenty calf. Good hoof. Moss. Little wolf. Herds fat. This year—she peach!"

After this opening of the matter in hand Alan buried himself in the affairs of the range, and the old thrill, the glow which comes through achievement, and the pioneer's pride in marking a new frontier with the creative forces of success rose uppermost in him, and he forgot the passing of time. A hundred questions he had to ask, and the tongues of Tautuk and Amuk Toolik were crowded with the things they desired to tell him. Their voices filled the room with a paean of triumph. His herds had increased by a thousand head during the fawning months of April and May, and interbreeding of the Asiatic stock with wild, woodland caribou had produced a hundred calves of the super-animal whose flesh was bound to fill the markets of the States within a few years. Never had the moss been thicker under the winter snow; there had been no destructive fires; soft-hoof had escaped them; breeding records had been beaten, and dairying in the edge of the Arctic was no longer an experiment, but an established fact, for Tautuk now had seven deer giving a pint and a half of milk each twice a day, nearly as rich as the best of cream from cattle, and more than twenty that were delivering from a cupful to a pint at a milking. And to this Amuk Toolik added the amazing record of their running-deer, Kauk, the three-year-old, had drawn a sledge five miles over unbeaten snow in thirteen minutes and forty-seven seconds; Kauk and Olo, in team, had drawn the same sledge ten miles in twenty-six minutes and forty seconds, and one day he had driven the two ninety-eight miles in a mighty endurance test; and with Eno and Sutka, the first of their inter-breed with the wild woodland caribou, and heavier beasts, he had drawn a load of eight hundred pounds for three consecutive days at the rate of forty miles a day. From Fairbanks, Tanana, and the ranges of the Seward Peninsula agents of the swiftly spreading industry had offered as high as a hundred and ten dollars a head for breeding stock with the blood of the woodland caribou, and of these native and larger caribou of the tundras and forests seven young bulls and nine female calves had been captured and added to their own propagative forces.

For Alan this was triumph. He saw nothing of what it all meant in the way of ultimate personal fortune. It was the earth under his feet, the vast expanse of unpeopled waste traduced and scorned in the blindness of a hundred million people, which he saw fighting itself on the glory and reward of the conqueror through such achievement as this; a land betrayed rising at last out of the slime of political greed and ignorance; a giant irresistible in its awakening, that was destined in his lifetime to rock the destiny of a continent. It was Alaska rising up slowly but inexorably out of its eternity of sleep, mountain-sealed forces of a great land that was once the cradle of the earth coming into possession of life and power again; and his own feeble efforts in that long and fighting process of planting the seeds which meant its ultimate ascendancy possessed in themselves their own reward.

Long after Tautuk and Amuk Toolik had gone, his heart was filled with the song of success.

He was surprised at the swiftness with which time had gone, when he looked at his watch. It was almost dinner hour when he had finished with his papers and books and went outside. He heard Wegaruk's voice coming from the dark mouth of the underground icebox dug into the frozen subsoil of the tundra, and pausing at the glimmer of his old housekeeper's candle, he turned aside, descended the few steps, and entered quietly into the big, square chamber eight feet under the surface, where the earth had remained steadfastly frozen for some hundreds of thousands of years. Wegaruk had a habit of talking when alone, but Alan thought it odd that she should be explaining to herself that the tundra-soil, in spite of its almost tropical summer richness and luxuriance, never thawed deeper than three or four feet, below which point remained the icy cold placed there so long ago that "even the spirits did not know." He smiled when he heard Wegaruk measuring time and faith in terms of "spirits," which she had never quite given up for the missionaries, and was about to make his presence known when a voice interrupted him, so close at his side that the speaker, concealed in the shadow of the wall, could have reached out a hand and touched him.

"Good morning, Mr. Holt!"

It was Mary Standish, and he stared rather foolishly to make her out in the gloom.

"Good morning," he replied. "I was on my way to your place when Wegaruk's voice brought me here. You see, even this icebox seems like a friend after my experience in the States. Are you after a steak, Mammy?" he called.

Wegaruk's strong, squat figure turned as she answered him, and the light from her candle, glowing brightly in a split tomato can, fell clearly upon Mary Standish as the old woman waddled toward them. It was as if a spotlight had been thrown upon the girl suddenly out of a pit of darkness, and something about her, which was not her prettiness or the beauty that was in her eyes and hair, sent a sudden and unaccountable thrill through Alan. It remained with him when they drew back out of gloom and chill into sunshine and warmth, leaving Wegaruk to snuff her tomato-can lantern and follow with the steak, and it did not leave him when they walked over the tundra together toward Sokwenna's cabin. It was a puzzling thrill, stirring an emotion which it was impossible for him to subdue or explain; something which he knew he should understand but could not. And it seemed to him that knowledge of this mystery was in the girl's face, glowing in a gentle embarrassment, as she told him she had been expecting him, and that Keok and Nawadlook had given up the cabin to them, so that he might question her uninterrupted. But with this soft flush of her uneasiness, revealing itself in her eyes and cheeks, he saw neither fear nor hesitation.

In the "big room" of Sokwenna's cabin, which was patterned after his own, he sat down amid the color and delicate fragrance of masses of flowers, and the girl seated herself near him and waited for him to speak.

"You love flowers," he said lamely. "I want to thank you for the flowers you placed in my cabin. And the other things."

"Flowers are a habit with me," she replied, "and I have never seen such flowers as these. Flowers—and birds. I never dreamed that there were so many up here."

"Nor the world," he added. "It is ignorant of Alaska."

He was looking at her, trying to understand the inexplicable something about her. She knew what was in his mind, because the strangely thrilling emotion that possessed him could not keep its betrayal from his eyes. The color was fading slowly out of her cheeks; her lips grew a little tense, yet in her attitude of suspense and of waiting there was no longer a suspicion of embarrassment, no trace of fear, and no sign that a moment was at hand when her confidence was on the ebb. In this moment Alan did not think of John Graham. It seemed to him that she was like a child again, the child who had come to him in his cabin, and who had stood with her back against his cabin door, entreating him to achieve the impossible; an angel, almost, with her smooth, shining hair, her clear, beautiful eyes, her white throat which waited with its little heart-throb for him to beat down the fragile defense which now lay in the greater power of his own hands. The inequality of it, and the pitilessness of what had been in his mind to say and do, together with an inundating sense of his own brute mastery, swept over him, and in sudden desperation he reached out his hands toward her and cried:

"Mary Standish, in God's name tell me the truth. Tell me why you have come up here!"

"I have come," she said, looking at him steadily, "because I know that a man like you, when he loves a woman, will fight for her and protect her even though he may not possess her."

"But you didn't know that—not until—the cottonwoods!" he protested.

"Yes, I did. I knew it in Ellen McCormick's cabin."

She rose slowly before him, and he, too, rose to his feet, staring at her like a man who had been struck, while intelligence—a dawning reason—an understanding of the strange mystery of her that morning, sent the still greater thrill of its shock through him. He gave an exclamation of amazement.

"You were at Ellen McCormick's! She gave you—*that!*"

She nodded. "Yes, the dress you brought from the ship. Please don't scold me, Mr. Holt. Be a little kind with me when you have heard what I am going to tell you. I was in the cabin that last day, when you returned from searching for me in the sea. Mr. McCormick didn't know. But *she* did. I lied a little, just a little, so that she, being a woman, would promise

152

not to tell you I was there. You see, I had lost a great deal of my faith, and my courage was about gone, and I was afraid of you."

"Afraid of me?"

"Yes, afraid of everybody. I was in the room behind Ellen McCormick when she asked you—that question; and when you answered as you did, I was like stone. I was amazed and didn't believe, for I was certain that after what had happened on the ship you despised me, and only through a peculiar sense of honor were making the search for me. Not until two days later, when your letters came to Ellen McCormick, and we read them—"

"You opened both?"

"Of course. One was to be read immediately, the other when I was found—and I had found myself. Maybe it wasn't exactly fair, but you couldn't expect two women to resist a temptation like that. And—*I wanted to know.*"

She did not lower her eyes or turn her head aside as she made the confession. Her gaze met Alan's with beautiful steadiness.

"And then I believed. I knew, because of what you said in that letter, that you were the one man in all the world who would help me and give me a fighting chance if I came to you. But it has taken all my courage—and in the end you will drive me away—"

Again he looked upon the miracle of tears in wide-open, unfaltering eyes, tears which she did not brush away, but through which, in a moment, she smiled at him as no woman had ever smiled at him before. And with the tears there seemed to possess her a pride which lifted her above all confusion, a living spirit of will and courage and womanhood that broke away the dark clouds of suspicion and fear that had gathered in his mind. He tried to speak, and his lips were thick.

"You have come—because you know I love you, and you—"

"Because, from the beginning, it must have been a great faith in you that inspired me, Alan Holt."

"There must have been more than that," he persisted. "Some other reason."

"Two," she acknowledged, and now he noticed that with the dissolution of tears a flush of color was returning into her cheeks.

"And those—"

"One it is impossible for you to know; the other, if I tell you, will make you despise me. I am sure of that."

"It has to do with John Graham?"

She bowed her head. "Yes, with John Graham."

For the first time long lashes hid her eyes from him, and for a moment it seemed that her resolution was gone and she stood stricken by the import of the thing that lay behind his question; yet her cheeks flamed red instead of paling, and when she looked at him again, her eyes burned with a lustrous fire.

"John Graham," she repeated. "The man you hate and want to kill."

Slowly he turned toward the door. "I am leaving immediately after dinner to inspect the herds up in the foothills," he said. "And you—*are welcome here.*"

He caught the swift intake of her breath as he paused for an instant at the door, and saw the new light that leaped into her eyes.

"Thank you, Alan Holt," she cried softly, "*Oh, I thank you!*"

And then, suddenly, she stopped him with a little cry, as if at last something had broken away from her control. He faced her, and for a moment they stood in silence.

"I'm sorry—sorry I said to you what I did that night on the *Nome*," she said. "I accused you of brutality, of unfairness, of—of even worse than that, and I want to take it all back. You are big and clean and splendid, for you would go away now, knowing I am poisoned by an association with the man who has injured you so terribly, *and you say I am welcome!* And I don't want you to go. You have made me *want* to tell you who I am, and why I have come to you, and I pray God you will think as kindly of me as you can when you have heard."

* * * * *

154

CHAPTER XVIII

It seemed to Alan that in an instant a sudden change had come over the world. There was silence in the cabin, except for the breath which came like a sob to the girl's lips as she turned to the window and looked out into the blaze of golden sunlight that filled the tundra. He heard Tautuk's voice, calling to Keok away over near the reindeer corral, and he heard clearly Keok's merry laughter as she answered him. A gray-cheeked thrush flew up to the roof of Sokwenna's cabin and began to sing. It was as if these things had come as a message to both of them, relieving a tension, and significant of the beauty and glory and undying hope of life. Mary Standish turned from the window with shining eyes.

"Every day the thrush comes and sings on our cabin roof," she said.

"It is—possibly—because you are here," he replied.

She regarded him seriously. "I have thought of that. You know, I have faith in a great many unbelievable things. I can think of nothing more beautiful than the spirit that lives in the heart of a bird. I am sure, if I were dying, I would like to have a bird singing near me. Hopelessness cannot be so deep that bird-song will not reach it."

He nodded, trying to answer in that way. He felt uncomfortable. She closed the door which he had left partly open, and made a little gesture for him to resume the chair which he had left a few moments before. She seated herself first and smiled at him wistfully, half regretfully, as she said:

"I have been very foolish. What I am going to tell you now I should have told you aboard the *Nome*. But I was afraid. Now I am not afraid, but ashamed, terribly ashamed, to let you know the truth. And yet I am not sorry it happened so, because otherwise I would not have come up here, and all this—your world, your people, and you—have meant a great deal to me. You will understand when I have made my confession."

"No, I don't want that," he protested almost roughly. "I don't want you to put it that way. If I can help you, and if you wish to tell me as a friend, that's different. I don't want a confession, which would imply that I have no faith in you."

"And you have faith in me?"

"Yes; so much that the sun will darken and bird-song never seem the same if I lose you again, as I thought I had lost you from the ship."

"Oh, *you mean that!*"

The words came from her in a strange, tense, little cry, and he seemed to see only her eyes as he looked at her face, pale as the petals of the tundra daises behind her. With the thrill of what he had dared to say tugging at his heart, he wondered why she was so white.

"You mean that," her lips repeated slowly, "after all that has happened— even after—that part of a letter—which Stampede brought to you last night—"

He was surprised. How had she discovered what he thought was a secret between himself and Stampede? His mind leaped to a conclusion, and she saw it written in his face.

"No, it wasn't Stampede," she said. "He didn't tell me. It—just happened. And after this letter—you still believe in me?"

"I must. I should be unhappy if I did not. And I am—most perversely hoping for happiness. I have told myself that what I saw over John Graham's signature was a lie."

"It wasn't that—quite. But it didn't refer to you, or to me. It was part of a letter written to Rossland. He sent me some books while I was on the ship, and inadvertently left a page of this letter in one of them as a marker. It was really quite unimportant, when one read the whole of it. The other half of the page is in the toe of the slipper which you did not return to Ellen McCormick. You know that is the conventional thing for a woman to do—to use paper for padding in a soft-toed slipper."

He wanted to shout; he wanted to throw up his arms and laugh as Tautuk and Amuk Toolik and a score of others had laughed to the beat of the tom-toms last night, not because he was amused, but out of sheer happiness. But Mary Standish's voice, continuing in its quiet and matter-of-fact way, held him speechless, though she could not fail to see the effect upon him of this simple explanation of the presence of Graham's letter.

"I was in Nawadlook's room when I saw Stampede pick up the wad of paper from the floor," she was saying. "I was looking at the slipper a few minutes before, regretting that you had left its mate in my cabin on the ship, and the paper must have dropped then. I saw Stampede read it, and the shock that came in his face. Then he placed it on the table and went out. I hurried to see what he had found and had scarcely read the few words when I heard him returning. I returned the paper where he had laid it, hid myself in Nawadlook's room, and saw Stampede when he carried it to you. I don't know why I allowed it to be done. I had no reason. Maybe it was just—intuition, and maybe it was because—just in that hour—I so hated myself that I wanted someone to flay me alive, and I thought that what Stampede had found would make you do it. And I deserve it! I deserve nothing better at your hands."

"But it isn't true," he protested. "The letter was to Rossland."

There was no responsive gladness in her eyes. "Better that it were true, and all that *is* true were false," she said in a quiet, hopeless voice. "I would almost give my life to be no more than what those words implied, dishonest, a spy, a criminal of a sort; almost any alternative would I accept in place of what I actually am. Do you begin to understand?"

"I am afraid—I can not." Even as he persisted in denial, the pain which had grown like velvety dew in her eyes clutched at his heart, and he felt dread of what lay behind it. "I understand—only—that I am glad you are here, more glad than yesterday, or this morning, or an hour ago."

She bowed her head, so that the bright light of day made a radiance of rich color in her hair, and he saw the sudden tremble of the shining lashes that lay against her cheeks; and then, quickly, she caught her breath, and her hands grew steady in her lap.

"Would you mind—if I asked you first—to tell me *your* story of John Graham?" she spoke softly. "I know it, a little, but I think it would make everything easier if I could hear it from you—now."

He stood up and looked down upon her where she sat, with the light playing in her hair; and then he moved to the window, and back, and she had not changed her position, but was waiting for him to speak. She raised her eyes, and the question her lips had formed was glowing in them as clearly as if she had voiced it again in words. A desire rose in him to speak to her as he had never spoken to another human being, and to reveal for her—and for her alone—the thing that had harbored itself in his soul for many years. Looking up at him, waiting, partial understanding softening her sweet face, a dusky glow in her eyes, she was so beautiful that he cried out softly and then laughed in a strange repressed sort of way as he half held out his arms toward her.

"I think I know how my father must have loved my mother," he said. "But I can't make you feel it. I can't hope for that. She died when I was so young that she remained only as a beautiful dream for me. But for my father she *never* died, and as I grew older she became more and more alive for me, so that in our journeys we would talk about her as if she were waiting for us back home and would welcome us when we returned. And never could my father remain away from the place where she was buried very long at a time. He called it *home*, that little cup at the foot of the mountain, with the waterfall singing in summer, and a paradise of birds and flowers keeping her company, and all the great, wild world she loved about her. There was the cabin, too; the little cabin where I was born, with its back to the big mountain, and filled with the handiwork of my mother as she had left it when she died. And my father too used to laugh and sing there—he had a clear voice that would roll half-way up the mountain; and as I grew older the miracle at times stirred me with a strange fear, so real to my father did my dead mother seem when he was home. But you look frightened, Miss Standish! Oh, it may seem weird and ghostly now, but it was *true*—so true that I have lain awake nights thinking of it and wishing that it had never been so!"

"Then you have wished a great sin," said the girl in a voice that seemed scarcely to whisper between her parted lips. "I hope someone will feel toward me—some day—like that."

"But it was this which brought the tragedy, the thing you have asked me to tell you about," he said, unclenching his hands slowly, and then tightening them again until the blood ebbed from their veins. "Interests were coming in; the tentacles of power and greed were reaching out, encroaching steadily a little nearer to our cup at the foot of the mountain. But my father did not dream of what might happen. It came in the spring of the year he took me on my first trip to the States, when I was eighteen. We were gone five months, and they were five months of hell for him. Day and night he grieved for my mother and the little home under the mountain. And when at last we came back—"

He turned again to the window, but he did not see the golden sun of the tundra or hear Tautuk calling from the corral.

"When we came back," he repeated in a cold, hard voice, "a construction camp of a hundred men had invaded my father's little paradise. The cabin was gone; a channel had been cut from the waterfall, and this channel ran where my mother's grave had been. They had treated it with that same desecration with which they have destroyed ten thousand Indian graves since then. Her bones were scattered in the sand and mud. And from the moment my father saw what had happened, never another sun rose in the heavens for him. His heart died, yet he went on living—for a time."

Mary Standish had bowed her face in her hands. He saw the tremor of her slim shoulders; and when he came back, and she looked up at him, it was as if he beheld the pallid beauty of one of the white tundra flowers.

"And the man who committed that crime—was John Graham," she said, in the strangely passionless voice of one who knew what his answer would be.

"Yes, John Graham. He was there, representing big interests in the States. The foreman had objected to what happened; many of the men had protested; a few of them, who knew my father, had thrown up their work rather than be partners to that crime. But Graham had the legal power; they say he laughed as if he thought it a great joke that a cabin and a grave should be considered obstacles in his way. And he laughed when my father and I went to see him; yes, *laughed*, in that noiseless, oily, inside way of his, as you might think of a snake laughing.

"We found him among the men. My God, you don't know how I hated him!—Big, loose, powerful, dangling the watch-fob that hung over his vest, and looking at my father in that way as he told him what a fool he was to think a worthless grave should interfere with his work. I wanted to kill him, but my father put a hand on my shoulder, a quiet, steady hand, and said: 'It is my duty, Alan. *My duty.*'

"And then—it happened. My father was older, much older than Graham, but God put such strength in him that day as I had never seen before, and with his naked hands he would have killed the brute if I had not unlocked them with my own. Before all his men Graham became a mass of helpless pulp, and from the ground, with the last of the breath that was in him, he cursed my father, and he cursed me. He said that all the days of his life he would follow us, until we paid a thousand times for what we had done. And then my father dragged him as he would have dragged a rat to the edge of a piece of bush, and there he tore his clothes from him until the brute was naked; and in that nakedness he scourged him with whips until his arms were weak, and John Graham was unconscious and like a great hulk of raw beef. When it was over, we went into the mountains."

During the terrible recital Mary Standish had not looked away from him, and now her hands were clenched like his own, and her eyes and face were aflame, as if she wanted to leap up and strike at something unseen between them.

"And after that, Alan; after that—"

She did not know that she had spoken his name, and he, hearing it, scarcely understood.

"John Graham kept his promise," he answered grimly. "The influence and money behind him haunted us wherever we went. My father had been successful, but one after another the properties in which he was interested were made worthless. A successful mine in which he was most heavily interested was allowed to become abandoned. A hotel which he partly owned in Dawson was bankrupted. One after another things happened, and after each happening my father would receive a polite note of regret from Graham, written as if the word actually came from a friend. But my father cared little for money losses now. His heart was drying up and his life ebbing away for the little cabin and the grave that were gone from the foot of the mountain. It went on this way for three years, and then, one morning, my father was found on the beach at Nome, dead."

"*Dead!*"

Alan heard only the gasping breath in which the word came from Mary Standish, for he was facing the window, looking steadily away from her.

"Yes—murdered. I know it was the work of John Graham. He didn't do it personally, but it was *his money* that accomplished the end. Of course nothing ever came of it. I won't tell you how his influence and power have dogged me; how they destroyed the first herd of reindeer I had, and how they filled the newspapers with laughter and lies about me when I was down in the States last winter in an effort to make *your* people see a little something of the truth about Alaska. I am waiting. I know the day is coming when I shall have John Graham as my father had him under our mountain twenty years ago. He must be fifty now. But that won't save him when the time comes. No one will loosen my hands as I loosened my father's. And all Alaska will rejoice, for his power and his money have become twin monsters that are destroying Alaska just as he destroyed the life of my father. Unless he dies, and his money-power ends, he will make of this great land nothing more than a shell out of which he and his kind have taken all the meat. And the hour of deadliest danger is now upon us."

He looked at Mary Standish, and it was as if death had come to her where she sat. She seemed not to breathe, and her face was so white it frightened him. And then, slowly, she turned her eyes upon him, and never had he seen such living pools of torture and of horror. He was amazed at the quietness of her voice when she began to speak, and startled by the almost deadly coldness of it.

"I think you can understand—now—why I leaped into the sea, why I wanted the world to think I was dead, and why I have feared to tell you the truth," she said. "*I am John Graham's wife.*"

* * * * *

CHAPTER XIX

Alan's first thought was of the monstrous incongruity of the thing, the almost physical impossibility of a mésalliance of the sort Mary Standish had revealed to him. He saw her, young and beautiful, with face and eyes that from the beginning had made him feel all that was good and sweet in life, and behind her he saw the shadow-hulk of John Graham, the pitiless iron-man, without conscience and without soul, coarsened by power, fiendish in his iniquities, and old enough to be her father!

A slow smile twisted his lips, but he did not know he smiled. He pulled himself together without letting her see the physical part of the effort it was taking. And he tried to find something to say that would help clear her eyes of the agony that was in them.

"That—is a most unreasonable thing—to be true," he said.

It seemed to him his lips were making words out of wood, and that the words were fatuously inefficient compared with what he should have said, or acted, under the circumstances.

She nodded. "It is. But the world doesn't look at it in that way. Such things just happen."

She reached for a book which lay on the table where the tundra daisies were heaped. It was a book written around the early phases of pioneer life in Alaska, taken from his own library, a volume of statistical worth, dryly but carefully written—and she had been reading it. It struck him as a symbol of the fight she was making, of her courage, and of her desire to triumph in the face of tremendous odds that must have beset her. He still could not associate her completely with John Graham. Yet his face was cold and white.

Her hand trembled a little as she opened the book and took from it a newspaper clipping. She did not speak as she unfolded it and gave it to him.

At the top of two printed columns was the picture of a young and beautiful girl; in an oval, covering a small space over the girl's shoulder, was a picture of a man of fifty or so. Both were strangers to him. He read their names, and then the headlines. "A Hundred-Million-Dollar Love" was the caption, and after the word love was a dollar sign. Youth and age, beauty and the other thing, two great fortunes united. He caught the idea and looked at Mary Standish. It was impossible for him to think of her as Mary Graham.

"I tore that from a paper in Cordova," she said. "They have nothing to do with me. The girl lives in Texas. But don't you see something in her eyes? Can't you see it, even in the picture? She has on her wedding things. But it seemed to me—when I saw her face—that in her eyes were agony and despair and hopelessness, and that she was bravely trying to hide them from the world. It's just another proof, one of thousands, that such unreasonable things do happen."

He was beginning to feel a dull and painless sort of calm, the stoicism which came to possess him whenever he was confronted by the inevitable. He sat down, and with his head bowed over it took one of the limp, little hands that lay in Mary Standish's lap. The warmth had gone out of it. It was cold and lifeless. He caressed it gently and held it between his brown, muscular hands, staring at it, and yet seeing nothing in particular. It was only the ticking of Keok's clock that broke the silence for a time. Then he released the hand, and it dropped in the girl's lap again. She had been looking steadily at the streak of gray in his hair. And a light came into her eyes, a light which he did not see, and a little tremble of her lips, and an almost imperceptible inclination of her head toward him.

"I'm sorry I didn't know," he said. "I realize now how you must have felt back there in the cottonwoods."

"No, you don't realize—*you don't!*" she protested.

In an instant, it seemed to him, a vibrant, flaming life swept over her again. It was as if his words had touched fire to some secret thing, as if he had unlocked a door which grim hopelessness had closed. He was amazed at the swiftness with which color came into her cheeks.

"You don't understand, and I am determined that you *shall*," she went on. "I would die before I let you go away thinking what is now in your mind. You will despise me, but I would rather be hated for the truth than because of the horrible thing which you must believe if I remain silent." She forced a wan smile to her lips. "You know, Belinda Mulrooneys were very well in their day, but they don't fit in now, do they? If a woman makes a mistake and tries to remedy it in a fighting sort of way, as Belinda Mulrooney might have done back in the days when Alaska was young—"

She finished with a little gesture of despair.

"I have committed a great folly," she said, hesitating an instant in his silence. "I see very clearly now the course I should have taken. You will advise me that it is still not too late when you have heard what I am going to say. Your face is like—a rock."

"It is because your tragedy is mine," he said.

She turned her eyes from him. The color in her cheeks deepened. It was a vivid, feverish glow. "I was born rich, enormously, hatefully rich," she said in the low, unimpassioned voice of a confessional. "I don't remember father or mother. I lived always with my Grandfather Standish and my Uncle Peter Standish. Until I was thirteen I had my Uncle Peter, who was grandfather's brother, and lived with us. I worshiped Uncle Peter. He was a cripple. From young manhood he had lived in a wheel-chair, and he was nearly seventy-five when he died. As a baby that wheel-chair, and my rides in it with him about the great house in which we lived, were my delights. He was my father and mother, everything that was good and sweet in life. I remember thinking, as a child, that if God was as good as Uncle Peter, He was a wonderful God. It was Uncle Peter who told me, year after year, the old stories and legends of the Standishes. And he was always happy—always happy and glad and seeing nothing but sunshine though he hadn't stood on his feet for nearly sixty years. And my Uncle Peter died when I was thirteen, five days before my birthday came. I think he must have been to me what your father was to you."

He nodded. There was something that was not the hardness of rock in his face now, and John Graham seemed to have faded away.

"I was left, then, alone with my Grandfather Standish," she went on. "He didn't love me as my Uncle Peter loved me, and I don't think I loved him. But I was proud of him. I thought the whole world must have stood in awe of him, as I did. As I grew older I learned the world *was* afraid of him—bankers, presidents, even the strongest men in great financial interests; afraid of him, and of his partners, the Grahams, and of Sharpleigh, who my Uncle Peter had told me was the cleverest lawyer in the nation, and who had grown up in the business of the two families. My grandfather was sixty-eight when Uncle Peter died, so it was John Graham who was the actual working force behind the combined fortunes of the two families. Sometimes, as I now recall it, Uncle Peter was like a little child. I remember how he tried to make me understand just how big my grandfather's interests were by telling me that if two dollars were taken from every man, woman, and child in the United States, it would just about add up to what he and the Grahams possessed, and my Grandfather Standish's interests were three-quarters of the whole. I remember how a hunted look would come into my Uncle Peter's face at times when I asked him how all this money was used, and where it was. And he never answered me as I wanted to be answered, and I never understood. I didn't know *why* people feared my grandfather and John Graham. I didn't know of the stupendous power my grandfather's money had rolled up for them. I didn't know"—her voice sank to a shuddering whisper—"I didn't know how they were using it in Alaska, for instance. I didn't know it was feeding upon starvation and ruin and death. I don't think even Uncle Peter knew *that*."

She looked at Alan steadily, and her gray eyes seemed burning up with a slow fire.

"Why, even then, before Uncle Peter died, I had become one of the biggest factors in all their schemes. It was impossible for me to suspect that John Graham was *anticipating* a little girl of thirteen, and I didn't guess that my Grandfather Standish, so straight, so grandly white of beard and hair, so like a god of power when he stood among men, was even then planning that I should be given to him, so that a monumental combination of wealth might increase itself still more in that juggernaut of financial achievement for which he lived. And to bring about my sacrifice, to make sure it would not fail, they set Sharpleigh to the task, because Sharpleigh was sweet and good of face, and gentle like Uncle Peter, so that I loved him and had confidence in him, without a suspicion that under his white hair lay a brain which matched in cunning and mercilessness that of John Graham himself. And he did his work well, Alan."

A second time she had spoken his name, softly and without embarrassment. With her nervous fingers tying and untying the two corners of a little handkerchief in her lap, she went on, after a moment of silence in which the ticking of Keok's clock seemed tense and loud.

"When I was seventeen, Grandfather Standish died. I wish you could understand all that followed without my telling you: how I clung to Sharpleigh as a father, how I trusted him, and how cleverly and gently he educated me to the thought that it was right and just, and my greatest duty in life, to carry out the stipulation of my grandfather's will and marry John Graham. Otherwise, he told me—if that union was not brought about before I was twenty-two—not a dollar of the great fortune would go to the house of Standish; and because he was clever enough to know that money alone would not urge me, he showed me a letter which he said my Uncle Peter had written, and which I was to read on my seventeenth birthday, and in that letter Uncle Peter urged me to live up to the Standish name and join in that union of the two great fortunes which he and Grandfather Standish had always planned. I didn't dream the letter was a forgery. And in the end they won—and I promised."

She sat with bowed head, crumpling the bit of cambric between her fingers. "Do you despise me?" she asked.

"No," he replied in a tense, unimpassioned voice. "I love you."

She tried to look at him calmly and bravely. In his face again lay the immobility of rock, and in his eyes a sullen, slumbering fire.

"I promised," she repeated quickly, as if regretting the impulse that had made her ask him the question. "But it was to be business, a cold, unsentimental business. I disliked John Graham. Yet I would marry him. In the eyes of the law I would be his wife; in the eyes of the world I would remain his wife—but never more than that. They agreed, and I in my ignorance believed.

"I didn't see the trap. I didn't see the wicked triumph in John Graham's heart. No power could have made me believe then that he wanted to possess only *me*; that he was horrible enough to want me even without love; that he was a great monster of a spider, and I the fly lured into his web. And the agony of it was that in all the years since Uncle Peter died I had dreamed strange and beautiful dreams. I lived in a make-believe world of my own, and I read, read, read; and the thought grew stronger and stronger in me that I had lived another life somewhere, and that I belonged back in the years when the world was clean, and there was love, and vast reaches of land wherein money and power were little guessed of, and where romance and the glory of manhood and womanhood rose above all other things. Oh, I wanted these things, and yet because others had molded me, and because of my misguided Standish sense of pride and honor, I was shackling myself to John Graham.

"In the last months preceding my twenty-second birthday I learned more of the man than I had ever known before; rumors came to me; I investigated a little, and I began to find the hatred, and the reason for it, which has come to me so conclusively here in Alaska. I almost knew, at the last, that he was a monster, but the world had been told I was to marry him, and Sharpleigh with his fatherly hypocrisy was behind me, and John Graham treated me so courteously and so coolly that I did not suspect the terrible things in his heart and mind—and I went on with the bargain. *I married him.*"

She drew a sudden, deep breath, as if she had passed through the ordeal of what she had most dreaded to say, and now, meeting the changeless expression of Alan's face with a fierce, little cry that leaped from her like a flash of gun-fire, she sprang to her feet and stood with her back crushed against the tundra flowers, her voice trembling as she continued, while he stood up and faced her.

"You needn't go on," he interrupted in a voice so low and terribly hard that she felt the menacing thrill of it. "You needn't. I will settle with John Graham, if God gives me the chance."

"You would have me stop *now*—before I have told you of the only shred of triumph to which I may lay claim!" she protested. "Oh, you may be sure that I realize the sickening folly and wickedness of it all, but I swear before my God that I didn't realize it then, until it was too late. To you, Alan, clean as the great mountains and plains that have been a part of you, I know how impossible this must seem—that I should marry a man I at first feared, then loathed, then came to hate with a deadly hatred; that I should sacrifice myself because I thought it was a duty; that I should be so weak, so ignorant, so like soft clay in the hands of those I trusted. Yet I tell you that at no time did I think or suspect that I was sacrificing *myself*; at no time, blind though you may call me, did I see a hint of that sickening danger into which I was voluntarily going. No, not even an hour before the wedding did I suspect that, for it had all been so coldly planned, like a great deal in finance—so carefully adjudged by us all as a business affair, that I felt no fear except that sickness of soul which comes of giving up one's life. And no hint of it came until the last of the few words were spoken which made us man and wife, and then I saw in John Graham's eyes something which I had never seen there before. And Sharpleigh—"

Her hands caught at her breast. Her gray eyes were pools of flame.

"I went to my room. I didn't lock my door, because never had it been necessary to do that. I didn't cry. No, I didn't cry. But something strange was happening to me which tears might have prevented. It seemed to me there were many walls to my room; I was faint; the windows seemed to appear and disappear, and in that sickness I reached my bed. Then I saw the door open, and John Graham came in, and closed the door behind him, and locked it. My room. He had come into *my room!* The unexpectedness of it—the horror—the insult roused me from my stupor. I sprang up to face him, and there he stood, within arm's reach of me, a look in his face which told me at last the truth which I had failed to suspect—or fear. His arms were reaching out—

"'You are my wife,' he said.

"Oh, I knew, then. '*You are my wife,*' he repeated. I wanted to scream, but I couldn't; and then—then—his arms reached me; I felt them crushing around me like the coils of a great snake; the poison of his lips was at my face—and I believed that I was lost, and that no power could save me in this hour from the man who had come to my room—the man who was my husband. I think it was Uncle Peter who gave me voice, who put the right words in my brain, who made me laugh—yes, laugh, and almost caress him with my hands. The change in me amazed him, stunned him, and he freed me—while I told him that in these first few hours of wifehood I wanted to be alone, and that he should come to me that evening, and that I would be waiting for him. And I smiled at him as I said these things, smiled while I wanted to kill him, and he went, a great, gloating, triumphant beast, believing that the obedience of wifehood was about to give him what he had expected to find through dishonor—and I was left alone.

"I thought of only one thing then—escape. I saw the truth. It swept over me, inundated me, roared in my ears. All that I had ever lived with Uncle Peter came back to me. This was not his world; it had never been— and it was not mine. It was, all at once, a world of monsters. I wanted never to face it again, never to look into the eyes of those I had known.

And even as these thoughts and desires swept upon me, I was filling a traveling bag in a fever of madness, and Uncle Peter was at my side, urging me to hurry, telling me I had no minutes to lose, for the man who had left me was clever and might guess the truth that lay hid behind my smiles and cajolery.

"I stole out through the back of the house, and as I went I heard Sharpleigh's low laughter in the library. It was a new kind of laughter, and with it I heard John Graham's voice. I was thinking only of the sea—to get away on the sea. A taxi took me to my bank, and I drew money. I went to the wharves, intent only on boarding a ship, any ship, and it seemed to me that Uncle Peter was leading me; and we came to a great ship that was leaving for Alaska—and you know—what happened then—Alan Holt."

With a sob she bowed her face in her hands, but only an instant it was there, and when she looked at Alan again, there were no tears in her eyes, but a soft glory of pride and exultation.

"I am clean of John Graham," she cried. "*Clean!*"

He stood twisting his hands, twisting them in a helpless, futile sort of way, and it was he, and not the girl, who felt like bowing his head that the tears might come unseen. For her eyes were bright and shining and clear as stars.

"Do you despise me now?"

"I love you," he said again, and made no movement toward her.

"I am glad," she whispered, and she did not look at him, but at the sunlit plain which lay beyond the window.

"And Rossland was on the *Nome*, and saw you, and sent word back to Graham," he said, fighting to keep himself from going nearer to her.

She nodded. "Yes; and so I came to you, and failing there, I leaped into the sea, for I wanted them to think I was dead."

"And Rossland was hurt."

"Yes. Strangely. I heard of it in Cordova. Men like Rossland frequently come to unexpected ends."

He went to the door which she had closed, and opened it, and stood looking toward the blue billows of the foothills with the white crests of the mountains behind them. She came, after a moment, and stood beside him.

"I understand," she said softly, and her hand lay in a gentle touch upon his arm. "You are trying to see some way out, and you can see only one. That is to go back, face the creatures I hate, regain my freedom in the old way. And I, too, can see no other way. I came on impulse; I must return with impulse and madness burned out of me. And I am sorry. I dread it. I—would rather die."

"And I—" he began, then caught himself and pointed to the distant hills and mountains. "The herds are there," he said. "I am going to them. I may be gone a week or more. Will you promise me to be here when I return?"

"Yes, if that is your desire."

"It is."

She was so near that his lips might have touched her shining hair.

"And when you return, I must go. That will be the only way."

"I think so."

"It will be hard. It may be, after all, that I am a coward. But to face all that—alone—"

"You won't be alone," he said quietly, still looking at the far-away hills. "If you go, I am going with you."

It seemed as if she had stopped breathing for a moment at his side, and then, with a little, sobbing cry she drew away from him and stood at the half-opened door of Nawadlook's room, and the glory in her eyes was the glory of his dreams as he had wandered with her hand in hand over the tundras in those days of grief and half-madness when he had thought she was dead.

"I am glad I was in Ellen McCormick's cabin the day you came," she was saying. "And I thank God for giving me the madness and courage to come to *you*. I am not afraid of anything in the world now—because—*I love you, Alan!*"

And as Nawadlook's door closed behind her, Alan stumbled out into the sunlight, a great drumming in his heart, and a tumult in his brain that twisted the world about him until for a little it held neither vision nor space nor sound.

* * * * *

CHAPTER XX

In that way, with the beautiful world swimming in sunshine and golden tundra haze until foothills and mountains were like castles in a dream, Alan Holt set off with Tautuk and Amuk Toolik, leaving Stampede and Keok and Nawadlook at the corral bars, with Stampede little regretting that he was left behind to guard the range. For a mighty resolution had taken root in the prospector's heart, and he felt himself thrilled and a bit trembling at the nearness of the greatest drama that had ever entered his life. Alan, looking back after the first few minutes, saw that Keok and Nawadlook stood alone. Stampede was gone.

The ridge beyond the coulée out of which Mary Standish had come with wild flowers soon closed like a door between him and Sokwenna's cabin, and the straight trail to the mountains lay ahead, and over this Alan set the pace, with Tautuk and Amuk Toolik and a caravan of seven pack-deer behind him, bearing supplies for the herdsmen.

Alan had scarcely spoken to the two men. He knew the driving force which was sending him to the mountains was not only an impulse, but almost an inspirational thing born of necessity. Each step that he took, with his head and heart in a swirl of intoxicating madness, was an effort behind which he was putting a sheer weight of physical will. He wanted to go back. The urge was upon him to surrender utterly to the weakness of forgetting that Mary Standish was a wife. He had almost fallen a victim to his selfishness and passion in the moment when she stood at Nawadlook's door, telling him that she loved him. An iron hand had drawn him out into the day, and it was the same iron hand that kept his face to the mountains now, while in his brain her voice repeated the words that had set his world on fire.

He knew what had happened this morning was not the merely important and essential incident of most human lives; it had been a cataclysmic thing with him. Probably it would be impossible for even the girl ever fully to understand. And he needed to be alone to gather strength and mental calmness for the meeting of the problem ahead of him, a complication so unexpected that the very foundation of that stoic equanimity which the mountains had bred in him had suffered a temporary upsetting. His happiness was almost an insanity. The dream wherein he had wandered with a spirit of the dead had come true; it was the old idyl in the flesh again, his father, his mother—and back in the cabin beyond the ridge such a love had cried out to him. And he was afraid to return. He laughed the fact aloud, happily and with an unrepressed exultation as he strode ahead of the pack-train, and with that exultation words came to his lips, words intended for himself alone, telling him that Mary Standish belonged to him, and that until the end of eternity he would fight for her and keep her. Yet he kept on, facing the mountains, and he walked so swiftly that Tautuk and Amuk Toolik fell steadily behind with the deer, so that in time long dips and swells of the tundra lay between them.

With grim persistence he kept at himself, and at last there swept over him in its ultimate triumph a compelling sense of the justice of what he had done—justice to Mary Standish. Even now he did not think of her as Mary Graham. But she was Graham's wife. And if he had gone to her in that moment of glorious confession when she had stood at Nawadlook's door, if he had violated her faith when, because of faith, she had laid the world at his feet, he would have fallen to the level of John Graham himself. Thought of the narrowness of his escape and of the first mad desire to call her back from Nawadlook's room, to hold her in his arms again as he had held her in the cottonwoods, brought a hot fire into his face. Something greater than his own fighting instinct had turned him to the open door of the cabin. It was Mary Standish—her courage, the-glory of faith and love shining in her eyes, her measurement of him as a man. She had not been afraid to say what was in her heart, because she knew what he would do.

Mid-afternoon found him waiting for Tautuk and Amuk Toolik at the edge of a slough where willows grew deep and green and the crested billows of sedge-cotton stood knee-high. The faces of the herdsmen were sweating. Thereafter Alan walked with them, until in that hour when the sun had sunk to its lowest plane they came to the first of the Endicott foothills. Here they rested until the coolness of deeper evening, when a golden twilight filled the land, and then resumed the journey toward the mountains.

Midsummer heat and the winged pests of the lower lands had driven the herds steadily into the cooler altitudes of the higher plateaux and valleys. Here they had split into telescoping columns which drifted in slowly moving streams wherever the doors of the hills and mountains opened into new grazing fields, until Alan's ten thousand reindeer were in three divisions, two of the greatest traveling westward, and one, of a thousand head, working north and east. The first and second days Alan remained with the nearest and southward herd. The third day he went on with Tautuk and two pack-deer through a break in the mountains and joined the herdsmen of the second and higher multitude of feeding animals. There began to possess him a curious disinclination to hurry, and this aversion grew in a direct ratio with the thought which was becoming stronger in him with each mile and hour of his progress. A multitude of emotions were buried under the conviction that Mary Standish must leave the range when he returned. He had a grim sense of honor, and a particularly devout one when it had to do with women, and though he conceded nothing of right and justice in the relationship which existed between the woman he loved and John Graham, he knew that she must go. To remain at the range was the one impossible thing for her to do. He would take her to Tanana. He would go with her to the States. The matter would be settled in a reasonable and intelligent way, and when he came back, he would bring her with him.

But beneath this undercurrent of decision fought the thing which his will held down, and yet never quite throttled completely—that something which urged him with an unconquerable persistence to hold with his own hands what a glorious fate had given him, and to finish with John Graham, if it ever came to that, in the madly desirable way he visioned for himself in those occasional moments when the fires of temptation blazed hottest.

The fourth night he said to Tautuk:

"If Keok should marry another man, what would you do?"

It was a moment before Tautuk looked at him, and in the herdsman's eyes was a wild, mute question, as if suddenly there had leaped into his stolid mind a suspicion which had never come to him before. Alan laid a reassuring hand upon his arm.

"I don't mean she's going to, Tautuk," he laughed. "She loves you. I know it. Only you are so stupid, and so slow, and so hopeless as a lover that she is punishing you while she has the right—before she marries you. But if she *should* marry someone else, what would you do?"

"My brother?" asked Tautuk.

"No."

"A relative?"

"No."

"A friend?"

"No. A stranger. Someone who had injured you, for instance; someone Keok hated, and who had cheated her into marrying him."

"I would kill him," said Tautuk quietly.

It was this night the temptation was strongest upon Alan. Why should Mary Standish go back, he asked himself. She had surrendered everything to escape from the horror down there. She had given up fortune and friends. She had scattered convention to the four winds, had gambled her life in the hazard, and in the end had come to him! Why should he not keep her? John Graham and the world believed she was dead. And he was master here. If—some day—Graham should happen to cross his path, he would settle the matter in Tautuk's way. Later, while Tautuk slept, and the world lay about him in a soft glow, and the valley below was filled with misty billows of twilight out of which came to him faintly the curious, crackling sound of reindeer hoofs and the grunting contentment of the feeding herd, the reaction came, as he had known it would come in the end.

The morning of the fifth day he set out alone for the eastward herd, and on the sixth overtook Tatpan and his herdsmen. Tatpan, like Sokwenna's foster-children, Keok and Nawadlook, had a quarter-strain of white in him, and when Alan came up to him in the edge of the valley where the deer were grazing, he was lying on a rock, playing Yankee Doodle on a mouth-organ. It was Tatpan who told him that an hour or two before an exhausted stranger had come into camp, looking for him, and that the man was asleep now, apparently more dead than alive, but had given instructions to be awakened at the end of two hours, and not a minute later. Together they had a look at him.

He was a small, ruddy-faced man with carroty blond hair and a peculiarly boyish appearance as he lay doubled up like a jack-knife, profoundly asleep. Tatpan looked at his big, silver watch and in a low voice described how the stranger had stumbled into camp, so tired he could scarcely put one foot ahead of the other; and that he had dropped down where he now lay when he learned Alan was with one of the other herds.

The man wore a gun. . . within reach of his hand.

"He must have come a long distance," said Tatpan, "and he has traveled fast."

Something familiar about the man grew upon Alan. Yet he could not place him. He wore a gun, which he had unbelted and placed within reach of his hand on the grass. His chin was pugnaciously prominent, and in sleep the mysterious stranger had crooked a forefinger and thumb about his revolver in a way that spoke of caution and experience.

"If he is in such a hurry to see me, you might awaken him," said Alan.

He turned a little aside and knelt to drink at a tiny stream of water that ran down from the snowy summits, and he could hear Tatpan rousing the stranger. By the time he had finished drinking and faced about, the little man with the carroty-blond hair was on his feet. Alan stared, and the little man grinned. His ruddy cheeks grew pinker. His blue eyes twinkled, and in what seemed to be a moment of embarrassment he gave his gun a sudden snap that drew an exclamation of amazement from Alan. Only one man in the world had he ever seen throw a gun into its holster like that. A sickly grin began to spread over his own countenance, and all at once Tatpan's eyes began to bulge.

"Stampede!" he cried.

Stampede rubbed a hand over his smooth, prominent chin and nodded apologetically.

"It's me," he conceded. "I had to do it. It was give one or t'other up—my whiskers *or her*. They went hard, too. I flipped dice, an' the whiskers won. I cut cards, an' the whiskers won. I played Klondike ag'in' 'em, an' the whiskers busted the bank. Then I got mad an' shaved 'em. Do I look so bad, Alan?"

"You look twenty years younger," declared Alan, stifling his desire to laugh when he saw the other's seriousness.

Stampede was thoughtfully stroking his chin. "Then why the devil did they laugh!" he demanded. "Mary Standish didn't laugh. She cried. Just stood an' cried, an' then sat down an' cried, she thought I was that blamed funny! And Keok laughed until she was sick an' had to go to bed. That little devil of a Keok calls me Pinkey now, and Miss Standish says it wasn't because I was funny that she laughed, but that the change in me was so sudden she couldn't help it. Nawadlook says I've got a character-ful chin—"

Alan gripped his hand, and a swift change came over Stampede's face. A steely glitter shot into the blue of his eyes, and his chin hardened.

Nature no longer disguised the Stampede Smith of other days, and Alan felt a new thrill and a new regard for the man whose hand he held. This, at last, was the man whose name had gone before him up and down the old trails; the man whose cool and calculating courage, whose fearlessness of death and quickness with the gun had written pages in Alaskan history which would never be forgotten. Where his first impulse had been to laugh, he now felt the grim thrill and admiration of men of other days, who, when in Stampede's presence, knew they were in the presence of a master. The old Stampede had come to life again. And Alan knew why. The grip of his hand tightened, and Stampede returned it.

"Some day, if we're lucky, there always comes a woman to make the world worth living in, Stampede," he said.

"There does," replied Stampede.

He looked steadily at Alan.

"And I take it you love Mary Standish," he added, "and that you'd fight for her if you had to."

"I would," said Alan.

"Then it's time you were traveling," advised Stampede significantly. "I've been twelve hours on the trail without a rest. She told me to move fast, and I've moved. I mean Mary Standish. She said it was almost a matter of life and death that I find you in a hurry. I wanted to stay, but she wouldn't let me. It's *you* she wants. Rossland is at the range."

"*Rossland!*"

"Yes, Rossland. And it's my guess John Graham isn't far away. I smell happenings, Alan. We'd better hurry."

* * * * *

CHAPTER XXI

Stampede had started with one of the two saddle-deer left at the range, but to ride deer-back successfully and with any degree of speed and specific direction was an accomplishment which he had neglected, and within the first half-dozen miles he had abandoned the adventure to continue his journey on foot. As Tatpan had no saddle-deer in his herd, and the swiftest messenger would require many hours in which to reach Amuk Toolik, Alan set out for his range within half an hour after his arrival at Tatpan's camp. Stampede, declaring himself a new man after his brief rest and the meal which followed it, would not listen to Alan's advice that he follow later, when he was more refreshed.

A fierce and reminiscent gleam smoldered in the little gun-fighter's eyes as he watched Alan during the first half-hour leg of their race through the foothills to the tundras. Alan did not observe it, or the grimness that had settled in the face behind him. His own mind was undergoing an upheaval of conjecture and wild questioning. That Rossland had discovered Mary Standish was not dead was the least astonishing factor in the new development. The information might easily have reached him through Sandy McCormick or his wife Ellen. The astonishing thing was that he had in some mysterious way picked up the trail of her flight a thousand miles northward, and the still more amazing fact that he had dared to follow her and reveal himself openly at his range. His heart pumped hard, for he knew Rossland must be directly under Graham's orders.

Then came the resolution to take Stampede into his confidence and to reveal all that had happened on the day of his departure for the mountains. He proceeded to do this without equivocation or hesitancy, for there now pressed upon him a grim anticipation of impending events ahead of them.

Stampede betrayed no astonishment at the other's disclosures. The smoldering fire remained in his eyes, the immobility of his face unchanged. Only when Alan repeated, in his own words, Mary Standish's confession of love at Nawadlook's door did the fighting lines soften about his comrade's eyes and mouth.

Stampede's lips responded with an oddly quizzical smile. "I knew that a long time ago," he said. "I guessed it that first night of storm in the coach up to Chitina. I knew it for certain before we left Tanana. She didn't tell me, but I wasn't blind. It was the note that puzzled and frightened me—the note she stuffed in her slipper. And Rossland told me, before I left, that going for you was a wild-goose chase, as he intended to take Mrs. John Graham back with him immediately."

"And you left her alone after *that?*"

Stampede shrugged his shoulders as he valiantly kept up with Alan's suddenly quickened pace.

"She insisted. Said it meant life and death for her. And she looked it. White as paper after her talk with Rossland. Besides—"

"What?"

"Sokwenna won't sleep until we get back. He knows. I told him. And he's watching from the garret window with a.303 Savage. I saw him pick off a duck the other day at two hundred yards."

They hurried on. After a little Alan said, with the fear which he could not name clutching at his heart, "Why did you say Graham might not be far away?"

"In my bones," replied Stampede, his face hard as rock again. "In my bones!"

"Is that all?"

"Not quite. I think Rossland told her. She was so white. And her hand cold as a lump of clay when she put it on mine. It was in her eyes, too.

Besides, Rossland has taken possession of your cabin as though he owns it. I take it that means somebody behind him, a force, something big to reckon with. He asked me how many men we had. I told him, stretching it a little. He grinned. He couldn't keep back that grin. It was as if a devil in him slipped out from hiding for an instant."

Suddenly he caught Alan's arm and stopped him. His chin shot out. The sweat ran from his face. For a full quarter of a minute the two men stared at each other.

"Alan, we're short-sighted. I'm damned if I don't think we ought to call the herdsmen in, and every man with a loaded gun!"

"You think it's that bad?"

"Might be. If Graham's behind Rossland and has men with him—"

"We're two and a half hours from Tatpan," said Alan, in a cold, unemotional voice. "He has only half a dozen men with him, and it will take at least four to make quick work in finding Tautuk and Amuk Toolik. There are eighteen men with the southward herd, and twenty-two with the upper. I mean, counting the boys. Use your own judgment. All are armed. It may be foolish, but I'm following your hunch."

They gripped hands.

"It's more than a hunch, Alan," breathed Stampede softly. "And for God's sake keep off the music as long as you can!"

He was gone, and as his agile, boyish figure started in a half-run toward the foothills, Alan set his face southward, so that in a quarter of an hour they were lost to each other in the undulating distances of the tundra.

Never had Alan traveled as on the last of this sixth day of his absence from the range. He was comparatively fresh, as his trail to Tatpan's camp had not been an exhausting one, and his more intimate knowledge of the country gave him a decided advantage over Stampede. He believed he could make the distance in ten hours, but to this he would be compelled to add a rest of at least three or four hours during the night. It was now eight o'clock. By nine or ten the next morning he would be facing Rossland, and at about that same hour Tatpan's swift messengers would be closing in about Tautuk and Amuk Toolik. He knew the speed with which his herdsmen would sweep out of the mountains and over the tundras. Two years ago Amuk Toolik and a dozen of his Eskimo people had traveled fifty-two hours without rest or food, covering a hundred and nineteen miles in that time. His blood flushed hot with pride. He couldn't do that. But his people could—and *would*. He could see them sweeping in from the telescoping segments of the herds as the word went among them; he could see them streaking out of the foothills; and then, like wolves scattering for freer air and leg-room, he saw them dotting the tundra in their race for home—and war, if it was war that lay ahead of them.

Twilight began to creep in upon him, like veils of cool, dry mist out of the horizons. And hour after hour he went on, eating a strip of pemmican when he grew hungry, and drinking in the spring coulées when he came to them, where the water was cold and clear. Not until a telltale cramp began to bite warningly in his leg did he stop for the rest which he knew he must take. It was one o'clock. Counting his journey to Tatpan's camp, he had been traveling almost steadily for seventeen hours.

Not until he stretched himself out on his back in a grassy hollow where a little stream a foot wide rippled close to his ears did he realize how tired he had become. At first he tried not to sleep. Rest was all he wanted; he dared not close his eyes. But exhaustion overcame him at last, and he slept. When he awoke, bird-song and the sun were taunting him. He sat up with a jerk, then leaped to his feet in alarm. His watch told the story. He had slept soundly for six hours, instead of resting three or four with his eyes open.

After a little, as he hurried on his way, he did not altogether regret what had happened. He felt like a fighting man. He breathed deeply, ate a breakfast of pemmican as he walked, and proceeded to make up lost time. The interval between fifteen minutes of twelve and twelve he almost ran. That quarter of an hour brought him to the crest of the ridge from which he could look upon the buildings of the range. Nothing had happened that he could see. He gave a great gasp of relief, and in his joy he laughed. The strangeness of the laugh told him more than anything else the tension he had been under.

Another half-hour, and he came up out of the dip behind Sokwenna's cabin and tried the door. It was locked. A voice answered his knock, and he called out his name. The bolt shot back, the door opened, and he stepped in. Nawadlook stood at her bedroom door, a gun in her hands. Keok faced him, holding grimly to a long knife, and between them, staring white-faced at him as he entered, was Mary Standish. She came forward to meet him, and he heard a whisper from Nawadlook, and saw Keok follow her swiftly through the door into the other room.

Mary Standish held out her hands to him a little blindly, and the tremble in her throat and the look in her eyes betrayed the struggle she was making to keep from breaking down and crying out in gladness at his coming. It was that look that sent a flood of joy into his heart, even when he saw the torture and hopelessness behind it. He held her hands close, and into her eyes he smiled in such a way that he saw them widen, as if she almost disbelieved; and then she drew in a sudden quick breath, and her fingers clung to him. It was as if the hope that had deserted her came in an instant into her face again. He was not excited. He was not even perturbed, now that he saw that light in her eyes and knew she was safe. But his love was there. She saw it and felt the force of it behind the deadly calmness with which he was smiling at her. She gave a little sob, so low it was scarcely more than a broken breath; a little cry that came of wonder—understanding—and unspeakable faith in this man who was smiling at her so confidently in the face of the tragedy that had come to destroy her.

"Rossland is in your cabin," she whispered. "And John Graham is back there—somewhere—coming this way. Rossland says that if I don't go to him of my own free will—"

He felt the shudder that ran through her.

"I understand the rest," he said. They stood silent for a moment. The gray-cheeked thrush was singing on the roof. Then, as if she had been a child, he took her face between his hands and bent her head back a little, so that he was looking straight into her eyes, and so near that he could feel the sweet warmth of her breath.

"You didn't make a mistake the day I went away?" he asked. "You— love me?"

"Yes."

For a moment longer he looked into her eyes. Then he stood back from her. Even Keok and Nawadlook heard his laugh. It was strange, they thought—Keok with her knife, and Nawadlook with her gun—for the bird was singing, and Alan Holt was laughing, and Mary Standish was very still.

Another moment later, from where he sat cross-legged at the little window in the attic, keeping his unsleeping vigil with a rifle across his knees, old Sokwenna saw his master walk across the open, and something in the manner of his going brought back a vision of another day long ago when Ghost Kloof had rung with the cries of battle, and the hands now gnarled and twisted with age had played their part in the heroic stand of his people against the oppressors from the farther north.

Then he saw Alan go into the cabin where Rossland was, and softly his fingers drummed upon the ancient tom-tom which lay at his side. His eyes fixed themselves upon the distant mountains, and under his breath he mumbled the old chant of battle, dead and forgotten except in Sokwenna's brain, and after that his eyes closed, and again the vision grew out of darkness like a picture for him, a vision of twisting trails and of fighting men gathering with their faces set for war.

* * * * *

CHAPTER XXII

At the desk in Alan's living-room sat Rossland, when the door opened behind him and the master of the range came in. He was not disturbed when he saw who it was, and rose to meet him. His coat was off, his sleeves rolled up, and it was evident he was making no effort to conceal his freedom with Alan's books and papers.

He advanced, holding out a hand. This was not the same Rossland who had told Alan to attend to his own business on board the *Nome*. His attitude was that of one greeting a friend, smiling and affable even before he spoke. Something inspired Alan to return the smile. Behind that smile he was admiring the man's nerve. His hand met Rossland's casually, but there was no uncertainty in the warmth of the other's grip.

"How d' do, Paris, old boy?" he greeted good-humoredly. "Saw you going in to Helen a few minutes ago, so I've been waiting for you. She's a little frightened. And we can't blame her. Menelaus is mightily upset. But mind me, Holt, I'm not blaming you. I'm too good a sport. Clever, I call it—damned clever. She's enough to turn any man's head. I only wish I were in your boots right now. I'd have turned traitor myself aboard the *Nome* if she had shown an inclination."

He proffered a cigar, a big, fat cigar with a gold band. It was inspiration again that made Alan accept it and light it. His blood was racing. But Rossland saw nothing of that. He observed only the nod, the cool smile on Alan's lips, the apparent nonchalance with which he was meeting the situation. It pleased Graham's agent. He reseated himself in the desk-chair and motioned Alan to another chair near him.

"I thought you were badly hurt," said Alan. "Nasty knife wound you got."

Rossland shrugged his shoulders. "There you have it again, Holt—the hell of letting a pretty face run away with you. One of the Thlinkit girls down in the steerage, you know. Lovely little thing, wasn't she? Tricked her into my cabin all right, but she wasn't like some other Indian girls I've known. The next night a brother, or sweetheart, or whoever it was got me through the open port. It wasn't bad. I was out of the hospital within a week. Lucky I was put there, too. Otherwise I wouldn't have seen Mrs. Graham one morning—through the window. What a little our fortunes hang to at times, eh? If it hadn't been for the girl and the knife and the hospital, I wouldn't be here now, and Graham wouldn't be bleeding his heart out with impatience—and you, Holt, wouldn't be facing the biggest opportunity that will ever come into your life."

"I'm afraid I don't understand," said Alan, hiding his face in the smoke of his cigar and speaking with an apparent indifference which had its effect upon Rossland. "Your presence inclines me to believe that luck has rather turned against me. Where can my advantage be?"

A grim seriousness settled in Rossland's eyes, and his voice became cool and hard. "Holt, as two men who are not afraid to meet unusual situations, we may as well call a spade a spade in this matter, don't you think so?"

"Decidedly," said Alan.

"You know that Mary Standish is really Mary Standish Graham, John Graham's wife?"

"Yes."

"And you probably know—now—why she jumped into the sea, and why she ran away from Graham."

"I do."

"That saves a lot of talk. But there is another side to the story which you probably don't know, and I am here to tell it to you. John Graham doesn't care for a dollar of the Standish fortune. It's the girl he wants,

189

and has always wanted. She has grown up under his eyes. From the day she was fourteen years old he has lived and planned with the thought of possessing her. You know how he got her to marry him, and you know what happened afterward. But it makes no difference to him whether she hates him or not. He *wants* her. And this"—he swept his arms out, "is the most beautiful place in the world in which to have her returned to him. I've been figuring from your books. Your property isn't worth over a hundred thousand dollars as it stands on hoof today. I'm here to offer you five times that for it. In other words, Graham is willing to forfeit all action he might have personally against you for stealing his wife, and in place of that will pay you five hundred thousand dollars for the privilege of having his honeymoon here, and making of this place a country estate where his wife may reside indefinitely, subject to her husband's visits when he is so inclined. There will be a stipulation, of course, requiring that the personal details of the deal be kept strictly confidential, and that you leave the country. Do I make myself clear?"

Alan rose to his feet and paced thoughtfully across the room. At least, Rossland measured his action as one of sudden, intensive reflection as he watched him, smiling complacently at the effect of his knock-out proposition upon the other. He had not minced matters. He had come to the point without an effort at bargaining, and he possessed sufficient dramatic sense to appreciate what the offer of half a million dollars meant to an individual who was struggling for existence at the edge of a raw frontier. Alan stood with his back toward him, facing a window. His voice was oddly strained when he answered. But that was quite natural, too, Rossland thought.

"I am wondering if I understand you," he said. "Do you mean that if I sell Graham the range, leave it bag and baggage, and agree to keep my mouth shut thereafter, he will give me half a million dollars?"

"That is the price. You are to take your people with you. Graham has his own."

Alan tried to laugh. "I think I see the point—now. He isn't paying five hundred thousand for Miss Standish—I mean Mrs. Graham. He's paying it for the *isolation*."

"Exactly. It was a last-minute hunch with him—to settle the matter peaceably. We started up here to get his wife. You understand, to *get* her, and settle the matter with you in a different way from the one we're using now. You hit the word when you said 'isolation.' What a damn fool a man can make of himself over a pretty face! Think of it—half a million dollars!"

"It sounds unreal," mused Alan, keeping his face to the window. "Why should he offer so much?"

"You must keep the stipulation in mind, Holt. That is an important part of the deal. You are to keep your mouth shut. Buying the range at a normal price wouldn't guarantee it. But when you accept a sum like that, you're a partner in the other end of the transaction, and your health depends upon keeping the matter quiet. Simple enough, isn't it?"

Alan turned back to the table. His face was pale. He tried to keep smoke in front of his eyes. "Of course, I don't suppose he'd allow Mrs. Graham to escape back to the States—where she might do a little upsetting on her own account?"

"He isn't throwing the money away," replied Rossland significantly.

"She would remain here indefinitely?"

"Indefinitely."

"Probably never would return."

"Strange how squarely you hit the nail on the head! Why should she return? The world believes she is dead. Papers were full of it. The little secret of her being alive is all our own. And this will be a beautiful summering place for Graham. Magnificent climate. Lovely flowers. Birds. And the girl he has watched grow up, and wanted, since she was fourteen."

"And who hates him."

"True."

"Who was tricked into marrying him, and who would rather die than live with him as his wife."

"But it's up to Graham to keep her alive, Holt. That's not our business. If she dies, I imagine you will have an opportunity to get your range back pretty cheap."

Rossland held a paper out to Alan.

"Here's partial payment—two hundred and fifty thousand. I have the papers here, on the desk, ready to sign. As soon as you give possession, I'll return to Tanana with you and make the remaining payment."

Alan took the check. "I guess only a fool would refuse an offer like this, Rossland."

"Yes, only a fool."

"*And I am that fool.*"

So quietly did Alan speak that for an instant the significance of his words did not fall with full force upon Rossland. The smoke cleared away from before Alan's face. His cigar dropped to the floor, and he stepped on it with his foot. The check followed it in torn scraps. The fury he had held back with almost superhuman effort blazed in his eyes.

"If I could have Graham where you are now—*in that chair*—I'd give ten years of my life, Rossland. I would kill him. And you—*you*—"

He stepped back a pace, as if to put himself out of striking distance of the beast who was staring at him in amazement.

"What you have said about her should condemn you to death. And I would kill you here, in this room, if it wasn't necessary for you to take my message back to Graham. Tell him that Mary Standish—*not* Mary Graham—is as pure and clean and as sweet as the day she was born. Tell him that she belongs to *me*. I love her. She is mine—do you understand? And all the money in the world couldn't buy one hair from her head. I'm going to take her back to the States. She is going to get a square deal, and the world is going to know her story. She has nothing to conceal. Absolutely nothing. Tell that to John Graham for me."

He advanced upon Rossland, who had risen from his chair; his hands were clenched, his face a mask of iron.

"Get out! Go before I flay you within an inch of your rotten life!"

The energy which every fiber in him yearned to expend upon Rossland sent the table crashing back in an overturned wreck against the wall.

"Go—before I kill you!"

He was advancing, even as the words of warning came from his lips, and the man before him, an awe-stricken mass of flesh that had forgotten power and courage in the face of a deadly and unexpected menace, backed quickly to the door and escaped. He made for the corrals, and Alan watched from his door until he saw him departing southward, accompanied by two men who bore packs on their shoulders. Not until then did Rossland gather his nerve sufficiently to stop and look back. His breathless voice carried something unintelligible to Alan. But he did not return for his coat and hat.

The reaction came to Alan when he saw the wreck he had made of the table. Another moment or two and the devil in him would have been at work. He hated Rossland. He hated him now only a little less than he hated John Graham, and that he had let him go seemed a miracle to him. He felt the strain he had been under. But he was glad. Some little god of common sense had overruled his passion, and he had acted wisely. Graham would now get his message, and there could be no misunderstanding of purpose between them.

He was staring at the disordered papers on his desk when a movement at the door turned him about. Mary Standish stood before him.

"You sent him away," she cried softly.

Her eyes were shining, her lips parted, her face lit up with a beautiful glow. She saw the overturned table, Rossland's hat and coat on a chair, the evidence of what had happened and the quickness of his flight; and then she turned her face to Alan again, and what he saw broke down the last of that grim resolution which he had measured for himself, so that in a moment he was at her side, and had her in his arms. She made no effort to free herself as she had done in the cottonwoods, but turned her mouth up for him to kiss, and then hid her face against his shoulder—while he, fighting vainly to find utterance for the thousand words in his throat, stood stroking her hair, and then buried his face in it, crying out at last in the warm sweetness of it that he loved her, and was going to fight for her, and that no power on earth could take her away from him now. And these things he repeated until she raised her flushed face from his breast, and let him kiss her lips once more, and then freed herself gently from his arms.

* * * *

CHAPTER XXIII

For a Space they stood apart, and in the radiant loveliness of Mary Standish's face and in Alan's quiet and unimpassioned attitude were neither shame nor regret. In a moment they had swept aside the barrier which convention had raised against them, and now they felt the inevitable thrill of joy and triumph, and not the humiliating embarrassment of dishonor. They made no effort to draw a curtain upon their happiness, or to hide the swift heart-beat of it from each other. It had happened, and they were glad. Yet they stood apart, and something pressed upon Alan the inviolableness of the little freedom of space between them, of its sacredness to Mary Standish, and darker and deeper grew the glory of pride and faith that lay with the love in her eyes when he did not cross it. He reached out his hand, and freely she gave him her own. Lips blushing with his kisses trembled in a smile, and she bowed her head a little, so that he was looking at her smooth hair, soft and sweet where he had caressed it a few moments before.

"I thank God!" he said.

He did not finish the surge of gratitude that was in his heart. Speech seemed trivial, even futile. But she understood. He was not thanking God for that moment, but for a lifetime of something that at last had come to him. This, it seemed to him, was the end, the end of a world as he had known it, the beginning of a new. He stepped back, and his hands trembled. For something to do he set up the overturned table, and Mary Standish watched him with a quiet, satisfied wonder. She loved him, and she had come into his arms. She had given him her lips to kiss. And he laughed softly as he came to her side again, and looked over the tundra where Rossland had gone.

"How long before you can prepare for the journey?" he asked.

"You mean—"

"That we must start tonight or in the morning. I think we shall go through the cottonwoods over the old trail to Nome. Unless Rossland lied, Graham is somewhere out there on the Tanana trail."

Her hand pressed his arm. "We are going—*back?* Is that it, Alan?"

"Yes, to Seattle. It is the one thing to do. You are not afraid?"

"With you there—no."

"And you will return with me—when it is over?"

He was looking steadily ahead over the tundra. But he felt her cheek touch his shoulder, lightly as a feather.

"Yes, I will come back with you."

"And you will be ready?"

"I am ready now."

The sun-fire of the plains danced in his eyes; a cob-web of golden mist rising out of the earth, beckoning wraiths and undulating visions—the breath of life, of warmth, of growing things—all between him and the hidden cottonwoods; a joyous sea into which he wanted to plunge without another minute of waiting, as he felt the gentle touch of her cheek against his shoulder, and the weight of her hand on his arm. That she had come to him utterly was in the low surrender of her voice. She had ceased to fight—she had given to him the precious right to fight for her.

It was this sense of her need and of her glorious faith in him, and of the obligation pressing with it that drove slowly back into him the grimmer realities of the day. Its horror surged upon him again, and the significance of what Rossland had said seemed fresher, clearer, even more terrible now that he was gone. Unconsciously the old lines of hatred crept into his face again as he looked steadily in the direction which the other man had taken, and he wondered how much of that same horror—of the unbelievable menace stealing upon her—Rossland had divulged to the girl who stood so quietly now at his side. Had he done right to let him go? Should he not have killed him, as he would have exterminated a serpent? For Rossland had exulted; he was of Graham's flesh and desires, a part of his foul soul, a defiler of womanhood and the one who had bargained to make possible the opportunity for an indescribable crime. It was not too late. He could still overtake him, out there in the hollows of the tundra—

The pressure on his arm tightened. He looked down. Mary Standish had seen what was in his face, and there was something in her calmness that brought him to himself. He knew, in that moment, that Rossland had told her a great deal. Yet she was not afraid, unless it was fear of what had been in his mind.

"I am ready," she reminded him.

"We must wait for Stampede," he said, reason returning to him. "He should be here sometime tonight, or in the morning. Now that Rossland is off my nerves, I can see how necessary it is to have someone like Stampede between us and—"

He did not finish, but what he had intended to say was quite clear to her. She stood in the doorway, and he felt an almost uncontrollable desire to take her in his arms again.

"He is between here and Tanana," she said with a little gesture of her head.

"Rossland told you that?"

"Yes. And there are others with him, so many that he was amused when I told him you would not let them take me away."

"Then you were not afraid that I—I might let them have you?"

"I have always been sure of what you would do since I opened that second letter at Ellen McCormick's, Alan!"

He caught the flash of her eyes, the gladness in them, and she was gone before he could find another word to say. Keok and Nawadlook were approaching hesitatingly, but now they hurried to meet her, Keok still grimly clutching the long knife; and beyond them, at the little window under the roof, he saw the ghostly face of old Sokwenna, like a death's-head on guard. His blood ran a little faster. The emptiness of the tundras, the illimitable spaces without sign of human life, the vast stage waiting for its impending drama, with its sunshine, its song of birds, its whisper and breath of growing flowers, struck a new note in him, and he looked again at the little window where Sokwenna sat like a spirit from another world, warning him in his silent and lifeless stare of something menacing and deadly creeping upon them out of that space which seemed so free of all evil. He beckoned to him and then entered his cabin, waiting while Sokwenna crawled down from his post and came hobbling over the open, a crooked figure, bent like a baboon, witch-like in his great age, yet with sunken eyes that gleamed like little points of flame, and a quickness of movement that made Alan shiver as he watched him through the window.

In a moment the old man entered. He was mumbling. He was saying, in that jumble of sound which it was difficult for even Alan to understand—and which Sokwenna had never given up for the missionaries' teachings—that he could hear feet and smell blood; and that the feet were many, and the blood was near, and that both smell and footfall were coming from the old kloof where yellow skulls still lay, dripping with the water that had once run red. Alan was one of the few who, by reason of much effort, had learned the story of the kloof from old Sokwenna; how, so long ago that Sokwenna was a young man, a hostile tribe had descended upon his people, killing the men and stealing the women; and how at last Sokwenna and a handful of his tribesmen fled south with what women were left and made a final stand in the kloof, and there, on a day that was golden and filled with the beauty of bird-song and flowers, had ambushed their enemies and killed them to a man. All were dead now, all but Sokwenna.

For a space Alan was sorry he had called Sokwenna to his cabin. He was no longer the cheerful and gentle "old man" of his people; the old man who chortled with joy at the prettiness and play of Keok and

Nawadlook, who loved birds and flowers and little children, and who had retained an impish boyhood along with his great age. He was changed. He stood before Alan an embodiment of fatalism, mumbling incoherent things in his breath, a spirit of evil omen lurking in his sunken eyes, and his thin hands gripping like bird-claws to his rifle. Alan threw off the uncomfortable feeling that had gripped him for a moment, and set him to an appointed task—the watching of the southward plain from the crest of a tall ridge two miles back on the Tanana trail. He was to return when the sun reached its horizon.

Alan was inspired now by a great caution, a growing premonition which stirred him with uneasiness, and he began his own preparations as soon as Sokwenna had started on his mission. The desire to leave at once, without the delay of an hour, pulled strong in him, but he forced himself to see the folly of such haste. He would be away many months, possibly a year this time. There was much to do, a mass of detail to attend to, a volume of instructions and advice to leave behind him. He must at least see Stampede, and it was necessary to write down certain laws for Tautuk and Amuk Toolik. As this work of preparation progressed, and the premonition persisted in remaining with him, he fell into a habit of repeating to himself the absurdity of fears and the impossibility of danger. He tried to make himself feel uncomfortably foolish at the thought of having ordered the herdsmen in. In all probability Graham would not appear at all, he told himself, or at least not for many days—or weeks; and if he did come, it would be to war in a legal way, and not with murder.

Yet his uneasiness did not leave him. As the hours passed and the afternoon lengthened, the invisible something urged him more strongly to take the trail beyond the cottonwoods, with Mary Standish at his side. Twice he saw her between noon and five o'clock, and by that time his writing was done. He looked at his guns carefully. He saw that his favorite rifle and automatic were working smoothly, and he called himself a fool for filling his ammunition vest with an extravagant number of cartridges.

He even carried an amount of this ammunition and two of his extra guns to Sokwenna's cabin, with the thought that it was this cabin on the edge of the ravine which was best fitted for defense in the event of necessity. Possibly Stampede might have use for it, and for the guns, if Graham should come after he and Mary were well on their way to Nome.

After supper, when the sun was throwing long shadows from the edge of the horizon, Alan came from a final survey of his cabin and the food which Wegaruk had prepared for his pack, and found Mary at the edge of the ravine, watching the twilight gathering where the coulée ran narrower and deeper between the distant breasts of the tundra.

"I am going to leave you for a little while," he said. "But Sokwenna has returned, and you will not be alone."

"Where are you going?"

"As far as the cottonwoods, I think."

"Then I am going with you."

"I expect to walk very fast."

"Not faster than I, Alan."

"But I want to make sure the country is clear in that direction before twilight shuts out the distances."

"I will help you." Her hand crept into his. "I am going with you, Alan," she repeated.

"Yes, I—think you are," he laughed joyously, and suddenly he bent his head and pressed her hand to his lips, and in that way, with her hand in his, they set out over the trail which they had not traveled together since the day he had come from Nome.

There was a warm glow in her face, and something beautifully soft and sweet in her eyes which she did not try to keep away from him. It made him forget the cottonwoods and the plains beyond, and his caution, and Sokwenna's advice to guard carefully against the hiding-places of Ghost Kloof and the country beyond.

"I have been thinking a great deal today," she was saying, "because you have left me so much alone. I have been thinking of *you*. And—my thoughts have given me a wonderful happiness."

"And I have been—in paradise," he replied.

"You do not think that I am wicked?"

"I could sooner believe the sun would never come up again."

"Nor that I have been unwomanly?"

"You are my dream of all that is glorious in womanhood."

"Yet I have followed you—have thrust myself at you, fairly at your head, Alan."

"For which I thank God," He breathed devoutly.

"And I have told you that I love you, and you have taken me in your arms, and have kissed me—"

"Yes."

"And I am walking now with my hand in yours—"

"And will continue to do so, if I can hold it."

"And I am another man's wife," she shuddered.

"You are mine," he declared doggedly. "You know it, and the Almighty God knows it. It is blasphemy to speak of yourself as Graham's wife. You are legally entangled with him, and that is all. Heart and soul and body you are free."

"No, I am not free."

"But you are!"

And then, after a moment, she whispered at his shoulder: "Alan, because you are the finest gentleman in all the world, I will tell you why I am not. It is because—heart and soul—I belong to you."

He dared not look at her, and feeling the struggle within him Mary Standish looked straight ahead with a wonderful smile on her lips and repeated softly, "Yes, the very finest gentleman in all the world!"

Over the breasts of the tundra and the hollows between they went, still hand in hand, and found themselves talking of the colorings in the sky, and the birds, and flowers, and the twilight creeping in about them, while Alan scanned the shortening horizons for a sign of human life. One mile, and then another, and after that a third, and they were looking into gray gloom far ahead, where lay the kloof.

It was strange that he should think of the letter now—the letter he had written to Ellen McCormick—but think of it he did, and said what was in his mind to Mary Standish, who was also looking with him into the wall of gloom that lay between them and the distant cottonwoods.

"It seemed to me that I was not writing it to her, but to *you*" he said. "And I think that if you hadn't come back to me I would have gone mad."

"I have the letter. It is here"—and she placed a hand upon her breast. "Do you remember what you wrote, Alan?"

"That you meant more to me than life."

"And that—particularly—you wanted Ellen McCormick to keep a tress of my hair for you if they found me."

He nodded. "When I sat across the table from you aboard the *Nome*, I worshiped it and didn't know it. And since then—since I've had you here—every time. I've looked at you—" He stopped, choking the words back in his throat.

"Say it, Alan."

"I've wanted to see it down," he finished desperately. "Silly notion, isn't it?"

"Why is it?" she asked, her eyes widening a little. "If you love it, why is it a silly notion to want to see it down?"

"Why, I though possibly you might think it so," he added lamely.

Never had he heard anything sweeter than her laughter as she turned suddenly from him, so that the glow of the fallen sun was at her back, and with deft, swift fingers began loosening the coils of her hair until its radiant masses tumbled about her, streaming down her back in a silken glory that awed him with its beauty and drew from his lips a cry of gladness.

She faced him, and in her eyes was the shining softness that glowed in her hair. "Do you think it is nice, Alan?"

He went to her and filled his hands with the heavy tresses and pressed them to his lips and face.

Thus he stood when he felt the sudden shiver that ran through her. It was like a little shock. He heard the catch of her breath, and the hand which she had placed gently on his bowed head fell suddenly away. When he raised his head to look at her, she was staring past him into the deepening twilight of the tundra, and it seemed as if something had stricken her so that for a space she was powerless to speak or move.

"What is it?" he cried, and whirled about, straining his eyes to see what had alarmed her; and as he looked, a deep, swift shadow sped over the earth, darkening the mellow twilight until it was somber gloom of night—and the midnight sun went out like a great, luminous lamp as a dense wall of purple cloud rolled up in an impenetrable curtain between it and the arctic world. Often he had seen this happen in the approach of summer storm on the tundras, but never had the change seemed so swift as now. Where there had been golden light, he saw his companion's face now pale in a sea of dusk. It was this miracle of arctic night, its suddenness and unexpectedness, that had startled her, he thought, and he laughed softly.

But her hand clutched his arm. "I saw them," she cried, her voice breaking. "I saw them—out there against the sun—before the cloud came—and some of them were running, like animals—"

"Shadows!" he exclaimed. "The long shadows of foxes running against the sun, or of the big gray rabbits, or of a wolf and her half-grown sneaking away—"

"No, no, they were not that," she breathed tensely, and her fingers clung more fiercely to his arm. "They were not shadows. *They were men!*"

* * * * *

CHAPTER XXIV

In the moment of stillness between them, when their hearts seemed to have stopped beating that they might not lose the faintest whispering of the twilight, a sound came to Alan, and he knew it was the toe of a boot striking against stone. Not a foot in his tribe would have made that sound; none but Stampede Smith's or his own.

"Were they many?" he asked.

"I could not see. The sun was darkening. But five or six were running—"

"Behind us?"

"Yes."

"And they saw us?"

"I think so. It was but a moment, and they were a part of the dusk."

He found her hand and held it closely. Her fingers clung to his, and he could hear her quick breathing as he unbuttoned the flap of his automatic holster.

"You think *they have come?*" she whispered, and a cold dread was in her voice.

"Possibly. My people would not appear from that direction. You are not afraid?"

"No, no, I am not afraid."

"Yet you are trembling."

"It is this strange gloom, Alan."

Never had the arctic twilight gone more completely. Not half a dozen times had he seen the phenomenon in all his years on the tundras, where thunder-storm and the putting out of the summer sun until twilight thickens into the gloom of near-night is an occurrence so rare that it is more awesome than the weirdest play of the northern lights. It seemed to him now that what was happening was a miracle, the play of a mighty hand opening their way to salvation. An inky wall was shutting out the world where the glow of the midnight sun should have been. It was spreading quickly; shadows became part of the gloom, and this gloom crept in, thickening, drawing nearer, until the tundra was a weird chaos, neither night nor twilight, challenging vision until eyes strained futilely to penetrate its mystery.

And as it gathered about them, enveloping them in their own narrowing circle of vision, Alan was thinking quickly. It had taken him only a moment to accept the significance of the running figures his companion had seen. Graham's men were near, had seen them, and were getting between them and the range. Possibly it was a scouting party, and if there were no more than five or six, the number which Mary had counted, he was quite sure of the situation. But there might be a dozen or fifty of them. It was possible Graham and Rossland were advancing upon the range with their entire force. He had at no time tried to analyze just what this force might be, except to assure himself that with the overwhelming influence behind him, both political and financial, and fired by a passion for Mary Standish that had revealed itself as little short of madness, Graham would hesitate at no convention of law or humanity to achieve his end. Probably he was playing the game so that he would be shielded by the technicalities of the law, if it came to a tragic end. His gunmen would undoubtedly be impelled to a certain extent by an idea of authority. For Graham was an injured husband "rescuing" his wife, while he—Alan Holt—was the woman's abductor and paramour, and a fit subject to be shot upon sight!

His free hand gripped the butt of his pistol as he led the way straight ahead. The sudden gloom helped to hide in his face the horror he felt of what that "rescue" would mean to Mary Standish; and then a cold and deadly definiteness possessed him, and every nerve in his body gathered itself in readiness for whatever might happen.

If Graham's men had seen them, and were getting between them and retreat, the neck of the trap lay ahead—and in this direction Alan walked so swiftly that the girl was almost running at his side. He could not hear her footsteps, so lightly they fell! her fingers were twined about his own, and he could feel the silken caress of her loose hair. For half a mile he kept on, watching for a moving shadow, listening for a sound. Then he stopped. He drew Mary into his arms and held her there, so that her head lay against his breast. She was panting, and he could feel and hear her thumping heart. He found her parted lips and kissed them.

"You are not afraid?" he asked again.

Her head made a fierce little negative movement against his breast. "No!"

He laughed softly at the beautiful courage with which she lied. "Even if they saw us, and are Graham's men, we have given them the slip," he comforted her. "Now we will circle eastward back to the range. I am sorry I hurried you so. We will go more slowly."

"We must travel faster," she insisted. "I want to run."

Her fingers sought his hand and clung to it again as they set out. At intervals they stopped, staring about them into nothingness, and listening. Twice Alan thought he heard sounds which did not belong to the night. The second time the little fingers tightened about his own, but his companion said no word, only her breath seemed to catch in her throat for an instant.

At the end of another half-hour it was growing lighter, yet the breath of storm seemed nearer. The cool promise of it touched their cheeks, and about them were gathering whispers and eddies of a thirsty earth rousing to the sudden change. It was lighter because the wall of cloud seemed to be distributing itself over the whole heaven, thinning out where its solid opaqueness had lain against the sun. Alan could see the girl's face and the cloud of her hair. Hollows and ridges of the tundra were taking more distinct shape when they came into a dip, and Alan recognized a thicket of willows behind which a pool was hidden.

The thicket was only half a mile from home. A spring was near the edge of the willows, and to this he led the girl, made her a place to kneel, and showed her how to cup the cool water in the palms of her hands. While she inclined her head to drink, he held back her hair and rested with his lips pressed to it. He heard the trickle of water running between her fingers, her little laugh of half-pleasure, half-fear, which in another instant broke into a startled scream as he half gained his feet to meet a crashing body that catapulted at him from the concealment of the willows.

A greater commotion in the thicket followed the attack; then another voice, crying out sharply, a second cry from Mary Standish, and he found himself on his knees, twisted backward and fighting desperately to loosen a pair of gigantic hands at his throat. He could hear the girl struggling, but she did not cry out again. In an instant, it seemed, his brain was reeling. He was conscious of a futile effort to reach his gun, and could see the face over him, grim and horrible in the gloom, as the merciless hands choked the life from him. Then he heard a shout, a loud shout, filled with triumph and exultation as he was thrown back; his head seemed leaving his shoulders; his body crumbled, and almost spasmodically his leg shot out with the last strength that was in him. He was scarcely aware of the great gasp that followed, but the fingers loosened at his throat, the face disappeared, and the man who was killing him sank back. For a precious moment or two Alan did not move as he drew great breaths of air into his lungs. Then he felt for his pistol. The holster was empty.

He could hear the panting of the girl, her sobbing breath very near him, and life and strength leaped back into his body. The man who had choked him was advancing again, on hands and knees. In a flash Alan was up and on him like a lithe cat. His fist beat into a bearded face; he called out to Mary as he struck, and through his blows saw her where she had fallen to her knees, with a second hulk bending over her, almost in the water of the little spring from which she had been drinking. A mad curse leaped from his lips. He was ready to kill now; he wanted to kill—to destroy what was already under his hands that he might leap upon this other beast, who stood over Mary Standish, his hands twisted in her long hair. Dazed by blows that fell with the force of a club the bearded man's head sagged backward, and Alan's fingers dug into his throat. It was a bull's neck. He tried to break it. Ten seconds—twenty—half a minute at the most—and flesh and bone would have given way—but before the bearded man's gasping cry was gone from his lips the second figure leaped upon Alan.

He had no time to defend himself from this new attack. His strength was half gone, and a terrific blow sent him reeling. Blindly he reached out and grappled. Not until his arms met those of his fresh assailant did he realize how much of himself he had expended upon the other. A sickening horror filled his soul as he felt his weakness, and an involuntary moan broke from his lips. Even then he would have cut out his tongue to have silenced that sound, to have kept it from the girl. She was creeping on her hands and knees, but he could not see. Her long hair trailed in the trampled earth, and in the muddied water of the spring, and her hands were groping—groping—until they found what they were seeking.

Then she rose to her feet, carrying the rock on which one of her hands had rested when she knelt to drink. The bearded man, bringing himself to his knees, reached out drunkenly, but she avoided him and poised herself over Alan and his assailant. The rock descended. Alan saw her then; he heard the one swift, terrible blow, and his enemy rolled away from him, limply and without sound. He staggered to his feet and for a moment caught the swaying girl in his arms.

The bearded man was rising. He was half on his feet when Alan was at his throat again, and they went down together. The girl heard blows, then a heavier one, and with an exclamation of triumph Alan stood up. By chance his hand had come in contact with his fallen pistol. He clicked the safety down; he was ready to shoot, ready to continue the fight with a gun.

"Come," he said.

His voice was gasping, strangely unreal and thick. She came to him and put her hand in his again, and it was wet and sticky with tundra mud from the spring. Then they climbed to the swell of the plain, away from the pool and the willows.

In the air about them, creeping up from the outer darkness of the strange twilight, were clearer whispers now, and with these sounds of storm, borne from the west, came a hallooing voice. It was answered from straight ahead. Alan held the muddied little hand closer in his own and set out for the range-houses, from which direction the last voice had come. He knew what was happening. Graham's men were cleverer than he had supposed; they had encircled the tundra side of the range, and some of them were closing in on the willow pool, from which the triumphant shout of the bearded man's companion had come. They were wondering why the call was not repeated, and were hallooing.

Every nerve in Alan's body was concentrated for swift and terrible action, for the desperateness of their situation had surged upon him like a breath of fire, unbelievable, and yet true. Back at the willows they would have killed him. The hands at his throat had sought his life. Wolves and not men were about them on the plain; wolves headed by two monsters of the human pack, Graham and Rossland. Murder and lust and mad passion were hidden in the darkness; law and order and civilization were hundreds of miles away. If Graham won, only the unmapped tundras would remember this night, as the deep, dark kloof remembered in its gloom the other tragedy of more than half a century ago. And the girl at his side, already disheveled and muddied by their hands—

His mind could go no farther, and angry protest broke in a low cry from his lips. The girl thought it was because of the shadows that loomed up suddenly in their path. There were two of them, and she, too, cried out as voices commanded them to stop. Alan caught a swift up-movement of an arm, but his own was quicker. Three spurts of flame darted in lightning flashes from his pistol, and the man who had raised his arm crumpled to the earth, while the other dissolved swiftly into the storm-gloom. A moment later his wild shouts were assembling the pack, while the detonations of Alan's pistol continued to roll over the tundra.

The unexpectedness of the shots, their tragic effect, the falling of the stricken man and the flight of the other, brought no word from Mary Standish. But her breath was sobbing, and in the lifting of the purplish gloom she turned her face for an instant to Alan, tensely white, with wide-open eyes. Her hair covered her like a shining veil, and where it clustered in a disheveled mass upon her breast Alan saw her hand thrusting itself forward from its clinging concealment, and in it—to his amazement—was a pistol. He recognized the weapon—one of a brace of light automatics which his friend, Carl Lomen, had presented to him several Christmas seasons ago. Pride and a strange exultation swept over him. Until now she had concealed the weapon, but all along she had prepared to fight—to fight with *him* against their enemies! He wanted to stop and take her in his arms, and with his kisses tell her how splendid she was. But instead of this he sped more swiftly ahead, and they came into the nigger-head bottom which lay in a narrow barrier between them and the range.

Through this ran a trail scarcely wider than a wagon-track, made through the sea of hummocks and sedge-boles and mucky pitfalls by the axes and shovels of his people; finding this, Alan stopped for a moment, knowing that safety lay ahead of them. The girl leaned against him, and then was almost a dead weight in his arms. The last two hundred yards had taken the strength from her body. Her pale face dropped back, and Alan brushed the soft hair away from it, and kissed her lips and her eyes, while the pistol lay clenched against his breast. Even then, too hard-run to speak, she smiled at him, and Alan caught her up in his arms and darted into the narrow path which he knew their pursuers would not immediately find if they could bet beyond their vision. He was joyously amazed at her lightness. She was like a child in his arms, a glorious little goddess hidden and smothered in her long hair, and he held her closer as he hurried toward the cabins, conscious of the soft tightening of her arms about his neck, feeling the sweet caress of her panting breath, strengthened and made happy by her helplessness.

Thus they came out of the bottom as the first mist of slowly approaching rain touched his face. He could see farther now—half-way back over the narrow trail. He climbed a slope, and here Mary Standish slipped from his arms and stood with new strength, looking into his face. His breath was coming in little breaks, and he pointed. Faintly they could make out the shadows of the corral buildings. Beyond them were no lights penetrating the gloom from the windows of the range of houses. The silence of the place was death-like.

And then something grew out of the earth almost at their feet. A hollow cry followed the movement, a cry that was ghostly and shivering, and loud enough only for them to hear, and Sokwenna stood at their side. He talked swiftly. Only Alan understood. There was something unearthly and spectral in his appearance; his hair and beard were wet; his eyes shot here and there in little points of fire; he was like a gnome, weirdly uncanny as he gestured and talked in his monotone while he watched the nigger-head bottom. When he had finished, he did not wait for an answer, but turned and led the way swiftly toward the range houses.

"What did he say?" asked the girl.

"That he is glad we are back. He heard the shots and came to meet us."

"And what else?" she persisted.

"Old Sokwenna is superstitious—and nervous. He said some things that you wouldn't understand. You would probably think him mad if he told you the spirits of his comrades slain in the kloof many years ago were here with him tonight, warning him of things about to happen. Anyway, he has been cautious. No sooner were we out of sight than he hustled every woman and child in the village on their way to the mountains. Keok and Nawadlook wouldn't go. I'm glad of that, for if they were pursued and overtaken by men like Graham and Rossland—"

"Death would be better," finished Mary Standish, and her hand clung more tightly to his arm.

"Yes, I think so. But that can not happen now. Out in the open they had us at a disadvantage. But we can hold Sokwenna's place until Stampede and the herdsmen come. With two good rifles inside, they won't dare to assault the cabin with their naked hands. The advantage is all ours now; we can shoot, but they won't risk the use of their rifles."

"Why?"

"Because you will be inside. Graham wants you alive, not dead. And bullets—"

They had reached Sokwenna's door, and in that moment they hesitated and turned their faces back to the gloom out of which they had fled. Voices came suddenly from beyond the corrals. There was no effort at concealment. The buildings were discovered, and men called out loudly and were answered from half a dozen points out on the tundra. They could hear running feet and sharp commands; some were cursing where they were entangled among the nigger-heads, and the sound of hurrying foes came from the edge of the ravine. Alan's heart stood still. There was something terribly swift and businesslike in this gathering of their enemies. He could hear them at his cabin. Doors opened. A window fell in with a crash. Lights flared up through the gray mist.

It was then, from the barricaded attic window over their heads, that Sokwenna's rifle answered. A single shot, a shriek, and then a pale stream of flame leaped out from the window as the old warrior emptied his gun. Before the last of the five swift shots were fired, Alan was in the cabin, barring the door behind him. Shaded candles burned on the floor, and beside them crouched Keok and Nawadlook. A glance told him what Sokwenna had done. The room was an arsenal. Guns lay there, ready to be used; heaps of cartridges were piled near them, and in the eyes of Keok and Nawadlook blazed deep and steady fires as they held shining cartridges between their fingers, ready to thrust them into the rifle chambers as fast as the guns were emptied.

In the center of the room stood Mary Standish. The candles, shaded so they would not disclose the windows, faintly illumined her pale face and unbound hair and revealed the horror in her eyes as she looked at Alan.

He was about to speak, to assure her there was no danger that Graham's men would fire upon the cabin—when hell broke suddenly loose out in the night. The savage roar of guns answered Sokwenna's fusillade, and a hail of bullets crashed against the log walls. Two of them found their way through the windows like hissing serpents, and with a single movement Alan was at Mary's side and had crumpled her down on the floor beside Keok and Nawadlook. His face was white, his brain a furnace of sudden, consuming fire.

"I thought they wouldn't shoot at women," he said, and his voice was terrifying in its strange hardness. "I was mistaken. And I am sure—now—that I understand."

With his rifle he cautiously approached the window. He was no longer guessing at an elusive truth. He knew what Graham was thinking, what he was planning, what he intended to do, and the thing was appalling. Both he and Rossland knew there would be some way of sheltering Mary Standish in Sokwenna's cabin; they were accepting a desperate gamble, believing that Alan Holt would find a safe place for her, while he fought until he fell. It was the finesse of clever scheming, nothing less than murder, and he, by this combination of circumstances and plot, was the victim marked for death.

The shooting had stopped, and the silence that followed it held a significance for Alan. They were giving him an allotted time in which to care for those under his protection. A trap-door was in the floor of Sokwenna's cabin. It opened into a small storeroom and cellar, which in turn possessed an air vent leading to the outside, overlooking the ravine. In the candle-glow Alan saw the door of this trap propped open with a stick. Sokwenna, too, was clever. Sokwenna had foreseen.

Crouched under the window, he looked at the girls. Keok, with a rifle in her hand, had crept to the foot of the ladder leading up to the attic, and began to climb it. She was going to Sokwenna, to load for him. Alan pointed to the open trap.

"Quick, get into that!" he cried. "It is the only safe place. You can load there and hand out the guns."

Mary Standish looked at him steadily, but did not move. She was clutching a rifle in her hands. And Nawadlook did not move. But Keok climbed steadily and disappeared in the darkness above.

"Go into the cellar!" commanded Alan. "Good God, if you don't—"

A smile lit up Mary's face. In that hour of deadly peril it was like a ray of glorious light leading the way through blackness, a smile sweet and gentle and unafraid; and slowly she crept toward Alan, dragging the rifle in one hand and holding the little pistol in the other, and from his feet she still smiled up at him through the dishevelment of her shining hair, and in a quiet, little voice that thrilled him, she said, "I am going to help you fight."

Mary sobbed as the man she loved faced winged death.

Nawadlook came creeping after her, dragging another rifle and bearing an apron heavy with the weight of cartridges.

And above, through the darkened loophole of the attic window, Sokwenna's ferret eyes had caught the movement of a shadow in the gray mist, and his rifle sent its death-challenge once more to John Graham and his men. What followed struck a smile from Mary's lips, and a moaning sob rose from her breast as she watched the man she loved rise up before the open window to face the winged death that was again beating a tattoo against the log walls of the cabin.

* * * * *

CHAPTER XXV

That in the lust and passion of his designs and the arrogance of his power John Graham was not afraid to overstep all law and order, and that he believed Holt would shelter Mary Standish from injury and death, there could no longer be a doubt after the first few swift moments following Sokwenna's rifle-shots from the attic window.

Through the window of the lower room, barricaded by the cautious old warrior until its aperture was not more than eight inches square, Alan thrust his rifle as the crash of gun-fire broke the gray and thickening mist of night. He could hear the thud and hiss of bullets; he heard them singing like angry bees as they passed with the swiftness of chain-lightning over the cabin roof, and their patter against the log walls was like the hollow drumming of knuckles against the side of a ripe watermelon. There was something fascinating and almost gentle about that last sound. It did not seem that the horror of death was riding with it, and Alan lost all sense of fear as he stared in the direction from which the firing came, trying to make out shadows at which to shoot. Here and there he saw dim, white streaks, and at these he fired as fast as he could throw cartridges into the chamber and pull the trigger. Then he crouched down with the empty gun. It was Mary Standish who held out a freshly loaded weapon to him. Her face was waxen in its deathly pallor. Her eyes, staring at him so strangely, never for an instant leaving his face, were lustrous with the agony of fear that flamed in their depths. She was not afraid for herself. It was for *him*. His name was on her lips, a whisper unspoken, a breathless prayer, and in that instant a bullet sped through the opening in front of which he had stood a moment before, a hissing, writing serpent of death that struck something behind them in its venomous wrath. With a cry she flung up her arms about his bent head.

"My God, they will kill you if you stand there!" she moaned. "Give me up to them, Alan. If you love me—give me up!"

A sudden spurt of white dust shot out into the dim candle-glow, and then another, so near Nawadlook that his blood went cold. Bullets were finding their way through the moss and earth chinking between the logs of the cabin. His arms closed in a fierce embrace about the girl's slim body, and before she could realize what was happening, he leaped to the trap with her and almost flung her into its protection. Then he forced Nawadlook down beside her, and after them he thrust in the empty gun and the apron with its weight of cartridges. His face was demoniac in its command.

"If you don't stay there, I'll open the door and go outside to fight! Do you understand? *Stay there!*"

His clenched fist was in their faces, his voice almost a shout. He saw another white spurt of dust; the bullet crashed in tinware, and following the crash came a shriek from Keok in the attic.

In that upper gloom Sokwenna's gun had fallen with a clatter. The old warrior bent himself over, nearly double, and with his two withered hands was clutching his stomach. He was on his knees, and his breath suddenly came in a panting, gasping cry. Then he straightened slowly and said something reassuring to Keok, and faced the window again with the gun which she had loaded for him.

The scream had scarcely gone from Keok's lips when Alan was at the top of the ladder, calling her. She came to him through the stark blackness of the room, sobbing that Sokwenna was hit; and Alan reached out and seized her, and dragged her down, and placed her with Nawadlook and Mary Standish.

From them he turned to the window, and his soul cried out madly for the power to see, to kill, to avenge. As if in answer to this prayer for light and vision he saw his cabin strangely illumined; dancing, yellow radiance

217

silhouetted the windows, and a stream of it billowed out through an open door into the night. It was so bright he could see the rain-mist, scarcely heavier than a dense, slowly descending fog, a wet blanket of vapor moistening the earth. His heart jumped as with each second the blaze of light increased. They had set fire to his cabin. They were no longer white men, but savages.

He was terribly cool, even as his heart throbbed so violently. He watched with the eyes of a deadly hunter, wide-open over his rifle-barrel. Sokwenna was still. Probably he was dead. Keok was sobbing in the cellar-pit. Then he saw a shape growing in the illumination, three or four of them, moving, alive. He waited until they were clearer, and he knew what they were thinking—that the bullet-riddled cabin had lost its power to fight. He prayed God it was Graham he was aiming at, and fired. The figure went down, sank into the earth as a dead man falls. Steadily he fired at the others—one, two, three, four—and two out of the four he hit, and the exultant thought flashed upon him that it was good shooting under the circumstances.

He sprang back for another gun, and it was Mary who was waiting for him, head and shoulders out of the cellar-pit, the rifle in her hands. She was sobbing as she looked straight at him, yet without moisture or tears in her eyes.

"Keep down!" he warned. "Keep down below the floor!"

He guessed what was coming. He had shown his enemies that life still existed in the cabin, life with death in its hands, and now—from the shelter of the other cabins, from the darkness, from beyond the light of his flaming home, the rifle fire continued to grow until it filled the night with a horrible din. He flung himself face-down upon the floor, so that the lower log of the building protected him. No living thing could have stood up against what was happening in these moments. Bullets tore through the windows and between the moss-chinked logs, crashing against metal and glass and tinware; one of the candles sputtered and went out, and in this hell Alan heard a cry and saw Mary Standish coming out of the cellar-pit toward him. He had flung himself down quickly, and she thought he was hit! He shrieked at her, and his heart froze with horror as he saw a heavy tress of her hair drop to the floor as she stood there in that frightful moment, white and glorious in the face of the gun-fire. Before she could move another step, he was at her side, and with her in his arms leaped into the pit.

A bullet sang over them. He crushed her so close that for a breath or two life seemed to leave her body.

A sudden draught of cool air struck his face. He missed Nawadlook. In the deeper gloom farther under the floor he heard her moving, and saw a faint square of light. She was creeping back. Her hands touched his arm.

"We can get away—there!" she cried in a low voice. "I have opened the little door. We can crawl through it and into the ravine."

Her words and the square of light were an inspiration. He had not dreamed that Graham would turn the cabin into a death-hole, and Nawadlook's words filled him with a sudden thrilling hope. The rifle fire was dying away again as he gave voice to his plan in sharp, swift words. He would hold the cabin. As long as he was there Graham and his men would not dare to rush it. At least they would hesitate a considerable time before doing that. And meanwhile the girls could steal down into the ravine. There was no one on that side to intercept them, and both Keok and Nawadlook were well acquainted with the trails into the mountains. It would mean safety for them. He would remain in the cabin, and fight, until Stampede Smith and the herdsmen came.

The white face against his breast was cold and almost expressionless. Something in it frightened him. He knew his argument had failed and that Mary Standish would not go; yet she did not answer him, nor did her lips move in the effort.

"Go—for *their* sakes, if not for your own and mine," he insisted, holding her away from him. "Good God, think what it will mean if beasts like those out there get hold of Keok and Nawadlook! Graham is your husband and will protect you for himself, but for them there will be no hope, no salvation, nothing but a fate more terrible than death. They will be like—like two beautiful lambs thrown among wolves—broken—destroyed—"

Her eyes were burning with horror. Keok was sobbing, and a moan which she bravely tried to smother in her breast came from Nawadlook.

"And *you!*" whispered Mary.

"I must remain here. It is the only way."

Dumbly she allowed him to lead her back with Keok and Nawadlook. Keok went through the opening first, then Nawadlook, and Mary Standish last. She did not touch him again. She made no movement toward him and said no word, and all he remembered of her when she was gone in the gloom was her eyes. In that last look she had given him her soul, and no whisper, no farewell caress came with it.

"Go cautiously until you are out of the ravine, then hurry toward the mountains," were his last words.

He saw their forms fade into dim shadows, and the gray mist swallowed them.

He hurried back, seized a loaded gun, and sprang to the window, knowing that he must continue to deal death until he was killed. Only in that way could he hold Graham back and give those who had escaped a chance for their lives. Cautiously he looked out over his gun barrel. His cabin was a furnace red with flame; streams of fire were licking out at the windows and through the door, and as he sought vainly for a movement of life, the crackling roar of it came to his ears, and so swiftly that his breath choked him, the pitch-filled walls became sheets of conflagration, until the cabin was a seething, red-hot torch of fire whose illumination was more dazzling than the sun of day.

Out into this illumination suddenly stalked a figure waving a white sheet at the end of a long pole. It advanced slowly, a little hesitatingly at first, as if doubtful of what might happen; and then it stopped, full in the light, an easy mark for a rifle aimed from Sokwenna's cabin. He saw who it was then, and drew in his rifle and watched the unexpected maneuver in amazement. The man was Rossland. In spite of the dramatic tenseness of the moment Alan could not repress the grim smile that came to his lips. Rossland was a man of illogical resource, he meditated. Only a short time ago he had fled ignominiously through fear of personal violence, while now, with a courage that could not fail to rouse admiration, he was exposing himself to a swift and sudden death, protected only by the symbol of truce over his head. That he owed this symbol either regard or honor did not for an instant possess Alan. A murderer held it, a man even more vile than a murderer if such a creature existed on earth, and for such a man death was a righteous end. Only Rossland's nerve, and what he might have to say, held back the vengeance within reach of Alan's hand.

He waited, and Rossland again advanced and did not stop until he was within a hundred feet of the cabin. A sudden disturbing thought flashed upon Alan as he heard his name called. He had seen no other figures, no other shadows beyond Rossland, and the burning cabin now clearly illumined the windows of Sokwenna's place. Was it conceivable that Rossland was merely a lure, and the instant he exposed himself in a parley a score of hidden rifles would reveal their treachery? He shuddered and held himself below the opening of the window. Graham and his men were more than capable of such a crime.

Rossland's voice rose above the crackle and roar of the burning cabin. "Alan Holt! Are you there?"

"Yes, I am here," shouted Alan, "and I have a line on your heart, Rossland, and my finger is on the trigger. What do you want?"

There was a moment of silence, as if the thought of what he was facing had at last stricken Rossland dumb. Then he said: "We are giving you a last chance, Holt. For God's sake, don't be a fool! The offer I made you today is still good. If you don't accept it—the law must take its course."

"*The law!*" Alan's voice was a savage cry.

"Yes, the law. The law is with us. We have the proper authority to recover a stolen wife, a captive, a prisoner held in restraint with felonious intent. But we don't want to press the law unless we are forced to do so. You and the old Eskimo have killed three of our men and wounded two others. That means the hangman, if we take you alive. But we are willing to forget that if you will accept the offer I made you today. What do you say?"

Alan was stunned. Speech failed him as he realized the monstrous assurance with which Graham and Rossland were playing their game. And when he made no answer Rossland continued to drive home his arguments, believing that at last Alan was at the point of surrender.

Up in the dark attic the voices had come like ghost-land whispers to old Sokwenna. He lay huddled at the window, and the chill of death was creeping over him. But the voices roused him. They were not strange voices, but voices which came up out of a past of many years ago, calling upon him, urging him, persisting in his ears with cries of vengeance and of triumph, the call of familiar names, a moaning of women, a sobbing of children. Shadowy hands helped him, and a last time he raised himself to the window, and his eyes were filled with the glare of the burning cabin. He struggled to lift his rifle, and behind him he heard the exultation of his people as he rested it over the sill and with gasping breath leveled it at something which moved between him and the blazing light of that wonderful sun which was the burning cabin. And then, slowly and with difficulty, he pressed the trigger, and Sokwenna's last shot sped on its mission.

At the sound of the shot Alan looked through the window. For a moment Rossland stood motionless. Then the pole in his hands wavered, drooped, and fell to the earth, and Rossland sank down after it making no sound, and lay a dark and huddled blot on the ground.

The appalling swiftness and ease with which Rossland had passed from life into death shocked every nerve in Alan's body. Horror for a brief space stupefied him, and he continued to stare at the dark and motionless blot, forgetful of his own danger, while a grim and terrible silence followed the shot. And then what seemed to be a single cry broke that silence, though it was made up of many men's voices. Deadly and thrilling, it was a message that set Alan into action. Rossland had been killed under a flag of truce, and even the men under Graham had something like respect for that symbol. He could expect no mercy—nothing now but the most terrible of vengeance at their hands, and as he dodged back from the window he cursed Sokwenna under his breath, even as he felt the relief of knowing he was not dead.

Before a shot had been fired from outside, he was up the ladder; in another moment he was bending over the huddled form of the old Eskimo.

"Come below!" he commanded. "We must be ready to leave through the cellar-pit."

His hand touched Sokwenna's face; it hesitated, groped in the darkness, and then grew still over the old warrior's heart. There was no tremor or beat of life in the aged beast. Sokwenna was dead.

The guns of Graham's men opened fire again. Volley after volley crashed into the cabin as Alan descended the ladder. He could hear bullets tearing through the chinks and windows as he turned quickly to the shelter of the pit.

He was amazed to find that Mary Standish had returned and was waiting for him there.

* * * * *

CHAPTER XXVI

In the astonishment with which Mary's unexpected presence confused him for a moment, Alan stood at the edge of the trap, staring down at her pale face, heedless of the terrific gun-fire that was assailing the cabin. That she had not gone with Keok and Nawadlook, but had come back to him, filled him with instant dread, for the precious minutes he had fought for were lost, and the priceless time gained during the parley with Rossland counted for nothing.

She saw his disappointment and his danger, and sprang up to seize his hand and pull him down beside her.

"Of course you didn't expect me to go," she said, in a voice that no longer trembled or betrayed excitement. "You didn't want me to be a coward. My place is with you."

He could make no answer to that, with her beautiful eyes looking at him as they were, but he felt his heart grow warmer and something rise up chokingly in his throat.

"Sokwenna is dead, and Rossland lies out there—shot under a flag of truce," he said. "We can't have many minutes left to us."

He was looking at the square of light where the tunnel from the cellar-pit opened into the ravine. He had planned to escape through it—alone—and keep up a fight in the open, but with Mary at his side it would be a desperate gantlet to run.

"Where are Keok and Nawadlook?" he asked.

"On the tundra, hurrying for the mountains. I told them it was your plan that I should return to you. When they doubted, I threatened to give myself up unless they did as I commanded them. And—Alan—the ravine is filled with the rain-mist, and dark—" She was holding his free hand closely to her breast.

"It is our one chance," he said.

"And aren't you glad—a little glad—that I didn't run away without you?"

Even then he saw the sweet and tremulous play of her lips as they smiled at him in the gloom, and heard the soft note in her voice that was almost playfully chiding; and the glory of her love as she had proved it to him there drew from him what he knew to be the truth.

"Yes—I am glad. It is strange that I should be so happy in a moment like this. If they will give us a quarter of an hour—"

He led the way quickly to the square of light and was first to creep forth into the thick mist. It was scarcely rain, yet he could feel the wet particles of it, and through this saturated gloom whining bullets cut like knives over his head. The blazing cabin illumined the open on each side of Sokwenna's place, but deepened the shadows in the ravine, and a few seconds later they stood hand in hand in the blanket of fog that hid the coulée.

Suddenly the shots grew scattering above them, then ceased entirely. This was not what Alan had hoped for. Graham's men, enraged and made desperate by Rossland's death, would rush the cabin immediately. Scarcely had the thought leaped into his mind when he heard swiftly approaching shouts, the trampling of feet, and then the battering of some heavy object at the barricaded door of Sokwenna's cabin. In another minute or two their escape would be discovered and a horde of men would pour down into the ravine.

Mary tugged at his hand. "Let us hurry," she pleaded.

What happened then seemed madness to the girl, for Alan turned and with her hand held tightly in his started up the side of the ravine, apparently in the face of their enemies. Her heart throbbed with sudden fear when their course came almost within the circle of light made by the burning cabin. Like shadows they sped into the deeper shelter of the corral buildings, and not until they paused there did she understand the significance of the hazardous chance they had taken. Already Graham's men were pouring into the ravine.

"They won't suspect we've doubled on them until it is too late," said Alan exultantly. "We'll make for the kloof. Stampede and the herdsmen should arrive within a few hours, and when that happens—"

A stifled moan interrupted him. Half a dozen paces away a crumpled figure lay huddled against one of the corral gates.

"He is hurt," whispered Mary, after a moment of silence.

"I hope so," replied Alan pitilessly. "It will be unfortunate for us if he lives to tell his comrades we have passed this way."

Something in his voice made the girl shiver. It was as if the vanishing point of mercy had been reached, and savages were at their backs. She heard the wounded man moan again as they stole through the deeper shadows of the corrals toward the nigger-head bottom. And then she noticed that the mist was no longer in her face. The sky was clearing. She could see Alan more clearly, and when they came to the narrow trail over which they had fled once before that night it reached out ahead of them like a thin, dark ribbon. Scarcely had they reached this point when a rifle shot sounded not far behind. It was followed by a second and a third, and after that came a shout. It was not a loud shout. There was something strained and ghastly about it, and yet it came distinctly to them.

"The wounded man," said Alan, in a voice of dismay. "He is calling the others. I should have killed him!"

He traveled at a half-trot, and the girl ran lightly at his side. All her courage and endurance had returned. She breathed easily and quickened her steps, so that she was setting the pace for Alan. They passed along the crest of the ridge under which lay the willows and the pool, and at the end of this they paused to rest and listen. Trained to the varied night whisperings of the tundras Alan's ears caught faint sounds which his companion did not hear. The wounded man had succeeded in giving his message, and pursuers were scattering over the plain behind them.

"Can you run a little farther?" he asked.

"Where?"

He pointed, and she darted ahead of him, her dark hair streaming in a cloud that began to catch a faint luster of increasing light. Alan ran a little behind her. He was afraid of the light. Only gloom had saved them this night, and if the darkness of mist and fog and cloud gave way to clear twilight and the sun-glow of approaching day before they reached the kloof he would have to fight in the open. With Stampede at his side he would have welcomed such an opportunity of matching rifles with their enemies, for there were many vantage points in the open tundra from which they might have defied assault. But the nearness of the girl frightened him. She, after all, was the hunted thing. He was only an incident. From him could be exacted nothing more than the price of death; he would be made to pay that, as Sokwenna had paid. For her remained the unspeakable horror of Graham's lust and passion. But if they could reach the kloof, and the hiding-place in the face of the cliff, they could laugh at Graham's pack of beasts while they waited for the swift vengeance that would come with Stampede and the herdsmen.

He watched the sky. It was clearing steadily. Even the mists in the hollows were beginning to melt away, and in place of their dissolution came faintly rose-tinted lights. It was the hour of dawn; the sun sent a golden glow over the disintegrating curtain of gloom that still lay between it and the tundras, and objects a hundred paces away no longer held shadow or illusionment.

The girl did not pause, but continued to run lightly and with surprising speed, heeding only the direction which he gave her. Her endurance amazed him. And he knew that without questioning him she had guessed the truth of what lay behind them. Then, all at once, she stopped, swayed like a reed, and would have fallen if his arms had not caught her.

"Splendid!" he cried.

She lay gasping for breath, her face against his breast. Her heart was a swiftly beating little dynamo.

They had gained the edge of a shallow ravine that reached within half a mile of the kloof. It was this shelter he had hoped for, and Mary's splendid courage had won it for them.

He picked her up in his arms and carried her again, as he had carried her through the nigger-head bottom. Every minute, every foot of progress, counted now. Range of vision was widening. Pools of sunlight were flecking the plains. In another quarter of an hour moving objects would be distinctly visible a mile away.

With his precious burden in his arms, her lips so near that he could feel their breath, her heart throbbing, he became suddenly conscious of the incongruity of the bird-song that was wakening all about them. It seemed inconceivable that this day, glorious in its freshness, and welcomed by the glad voice of all living things, should be a day of tragedy, of horror, and of impending doom for him. He wanted to shout out his protest and say that it was all a lie, and it seemed absurd that he should handicap himself with the weight and inconvenient bulk of his rifle when his arms wanted to hold only that softer treasure which they bore.

In a little while Mary was traveling at his side again. And from then on he climbed at intervals to the higher swellings of the gully edge and scanned the tundra. Twice he saw men, and from their movements he concluded their enemies believed they were hidden somewhere on the tundra not far from the range-houses.

Three-quarters of an hour later they came to the end of the shallow ravine, and half a mile of level plain lay between them and the kloof. For a space they rested, and in this interval Mary smoothed her long hair and plaited it in two braids. In these moments Alan encouraged her, but he did not lie. He told her the half-mile of tundra was their greatest hazard, and described the risks they would run. Carefully he explained what she was to do under certain circumstances. There was scarcely a chance they could cross it unobserved, but they might be so far ahead of the searchers that they could beat them out to the kloof. If enemies appeared between them and the kloof, it would be necessary to find a dip or shelter of rock, and fight; and if pursuers from behind succeeded in out-stripping them in the race, she was to continue in the direction of the kloof as fast as she could go, while he followed more slowly, holding Graham's men back with his rifle until she reached the edge of the gorge. After that he would come to her as swiftly as he could run.

They started. Within five minutes they were on the floor of the tundra. About them in all directions stretched the sunlit plains. Half a mile back toward the range were moving figures; farther west were others, and eastward, almost at the edge of the ravine, were two men who would have discovered them in another moment if they had not descended into the hollow. Alan could see them kneeling to drink at the little coulée which ran through it.

"Don't hurry," he said, with a sudden swift thought. "Keep parallel with me and a distance away. They may not discover you are a woman and possibly may think we are searchers like themselves. Stop when I stop. Follow my movements."

"Yes, sir!"

Now, in the sunlight, she was not afraid. Her cheeks were flushed, her eyes bright as stars as she nodded at him. Her face and hands were soiled with muck-stain, her dress spotted and torn, and looking at her thus Alan laughed and cried out softly:

"You beautiful little vagabond!"

She sent the laugh back, a soft, sweet laugh to give him courage, and after that she watched him closely, falling in with his scheme so cleverly that her action was better than his own—and so they had made their way over a third of the plain when Alan came toward her suddenly and cried, "Now, *run!*"

A glance showed her what was happening. The two men had come out of the ravine and were running toward them.

Swift as a bird she was ahead of Alan, making for a pinnacle of rock which he had pointed out to her at the edge of the kloof.

Close behind her, he said: "Don't hesitate a second. Keep on going. When they are a little nearer I am going to kill them. But you mustn't stop."

At intervals he looked behind him. The two men were gaining rapidly. He measured the time when less than two hundred yards would separate them. Then he drew close to Mary's side.

"See that level place ahead? We'll cross it in another minute or two. When they come to it I'm going to stop, and catch them where they can't find shelter. But you must keep on going. I'll overtake you by the time you reach the edge of the kloof."

She made no answer, but ran faster; and when they had passed the level space she heard his footsteps growing fainter, and her heart was ready to choke her when she knew the time had come for him to turn upon their enemies. But in her mind burned the low words of his command, his warning, and she did not look back, but kept her eyes on the pinnacle of rock, which was now very near. She had almost reached it when the first shot came from behind her.

Without making a sound that would alarm her, Alan had stumbled, and made pretense of falling. He lay upon his face for a moment, as if stunned, and then rose to his knees. An instant too late Graham's men saw his ruse when his leveled rifle gleamed in the sunshine. The speed of their pursuit was their undoing. Trying to catch themselves so that they might use their rifles, or fling themselves upon the ground, they brought themselves into a brief but deadly interval of inaction, and in that flash one of the men went down under Alan's first shot. Before he could fire again the second had flattened himself upon the earth, and swift as a fox Alan was on his feet and racing for the kloof. Mary stood with her back against the huge rock, gasping for breath, when he joined her. A bullet sang over their heads with its angry menace. He did not return the fire, but drew the girl quickly behind the rock.

"He won't dare to stand up until the others join him," he encouraged her. "We're beating them to it, little girl! If you can keep up a few minutes longer—"

She smiled at him, even as she struggled to regain her breath. It seemed to her there was no way of descending into the chaos of rock between the gloomy walls of the kloof, and she gave a little cry when Alan caught her by her hands and lowered her over the face of a ledge to a table-like escarpment below. He laughed at her fear when he dropped down beside her, and held her close as they crept back under the shelving face of the cliff to a hidden path that led downward, with a yawning chasm at their side. The trail widened as they descended, and at the last they reached the bottom, with the gloom and shelter of a million-year-old crevasse hovering over them. Grim and monstrous rocks, black and slippery with age, lay about them, and among these they picked their way, while the trickle and drip of water and the flesh-like clamminess of the air sent a strange shiver of awe through Mary Standish. There was no life here—only an age-old whisper that seemed a part of death; and when voices came from above, where Graham's men were gathering, they were ghostly and far away.

But here, too, was refuge and safety. Mary could feel it as they picked their way through the chill and gloom that lay in the silent passages between the Gargantuan rocks. When her hands touched their naked sides an uncontrollable impulse made her shrink closer to Alan, even though she sensed the protection of their presence. They were like colossi, carved by hands long dead, and now guarded by spirits whose voices guttered low and secretly in the mysterious drip and trickle of unseen water. This was the haunted place. In this chasm death and vengeance had glutted themselves long before she was born; and when a rock crashed behind them, accidentally sent down by one of the men above, a cry broke from her lips. She was frightened, and in a way she had never known before. It was not death she feared here, nor the horror from which she had escaped above, but something unknown and indescribable, for which she would never be able to give a reason. She clung to Alan, and when at last the narrow fissure widened over their heads, and light came down and softened their way, he saw that her face was deathly white.

"We are almost there," he comforted. "And—some day—you will love this gloomy kloof as I love it, and we will travel it together all the way to the mountains."

A few minutes later they came to an avalanche of broken sandstone that was heaped half-way up the face of the precipitous wall, and up this climbed until they came to a level shelf of rock, and back of this was a great depression in the rock, forty feet deep and half as wide, with a floor as level as a table and covered with soft white sand. Mary would never forget her first glimpse of this place; it was unreal, strange, as if a band of outlaw fairies had brought the white sand for a carpet, and had made this their hiding-place, where wind and rain and snow could never blow. And up the face of the cavern, as if to make her thought more real, led a ragged fissure which it seemed to her only fairies' feet could travel, and which ended at the level of the plain. So they were tundra fairies, coming down from flowers and sunlight through that fissure, and it was from the evil spirits in the kloof itself that they must have hidden themselves. Something in the humor and gentle thought of it all made her smile at Alan. But his face had turned suddenly grim, and she looked up the kloof, where they had traveled through danger and come to safety. And then she saw that which froze all thought of fairies out of her heart.

Men were coming through the chaos and upheaval of rock. There were many of them, appearing out of the darker neck of the gorge into the clearer light, and at their head was a man upon whom Mary's eyes fixed themselves in horror. White-faced she looked at Alan. He had guessed the truth.

"That man in front?" he asked.

She nodded. "Yes."

"Is John Graham."

He heard the words choking in her throat.

"Yes, John Graham."

He swung his rifle slowly, his eyes burning with a steely fire.

"I think," he said, "that from here I can easily kill him!"

Her hand touched his arm; she was looking into his eyes. Fear had gone out of them, and in its place was a soft and gentle radiance, a prayer to him.

"I am thinking of tomorrow—the next day—the years and years to come, *with you*," she whispered. "Alan, you can't kill John Graham—not until God shows us it is the only thing left for us to do. You can't—"

The crash of a rifle between the rock walls interrupted her. The snarl of a bullet followed the shot. She heard it strike, and her heart stopped beating, and the rigidity of death came into her limbs and body as she saw the swift and terrible change in the stricken face of the man she loved. He tried to smile at her, even as a red blot came where the streak of gray in his hair touched his forehead. And then he crumpled down at her feet, and his rifle rattled against the rocks.

She knew it was death. Something seemed to burst in her head and fill her brain with the roar of a flood. She screamed. Even the men below hesitated and their hearts jumped with a new sensation as the terrible cry of a woman rang between the rock walls of the chasm. And following the cry a voice came down to them.

"John Graham, I'm going to kill you—*kill you*—"

And snatching up the fallen rifle Mary Standish set herself to the task of vengeance.

* * * * *

233

CHAPTER XXVII

She waited. The ferocity of a mother defending her young filled her soul, and she moaned in her grief and despair as the seconds passed. But she did not fire blindly, for she knew she must kill John Graham. The troublesome thing was a strange film that persisted in gathering before her eyes, something she tried to brush away, but which obstinately refused to go. She did not know she was sobbing as she looked over the rifle barrel. The figures came swiftly, but she had lost sight of John Graham. They reached the upheaval of shattered rock and began climbing it, and in her desire to make out the man she hated she stood above the rampart that had sheltered her. The men looked alike, jumping and dodging like so many big tundra hares as they came nearer, and suddenly it occurred to her that *all* of them were John Grahams, and that she must kill swiftly and accurately. Only the hiding fairies might have guessed how her reason trembled and almost fell in those moments when she began firing. Certainly John Graham and his men did not, for her first shot was a lucky one, and a man slipped down among the rocks at the crack of it. After that she continued to fire until the responseless click of the hammer told her the gun was empty. The explosions and the shock against her slight shoulder cleared her vision and her brain. She saw the men still coming, and they were so near she could see their faces clearly. And again her soul cried out in its desire to kill John Graham.

She turned, and for an instant fell upon her knees beside Alan. His face was hidden in his arm. Swiftly she tore his automatic from its holster, and sprang back to her rock. There was no time to wait or choose now, for his murderers were almost upon her. With all her strength she tried to fire accurately, but Alan's big gun leaped and twisted in her hand as she poured its fire wildly down among the rocks until it was empty. Her own smaller weapon she had lost somewhere in the race to the kloof, and now when she found she had fired her last shot she waited through another instant of horror, until she was striking at faces that came within the reach of her arm. And then, like a monster created suddenly by an evil spirit, Graham was at her side. She had a moment's vision of his cruel, exultant face, his eyes blazing with a passion that was almost madness, his powerful body lunging upon her. Then his arms came about her. She could feel herself crushing inside them, and fought against their cruel pressure, then broke limply and hung a resistless weight against him. She was not unconscious, but her strength was gone, and if the arms had closed a little more they would have killed her.

And she could hear—clearly. She heard suddenly the shots that came from up the kloof, scattered shots, then many of them, and after that the strange, wild cries that only the Eskimo herdsmen make.

Graham's arms relaxed. His eyes swept the fairies' hiding-place with its white sand floor, and fierce joy lit up his face.

"Martens, it couldn't happen in a better place," he said to a man who stood near him. "Leave me five men. Take the others and help Schneider. If you don't clean them out, retreat this way, and six rifles from this ambuscade will do the business in a hurry."

Mary heard the names of the men called who were to stay. The others hurried away. The firing in the kloof was steady now. But there were no cries, no shouts—nothing but the ominous crack of the rifles.

Graham's arms closed about her again. Then he picked her up and carried her back into the cavern, and in a place where the rock wall sagged inward, making a pocket of gloom which was shut out from the light of day, he laid her upon the carpet of sand.

Where the erosion of many centuries of dripping water had eaten its first step in the making of the ragged fissure a fairy had begun to climb down from the edge of the tundra. He was a swift and agile fairy, very red in the face, breathing fast from hard running, but making not a sound as he came like a gopher where it seemed no living thing could find a hold. And the fairy was Stampede Smith.

From the lips of the kloof he had seen the last few seconds of the tragedy below, and where death would have claimed him in a more reasonable moment he came down in safety now. In his finger-ends was the old tingling of years ago, and in his blood the thrill which he had thought was long dead—the thrill of looking over leveled guns into the eyes of other men. Time had rolled back, and he was the old Stampede Smith. He saw under him lust and passion and murder, as in other days he had seen them, and between him and desire there was neither law nor conscience to bar the way, and his dream—a last great fight—was here to fill the final unwritten page of a life's drama that was almost closed. And what a fight, if he could make that carpet of soft, white sand unheard and unseen. Six to one! Six men with guns at their sides and rifles in their hands. What a glorious end it would be, for a woman—and Alan Holt!

He blessed the firing up the kloof which kept the men's faces turned that way; he thanked God for the sound of combat, which made the scraping of rock and the rattle of stones under his feet unheard. He was almost down when a larger rock broke loose, and fell to the ledge. Two of the men turned, but in that same instant came a more thrilling interruption. A cry, a shrill scream, a woman's voice filled with madness and despair, came from the depth of the cavern, and the five men stared in the direction of its agony. Close upon the cries came Mary Standish, with Graham behind her, reaching out his hands for her. The girl's hair was flying, her face the color of the white sand, and Graham's eyes were the eyes of a demon forgetful of all else but her. He caught her. The slim body crumpled in his arms again while pitifully weak hands beat futilely in his face.

And then came a cry such as no man had ever heard in Ghost Kloof before.

236

It was Stampede Smith. A sheer twenty feet he had leaped to the carpet of sand, and as he jumped his hands whipped out his two guns, and scarcely had his feet touched the floor of the soft pocket in the ledge when death crashed from them swift as lightning flashes, and three of the five were tottering or falling before the other two could draw or swing a rifle. Only one of them had fired a shot. The other went down as if his legs had been knocked from under him by a club, and the one who fired bent forward then, as if making a bow to death, and pitched on his face.

And then Stampede Smith whirled upon John Graham.

During these few swift seconds Graham had stood stunned, with the girl crushed against his breast. He was behind her, sheltered by her body, her head protecting his heart, and as Stampede turned he was drawing a gun, his dark face blazing with the fiendish knowledge that the other could not shoot without killing the girl. The horror of the situation gripped Stampede. He saw Graham's pistol rise slowly and deliberately. He watched it, fascinated. And the look in Graham's face was the cold and unexcited triumph of a devil. Stampede saw only that face. It was four inches—perhaps five—away from the girl's. There was only that—and the extending arm, the crooking finger, the black mouth of the automatic seeking his heart. And then, in that last second, straight into the girl's staring eyes blazed Stampede's gun, and the four inches of leering face behind her was suddenly blotted out. It was Stampede, and not the girl, who closed his eyes then; and when he opened them and saw Mary Standish sobbing over Alan's body, and Graham lying face down in the sand, he reverently raised the gun from which he had fired the last shot, and pressed its hot barrel to his thin lips.

Then he went to Alan. He raised the limp head, while Mary bowed her face in her hands. In her anguish she prayed that she, too, might die, for in this hour of triumph over Graham there was no hope or joy for her. Alan was gone. Only death could have come with that terrible red blot on his forehead, just under the gray streak in his hair. And without him there was no longer a reason for her to live.

She reached out her arms. "Give him to me," she whispered. "Give him to me."

Through the agony that burned in her eyes she did not see the look in Stampede's face. But she heard his voice.

"It wasn't a bullet that hit him," Stampede was saying. "The bullet hit a rock, an' it was a chip from the rock that caught him square between the eyes. He isn't dead, *and he ain't going to die!*"

How many weeks or months or years it was after his last memory of the fairies' hiding-place before he came back to life, Alan could make no manner of guess. But he did know that for a long, long time he was riding through space on a soft, white cloud, vainly trying to overtake a girl with streaming hair who fled on another cloud ahead of him; and at last this cloud broke up, like a great cake of ice, and the girl plunged into the immeasurable depths over which they were sailing, and he leaped after her. Then came strange lights, and darkness, and sounds like the clashing of cymbals, and voices; and after those things a long sleep, from which he opened his eyes to find himself in a bed, and a face very near, with shining eyes that looked at him through a sea of tears.

And a voice whispered to him, sweetly, softly, joyously, "Alan!"

He tried to reach up his arms. The face came nearer; it was pressed against his own, soft arms crept about him, softer lips kissed his mouth and eyes, and sobbing whispers came with their love, and he knew the end of the race had come, and he had won.

This was the fifth day after the fight in the kloof; and on the sixth he sat up in his bed, bolstered with pillows, and Stampede came to see him, and then Keok and Nawadlook and Tatpan and Topkok and Wegaruk, his old housekeeper, and only for a few minutes at a time was Mary away from him. But Tautuk and Amuk Toolik did not come, and he saw the strange change in Keok, and knew that they were dead. Yet he dreaded to ask the question, for more than any others of his people did he love these two missing comrades of the tundras.

It was Stampede who first told him in detail what had happened—but he would say little of the fight on the ledge, and it was Mary who told him of that.

"Graham had over thirty men with him, and only ten got away," he said. "We have buried sixteen and are caring for seven wounded at the corrals. Now that Graham is dead, they're frightened stiff—afraid we're going to hand them over to the law. And without Graham or Rossland to fight for them, they know they're lost."

"And our men—my people?" asked Alan faintly.

"Fought like devils."

"Yes, I know. But—"

"They didn't rest an hour in coming from the mountains."

"You know what I mean, Stampede."

"Not many, Alan. Seven were killed, including Sokwenna," and he counted over the names of the slain. Tautuk and Amuk Toolik were not among them.

"And Tautuk?"

"He is wounded. Missed death by an inch, and it has almost killed Keok. She is with him night and day, and as jealous as a little cat if anyone else attempts to do anything for him."

"Then—I am glad Tautuk was hit," smiled Alan. And he asked, "Where is Amuk Toolik?"

Stampede hung his head and blushed like a boy.

"You'll have to ask *her*, Alan."

And a little later Alan put the question to Mary.

She, too, blushed, and in her eyes was a mysterious radiance that puzzled him.

"You must wait," she said.

Beyond that she would say no word, though he pulled her head down, and with his hands in her soft, smooth hair threatened to hold her until she told him the secret. Her answer was a satisfied little sigh, and she nestled her pink face against his neck, and whispered that she was content to accept the punishment. So where Amuk Toolik had gone, and what he was doing, still remained a mystery.

A little later he knew he had guessed the truth.

"I don't need a doctor," he said, "but it was mighty thoughtful of you to send Amuk Toolik for one." Then he caught himself suddenly. "What a senseless fool I am! Of course there are others who need a doctor more than I do."

Mary nodded. "But I was thinking chiefly of you when I sent Amuk Toolik to Tanana. He is riding Kauk, and should return almost any time now." And she turned her face away so that he could see only the pink tip of her ear.

"Very soon I will be on my feet and ready for travel," he said. "Then we will start for the States, as we planned."

"You will have to go alone, Alan, for I shall be too busy fitting up the new house," she replied, in such a quiet, composed, little voice that he was stunned. "I have already given orders for the cutting of timber in the foothills, and Stampede and Amuk Toolik will begin construction very soon. I am sorry you find your business in the States so important, Alan. It will be a little lonesome with you away."

He gasped. "Mary!"

She did not turn. "*Mary!*"

He could see again that little, heart-like throb in her throat when she faced him.

And then he learned the secret, softly whispered, with sweet, warm lips pressed to his.

"It wasn't a doctor I sent for, Alan. It was a minister. We need one to marry Stampede and Nawadlook and Tautuk and Keok. Of course, you and I can wait—"

But she never finished, for her lips were smothered with a love that brought a little sob of joy from her heart.

And then she whispered things to him which he had never guessed of Mary Standish, and never quite hoped to hear. She was a little wild, a little reckless it may be, but what she said filled him with a happiness which he believed had never come to any other man in the world. It was not her desire to return to the States at all. She never wanted to return. She wanted nothing down there, nothing that the Standish fortune-builders had left her, unless he could find some way of using it for the good of Alaska. And even then she was afraid it might lead to the breaking of her dream. For there was only one thing that would make her happy, and that was *his* world. She wanted it just as it was—the big tundras, his people, the herds, the mountains—with the glory and greatness of God all about them in the open spaces. She now understood what he had meant when he said he was an Alaskan and not an American; she was that, too, an Alaskan first of all, and for Alaska she would go on fighting with him, hand in hand, until the very end. His heart throbbed until it seemed it would break, and all the time she was whispering her hopes and secrets to him he stroked her silken hair, until it lay spread over his breast, and against his lips, and for the first time in years a hot flood of tears filled his eyes.

So happiness came to them; and only strange voices outside raised Mary's head from where it lay, and took her quickly to the window where she stood a vision of sweet loveliness, radiant in the tumbled confusion and glory of her hair. Then she turned with a little cry, and her eyes were shining like stars as she looked at Alan.

"It is Amuk Toolik," she said. "He has returned."

"And—is he alone?" Alan asked, and his heart stood still while he waited for her answer.

Demurely she came to his side, and smoothed his pillow, and stroked back his hair. "I must go and do up my hair, Alan," she said then. "It would never do for them to find me like this."

And suddenly, in a moment, their fingers entwined and tightened, for on the roof of Sokwenna's cabin the little gray-cheeked thrush was singing again.

BIBLIOBAZAAR

The essential book market!

Did you know that you can get any of our titles in large print?

Did you know that we have an ever-growing collection of books in many languages?

Order online:
www.bibliobazaar.com

Find all of your favorite classic books!

Stay up to date with the latest government reports!

At BiblioBazaar, we aim to make knowledge more accessible by making thousands of titles available to you- *quickly and affordably*.

Contact us:
BiblioBazaar
PO Box 21206
Charleston, SC 29413